A Hero's Plight

Dark Beginnings

By Hammed Akbaryeh

authorHOUSE®

AuthorHouse™
1663 Liberty Drive
Bloomington, IN 47403
www.authorhouse.com
Phone: 1-800-839-8640

First published by AuthorHouse 3/15/2011

ISBN: 978-1-4567-5032-9 (e)
ISBN: 978-1-4567-5033-6 (sc)

Library of Congress Control Number: 2011904078

Printed in the United States of America

Special Thanks to the Loch Raven High School faculty who helped edit my novel, and supported my pursuits.

I couldn't have done it without all of you, thank you from the bottom of my heart.

My English teachers: Kathleen Maher-Baker, Tracy Mabe, Kelly Dougherty, Niamh McQuillan, and especially Gail Shaffer who gave me the extra push in the right direction.

My principal: Bonnie Lambert

To
Katie Brennan, my inspiration.

TABLE OF CONTENTS

PART 2: PARTING OF THE WAYS

CHAPTER 1:
THE THING IN THE WOODS

"No! The darkness is closing in on Nijad!" shouted a knight in the high tower of a pearly white castle. The castle glowed like a pale moon on a starry night. A mysterious fog was settling in on the land and an eerie feeling came with it. Strange shadows of people, lost, begging to find some sort of guiding light circled around the castle. As if an answer to their prayers, a light came through the sky. Inside the light was a blurry figure holding a sword. A teenager with thick black hair and hazel eyes held the sword. His name was Zanatose. He came closer to the ground, becoming clear against the fog, and the shadows soon began to engulf him. He gasped and his lungs stung with an icy feeling. Once again he was growing blurry becoming....

"WAKE UP!"

"No!" yelled Zanatose, clambering sleepily out of his straw bed, and falling painfully to the hard floor. Zanatose scratched his romantic nose and blinked in an attempt to clear his vision. He was flustered and could not understand where he was for a moment until he saw his friend Bill. "Why'd you wake me up Bill? It's only..." he looked outside and saw he had slept straight through last night to mid afternoon. "Oops," he muttered inaudibly after a yawn. "*Now I'm going to get it*," he thought to himself.

"Yeah, you nimrod, we're late because of you!" yelled his friend Bill. Bill was a bigger guy than Zanatose, but was far less agile due to size. He had black hair and powerful, dark brown eyes. Both of these friends were orphans. Bill's parents died mysteriously in the woods, and no one in the village could recall anything about Zanatose's parents.

"Calm down, Bill!" said Zanatose to his fuming friend. "I had a really weird dream last night!" Zanatose was hoping Bill would like his story enough to forget about how much time they wasted because of him; he was supposed to wake Bill up for a get-together with their friends.

The two friends wore tattered green tunics; both of them were almost eighteen. Their hut was wooden and strong, built with the help of their friends. There were just two straw beds to sleep on and there was only one cupboard for food. The two students were far from having a grand house. They had papers from their studies scattered all over the ground, and Zanatose's wooden sword and shield lay on the ground. It was, beyond doubt, not a high class hut, even for their small village of Sholkon.

"So, you had another weird dream?" asked Bill in a careless voice. "None of us have had a decent night's sleep in a while, Zanatose, you know that. We've both seen some creepy dreams like the one I had last night; a dream about…" he stopped to imitate small scurrying things with his hands. "Spiders! The dream had spiders! It was terrible; spiders were attacking me by the thousands!" gasped Bill.

"I had that one too," admitted Zanatose. "But this one was more like a vision than a dream; kind of like the villager who had the vision of a rainstorm."

"That was a coincidence. Nothing more than a coincidence," said Bill. "Anyway, just tell me your new and *amazing* dream." said Bill as he yawned. Zanatose told him his story and Bill listened with little curiosity or attention.

"Wo...w how a...a...amazing," yawned Bill. "Anyway, it's about time we go out a little. Go see our pals like *Katie*," remarked Bill with a chuckle.

Zanatose ignored him, "Yeah, good idea, I need to train some more." Zanatose grabbed his sword and brandished it. Katie was a girl Zanatose had been friends with since he was little. She was the reason he took up sword fighting; Sholkon village never really had any dangerous problems, but he wanted to impress her. Sholkon village was isolated from the rest of the world by a cave and a river. Sholkon village decided to isolate itself from all other villages and cities in an effort to retain peace. Zanatose's teachers were never clear about what the outside world had done to warrant the village's isolation.

"Zanatose, that's why she doesn't have any interest in you man; if you want a girl, it can't always be about you," said Bill as he shook his head.

"Fine, I'll drop my training for a day." Zanatose had felt that he was starting to make some great progress with his combat abilities and was disappointed to stop for even a day. The two friends went outside into the old, shabby village. The village was mainly contrived of straw and wooden huts. There were bunches of kids and men in tunics much like Zanatose and Bill's. Some of the villagers wore finely weaved tunics while others wore tunics with patches of dirt hardened into the weaving.

Up ahead sitting on some tree trunks were Katie, Alexis, and Edwin. Edwin was skinny, had long black hair, green eyes, and a set of bow and arrows with him. Alexis had dark skin, black eyes, and braided hair. Katie was relatively tall, had sleek blond hair, and bright blue eyes. In Zanatose's eyes there was no flaw to her beauty; her freckles only added to her beauty in his eyes. She rejoiced at the sight of Zanatose and Bill. "Finally, I thought you two were no shows!" she said.

"Sorry, but Zanatose here never woke me up!" replied Bill.

"Well you see I... um .... kind of fell asleep, yeah......" Zanatose knew he should turn the conversation. He remembered an old village legend about a great sword that was created by the village's founder in order to defend the village. He wanted to go after the sword ever since he had read about it in class. "Hey guys, who wants to go into the dark woods? The Sholkon sword is in there, it's the most amazing artifact of our village!"

"Yeah, great idea!" said Edwin sarcastically. "Let's go into the dark, treacherous woods near nightfall! Great idea, Zanatose!" laughed Edwin. "And why should we go? To find a sword that may or may not exist at all!"

"Hey, I'll go!" said Katie. "But only if you promise to stick by me Zanatose."

"Alright Kate, how about the rest of you?" asked Zanatose unsurely. Calling Katie Kate was his subtle attempt at endearment. Zanatose was shy with girls.

"Don't evil spirits slumber in there or something?" asked Bill.

"Bill, we have a trained swordsman!" said Katie, she was teasing Zanatose. Katie did not really think Zanatose was the best man to protect them, but thought it would be fun to play with the situation.

"Well, you know if we don't find that sword and something attacks us, we're as good as dead," said Edwin. Alexis had already left silently; she lost all of her courage with the setting sun.

"He's got it covered," said Bill. This time Bill said it, and meant it. He had real confidence in Zanatose. They had been best friends for years, and they trusted each other entirely.

"Er... yeah, Bill's right! I've got it covered!" said Zanatose trying to sound confident. He started to play around with his small wooden shield and miniscule dagger. Katie was starting to feel worried. She expected Bill to chicken out, because she had her doubts about Zanatose. He had always seemed strange to her, and she never knew exactly how she felt about him. Regardless, the four anxious friends entered the pitch black woods.

Once inside, it was near impossible to see. Zanatose suspiciously looked tree to tree and kept mumbling that he had seen something. After a short time that felt like years, they saw the legendary Sholkon sword, wielded by the village's founder, Sholk. The village was named after him to commemorate his bravery against a mysterious plague.

"Look out!" yelled a far off voice, then a huge crash shook the floor.

"BILL!" this time it was Zanatose who was yelling with his shield and dagger ready. He ran to the nearest fallen body, Edwin, and made sure he was alright. Zanatose blindly ran to Bill's yells and stumbled on tree roots on his way until he suddenly felt an abrupt pain hit him hard in the gut and he flew back, colliding with a tree. He tried to stand, but a hard body was tossed onto him. Zanatose thrust the body off and stood ready, his sword steady and shield up. He struggled to regain his breath.

A few silent seconds passed before he saw some movement heading toward a light patch in the forest. He ran toward the single patch of moonlight; he finally got a good view of the thing attacking them. It was a strange sight, and it brought an ice cold chill into his soul. It was taller than any human could ever be; the thing glimmered in the moon light, was black, and had many tentacles. Its head looked like some kind of mutant person or snake.

He looked around at his surroundings and realized that he was standing near the Sholkon sword. As he made a move for it he saw that the *thing* was holding a very scared and pale looking Katie.

"No! Are you alright?" He called. There was no reply, she just stared at him. Zanatose immediately lunged for the sword. He grabbed it, its fine leather snug in his hand, and he swung the great sword out of the rock and through the thing's tentacle.

It gave an unearthly roar of pain and Zanatose raised the sword and swung it again. The sword gleamed marvelously in the moonlight. Zanatose charged at the bizarre fiend, he was angrily slashing through the air with his sword. He cut Katie free and kept fighting with the sudden rage of hatred. He felt his anger taking over his mind, poisoning him. The *thing* lost its temper, launching a livid blow to Zanatose, slamming him into a tree with a bone crushing impact. The wounded *thing* ran away into the darkness.

Zanatose painfully got up and staggered to Katie's side. His anger disappeared just as quickly as the *thing* had. "Are you alright? I'm sorry I let this happen."

"I....I'm o...okay," stuttered Katie. She took deep breathes, trying to calm herself.

"We're fine too, I think," said Bill as he helped Edwin up.

"I told you it was a bad idea!" said Edwin, wearing a disgruntled expression.

Bill looked like he agreed until he saw Zanatose's hand. Bill's eyes widened and a grin spread across his face. "Oh really, that new sword begs to differ."

The four friends left those vile woods, shaken and stirred. After this event they wisely chose not to venture too close to the woods. Every time they went close to the wood's edge they saw a strange creature lurking in the shadows. Fortunately, Zanatose had a brand new, sharp edged sword ready for the toughest battles.

The next few days went by normally; they would go out

into the village square and have lunch or play sports with a small wooden ball. The village square was magnificent; it had scores of wooden huts and a wide open field in the middle of it all. Zanatose refused to play, training instead. No one argued with him this time; everyone understood why. Katie was jumpy, as were Bill and Edwin. About a week after the forest incident, Alexis saw something dark in the distance and asked, "Wow! What was that? It looked really ugly and it was heading toward the village square!"

Everyone except Alexis looked stunned; they knew what was out there. "I...i...it's here!?" Katie did not expect the thing to return.

Zanatose grabbed his sword and shield, and Edwin grabbed his bow and arrows. "Wait!" yelled Bill. "I'm coming too Zanatose." Bill grabbed Zanatose's old sword and his own shield which he had constructed as a child for fun. Bill nodded to Zanatose and they stared each other down for a moment. Zanatose did not feel that Bill was ready to take on the strange beast, but the look in Bill's eyes convinced him otherwise, a look of bold force.

"Alright guys, let's go! You all know what is going to happen," he looked at Bill and Edwin gravely. They nodded to each other and ran toward the center of the old moss covered village.

They followed the desperate screams and cries for help from their people. The three rushed there until they saw it. The *thing* stood at the center, unleashing its rage and darkness upon the village. There were demolished huts, and unconscious people lying on the ground. Everything was turning dark; a strange mist was covering the village. Everything seemed quiet except the *thing's* unearthly screeching.

The three heroes were starting to feel an eerie chill as if a cold mist was settling upon them. "Alright," said Zanatose. He could see his own breath in the cold. "We need to...." He stopped as Edwin broke under the pressure of the cold, he ran toward the thing to ram it. Before he even got close, the thing effortlessly slammed him into the ground, unconscious, with a single blow. "We need to not do that!" said Zanatose. He was stunned to see Edwin snap haphazardly.

The thing was starting to turn around toward them to attack him and Bill. "Alright, Bill, we need to stay calm and work together or else we'll end up like Edwin!"

"Right... you've got a plan, right!?" squeaked Bill. Seeing Edwin pummeled so easily was not consoling for him. The two friends brought up their weapons and got ready to face the unfolding conflict.

"Listen, just go on your instincts alright?" said Zanatose nervously.

"Alright, but my instincts tell me to *run!!!!*" yelled Bill. They relentlessly stood their ground, half because they could not move from fear as the *thing* approached.

A tentacle, like a speeding arrow, came and slapped Bill across the face while Zanatose acted on instinct and ducked. Bill fell, but got back up trembling from head to toe. The side of his face was bleeding. *"Bill!"* Zanatose rushed at the *thing*, he raised his sword and slashed madly in every direction.

The thing jumped over him and slapped him in the back. Zanatose fell and the thing was ready to give him one last punishing blow in his back.

Bill hastily threw his dagger straight into the side of the beast's head. Bill gave a final shutter and fell, shivering from a nonexistent cold. The thing did not bleed from the dagger, simply took it out and thrashed at where Zanatose lay on the ground.

The thing gave an earth-shaking blow to the ground, but there was nothing there to hit. It gave out a deafening screech as a sharp blade slashed off several of its tentacles from behind. "You should watch your back!" yelled Zanatose as he stabbed the sword into its back and tore straight down.

The thing still did not bleed; it turned into a cloud of black smoke. The strange mist left with it.

Zanatose, like Bill, gave a shutter and fell cold and shivering onto the ground. Bill and Edwin woke up, so did the town's people. "What just happened here?" yelled an old civilian dressed richly in a fur robe. "It suddenly became cold and then this thing starts wrecking our village!"

"We don't know!" yelled back Edwin. Just as he said it, Katie and Alexis came running toward them.

"You guys did it!" she yelled jubilantly. She was wearing a big smile until her eyes rested on Zanatose, shivering with his eyes closed, on the ground. "No," she whimpered.

"He did it all," said Bill sadly. "We owe our lives to him. I couldn't help him!" He yelled angrily. "For some reason I became all cold and fell."

"Me too!" said Edwin. This brought a question to all of their minds. "What was that mist? I don't think it was natural."

"Good point," said Bill.

"Hey!" yelled Katie. "You guys, help me get Zanatose to a fire or something!"

"Oh, right! Knew we forgot something," said Bill shaking his head. The two, Bill and Edwin, lifted Zanatose and took him inside his hut. "So... who's going to watch over him?" asked Bill as he looked over the group.

"Um... I will..." said Katie. She was taking courses in healing; although, that was not the only reason she wanted to stay. "So I'll watch over him. I'll need a thick fur blanket, a fire, and some water."

"Right..." replied Bill.

Bill and Edwin hurried off and got the materials expediently. Zanatose was soon wrapped tightly in a thick fur blanket near a warm crackling fire.

Katie stayed by his side for two days until he finally woke up. "*Zanatose, you're alive!*" she screamed gleefully.

CHAPTER 2:
THE SHOLKON SWORD

"Hey, Kate..." coughed Zanatose. "How did things go? Did it work?" he asked in a croaky voice.

"Yes, it worked Zanatose! You did it! We were worried you wouldn't wake up," she said grimly.

"What do you mean? How many days have gone by?" He asked worriedly.

"Er... It's been two days," she said quietly.

"Wow! I've been asleep that long?" Zanatose said. He thought back, but still it did not make sense why he was asleep that long.

"What a surprise. You're alive!" proclaimed Bill.

"Finally! You were asleep for a while," said Edwin scathingly.

"Are you okay now?" asked Alexis. "You were freezing."

"Yeah I'm alright now, but back when I was fighting that *thing* I felt so cold it stung! It seemed like that *thing* wanted to take me down with it!" He gave a shudder as he said this.

"At least it's gone now!" said Katie happily.

"Where's my sword?" asked Zanatose, suddenly sitting bolt upright on the bed.

"Right here, Zanatose," said Bill as he grabbed the sword near the fire and handed it to Zanatose. "It sure is a nice blade. It's sharp, light, elegant and..."

"Legendary," said a new voice. "Don't you know the great legend of the Sholkon sword and those creatures? I'll take a wild guess and say none of you know that old story."

Zanatose turned to see the newcomer. He wore a fine blue tunic; he was short, scrawny, and had combed brown hair. "Well, I guess you're right. I'm Zanatose and you are?"

"Oh yes, I know you! The whole village does after what you did for us. I'm Ethan and it's nice to meet you, Zanatose... and the rest of you." He eyed the rest in pity. This aggravated Bill.

"So what do you know about my sword, Ethan? Anything to concern us?" Zanatose asked.

"He seems too small to help in any fights," whispered Bill to Zanatose.

"At least I'm a lot smarter than some!" said Ethan. Ethan was a fellow student in Bill's school. Zanatose was not in all of Bill's classes so he had never met Ethan. Ethan was a top student and the son of the village's greatest mason.

As Bill was grinding his teeth Zanatose decided to ease the tension. "So what's your story Ethan?"

"Well, this is the legend I've heard, but the wise men know more; there was once an evil time over run by war, greed, and treachery. The era of war; the different races turned on each other. Each thought they were better than the rest. It was from the darkness in their hearts that a new race was born. A race that is not natural, God had not created this race of beings. The unholy race of pure evil was born from the darkness in the heart of the peoples of our world. They came from a kind of underworld. They destroyed many cities. This was when the wars stopped and the races of our world joined together. Many cities, I don't know how many, had their best craftsmen create mystical swords. The swords were then used against the beasts. After a period of time, the chosen ones were killed off by their own people. The people's greed drove them to kill their own heroes. Throughout the war, most swords had two heroes wield them. There were a few heroes who never died throughout the war; they were like Gods among men. Some say we haven't even fought half of those beasts."

"That's interesting... Do the beasts... *things* have a name?" asked Zanatose.

"They're monsters of the shadows; I don't know much more about them." Ethan stopped and thought for a moment then went on. "But I think the council of wise men may know."

"Where can I find the council?" asked Zanatose.

"I'll show you all soon."

"And you're saying the beasts were made from the evils of people?" asked Katie out of the blue.

"Not just people, but the whole planet. The era of war was a dark time filled with hatred and war. The greatest warriors of all time fought in the war against those beasts, but they failed!" Ethan was looking quite alarmed. "Those things have returned and the only ones willing to help are a few young teens! We're all going to die!" Ethan suddenly became wide eyed and had a nervous twitch.

Zanatose looked at Bill and nodded his head. "Snap out of it!" yelled Bill as he slapped Ethan hard in the face. Ethan swayed a little in place then shook his head and regained some color. "I'm sure others are willing to help in the outside world."

"Sorry about that." said Ethan in a faint voice.

"I have enough strength to take on the beasts!" said Zanatose in a booming voice of confidence.

Ethan laughed to himself. "Really, *hero?*" Once Ethan said this, he fell into a fit of laughter. "I fear even you don't have the power for this battle, *hero*. Many before you have tried to defeat these *things*, but all they could do is delay them. And now the delay has been breached, bypassed. Do you truly believe you can stop them.... *hero*."

"There has to be a way to defeat them!" said Katie with great dismay.

"If you expect to defeat them, you'll have to use all of the elemental swords if and when you find them," said Ethan.

Zanatose was sitting on a small fur bed, thinking. Bill turned to him and said, "Zanatose... It's your call. There must be others who know and are better trained than us. Do you think we should do something?" asked Bill.

Everyone looked at him and there was a tense silence for a while. Zanatose raised his head from his hands and said in a shaky voice, "Alright. We will leave Sholkon and we will head off into the world to find the elemental swords."

Alexis was about to protest, but decided not to in dismay. Ethan was ready to take them to the council of elders. Bill was standing, fixed in a trance. Edwin looked like he might puke, and Katie was just staring at Zanatose.

"I think it's wise that I give the sword to Bill," said Zanatose. He handed the prized Sholkon sword to Bill.

"Thanks man... Here's your dagger back." said Bill as he handed over Zanatose's old dagger. Bill was finally out of his daze and was focused. "Well, let's go to the council Ethan!" Bill said with a confident nod.

"Wait, there's something about the swords you may like to know!" said Ethan. "The swords each have their own elemental powers. Try to use it Bill."

"If it won't work, it means you are not destined to wield it, right?" asked Edwin.

"Right," said Ethan.

Bill focused with all his might and the sword slowly started to glow white. Bill's eyes opened wide and he waved it all around. This was the wrong thing to do. The sword's power made itself evident. The energy focused around the sword went flying. "**DUCK!**" yelled Zanatose as the sword wrecked the furniture.

A cloud of dust rose from the wreckage. "You might want

14

to learn how to use the power before you wave it around like that!" yelled Katie in a rage. Chunks of splintered wood hung from the ceiling. The bed Zanatose was sitting on seconds ago was shredded by the blast.

"Whoops" said Bill as he laughed. "I've got the power!" he said as he looked at all of the wreckage.

"Okay... I guess we should be going to the council now?" asked Ethan as he stared at all the damage, pondering Bill's idiocy.

"Umm... Yeah... let's go before the place crumbles on top of our heads!" said Zanatose. On their way out Zanatose glared at Bill and whispered to him, "You really shouldn't have done that. Now we have to leave." Bill simply laughed.

CHPT 3:
THE ELDERS OF SHOLKON

Ethan led the group out to a wooded path, heading into a thick over growth of trees. They followed the path with the sun rising behind them. The path had many stray tree roots and fallen, orange leaves. The little woods had scores of thorns and gave the group painful scratches.

After two hours Alexis asked, "How much further? I didn't even have breakfast."

"Don't remind me!" yelled Edwin as his stomach gave a roar of hunger.

"Not far now... A matter of fact, there it is!" said Ethan. They had finally reached a small, white hut in the middle of a clear plain of short grass. Odd smells came from within the mysterious hut.

Zanatose stepped up to the door and knocked using the heavy brass door knocker. There was no reply from inside, but there were rustling sounds. Zanatose wondered whether or not the old men had heard him. He raised the knocker one more time. Just as his hand came down for impact, the door burst into splinters. A body flew painfully into Zanatose and sent him crashing into the ground; this was followed by a huge shadow beast. "They beat us here," yelled Zanatose in anger.

"Weapons out, everyone!" yelled the body of the fallen elder, dusting off the splinters of the door. It seemed he was not speaking to the group, but the council of elders. The council all wore matching plain brown robes; some elders were bald and others had snow white hair.

Zanatose began to reach for his sword; one of the older elders on a cane said, "That will not be necessary. We are the wise council." The elder gave them a smile as the council jumped into action. Zanatose released his sword and stood back hesitantly.

A bald elder came at the beast from behind, and as the beast whirled around the rest drew their swords and slashed the beast in half with one smooth motion. The beast instantly disappeared into dust with one last scream.

The unearthly call of the beast echoed into the distance, shaking the earth they stood on. The trees swayed with the wind and the sun was blocked out. They all looked up to the sky, but could not see any clouds. Shadows crept out from the surrounding trees. They soon found themselves surrounded by unearthly shadows that swayed and moved with a will of their own.

"What is that?" asked Alexis. An elder slowly approached a shadow, not knowing what to expect. He was two steps away when the shadow began to rise, becoming a definite being. All of the shadows rose in unison, forming a large group of dark beasts.

The elders brought up their weapons and continued the fight against the beasts, uniting their attacks.

"It's our turn!" yelled Zanatose. Zanatose and Bill unsheathed their swords, and Edwin took out his bow. "Edwin, aim for a weak spot!"

"Like what!?" asked Edwin, mockingly.

"Well, it's not its head. Experience tells us that," said Bill.

"Charge now!" yelled Zanatose as Edwin shot several arrows which made the beast stagger. Zanatose and Bill charged at a beast, swords raised and shields up. Bill stopped short while Zanatose kept going.

The beast thrust a tentacle straight at Zanatose. Zanatose brought up his wooden shield, but the blow shattered the shield and hit Zanatose hard in the chest. The air was knocked out of Zanatose's lungs. He fell onto his knees with tears in his eyes, gasping for air.

"Zanatose!" yelled Katie. "Edwin, Bill, help him, you two!" she screamed at them with frustration.

"Right!" yelled Bill. Bill and Edwin charged in for help. A tentacle flew straight at Edwin's face, but he quickly ducked and shot several more arrows into the beast. The arrows immobilized the beast long enough for Zanatose to get up and Bill to cut off a few tentacles.

As the beast swung at Bill, a stray tentacle hit Edwin in the gut and he fell over out of breath as well. Bill ducked and ran as fast as he could, stopping abruptly to charge his sword. *"Come on, I can do this,"* he thought to himself. The sword glowed and he slashed straight at its chest. The blast cut through it and the beast blew up into dust.

"Yeah! Nice job, Bill!" yelled Zanatose; he felt Bill was lucky. The rest of the team congratulated him, but Katie didn't. She still thought he was too late for the fight and should have helped Zanatose from the start.

"Since when did you start caring about Zanatose that much?" asked Bill in indignation. This made Katie go silent and Zanatose dropped his gaze to the ground.

The elders dusted the dirt off their robes. "Yes, well done kids," said an elder with a particularly thick white mustache. "What brings you youngsters here?" he asked in a deep muffled voice. The elder was trying to seem amiable.

"We have seen another of these beasts, and we have decided to set out on a quest to stop them. A quest to the land of Nijad," said Zanatose. The others were not expecting such an exact answer. They had never heard of Nijad.

"How do you know the name of that place, child?" asked a wrinkly elder.

Zanatose went silent and then replied, "I saw it in a dream, and it was under attack."

The elders looked at each other gravely. "Come in... We should talk, but only you. The rest of you wait outside, please."

The group obeyed and Zanatose went inside the dark hut with the elders. The inside of the hut had simple wooden chairs arranged in a circle and one chair in the center which Zanatose sat on. There were many shelves of books and odd jars on the walls. A few jars looked like they had an ancient bug or herb in them. An elder pulled a curtain over the entrance to replace the broken door.

"What is your name?" asked the mustached elder.

"My name is Zanatose," replied Zanatose.

"So... Zanatose what do you need to know for your quest?" asked the head elder, an exceptionally old man with shaggy eyebrows and no hair.

"I need to know how to defeat those shadow beasts once and for all," Zanatose said.

"We know the location of a few elemental items, but not all of them," said the head elder gravely. "We see your friend has the Sholkon sword. This brings us hope for you Zanatose. It seems you are resourceful enough to have found an element sword in plain sight without assistance."

"Why are the swords even that important?" asked Zanatose. Zanatose wanted to know why a simple army was not enough to fight the beasts.

"You could just fight the beasts with simple swords; the problem is it would cost more lives than you can imagine. Those beasts are not just any adversary. The swords are needed to unlock something," said the elder quietly. He started to think to himself. "We, the elders of Sholkon, do not know what will be unlocked, but there is one who does in the land of Nijad; she is a fair princess."

"Alright, so my first plan should be to meet this princess," said Zanatose. The council nodded in agreement. "But for now the important part is: where can I find the swords?"

The elders laughed and said in guilty voices, "We do not know where any of the swords are except the Sholkon sword, although, we know another is in the cave at the northern trail." The elders now went silent, and the head elder spoke in a deep, serious voice of great importance.

"Know that some of the swords have souls of their own. Some of the swords are so powerful they will try to consume the wielder and control them."

"Why would a sword try to consume the one wielding it?" asked Zanatose out of curiosity.

"We do not know. We only know parts of the legend; only the true hero may wield the most powerful of the swords. We believe you are the destined hero."

"I don't think so. Back there I was fighting for your information, nothing else," said Zanatose in a worried voice. He was worried that if he was the hero, he might fail. It was too much pressure for him.

"Ah yes, but at last you couldn't have forgotten the woods could you? We've heard your story; that wasn't just for you, it was also for them." The elder gestured to the door where his team stood, waiting. "Friendship and love are the driving forces behind some of the greatest heroes; although, there are such heroes who have fallen because they lost their loved ones in battle." The elder grimaced at the thought.

"I still don't believe you, I am not an extraordinary warrior yet," said Zanatose nervously.

"Exactly Zanatose, you are not an extraordinary warrior *yet*. And if you are not the hero, then why do they follow your command so devotedly?" The elder paused for Zanatose to soak it all in; then he continued once more, "Zanatose they believe in *you!* One day, you shall be certain that you are the hero."

Zanatose was starting to feel uneasy and felt he had

already received all the information the elders had. "Alright, I appreciate all of your kind words and help, but I think I should be leaving. Goodbye elders." Zanatose gave a bow and walked to the curtain, but before he reached the curtain an elder stopped him.

"Zanatose, you really don't think we would let you leave the council for an adventure without gifts?" The fat elder laughed as his long beard wagged side to side. "I think we should give gifts to all of them!" he said gladly. He pushed aside the curtain, and all the elders, with Zanatose, went outside. The last few elders were carrying long packages.

"Gather round, all of you!" called the gay, fat elder. The council and group gathered in a circle around the head elder who had the stack of packages at his feet.

"For all of you brave souls who are about to embark upon this quest, we bring you gifts and weapons to aid you on your trip," said the head elder. He picked up a package and opened it to reveal a bronze-looking sword. It had a leather handle and a shined magnificently in the morning sunlight. "This sword is the sword of earth. The earth element is a two part weapon and this requires an earth gem for power." He cleared his voice and spoke more formally now. "We, the council of elders, bestow this sword on Edwin."

The group gave Edwin a huge round of applause as he walked up and received the sword. Edwin went back into the circle as the next gift was handed out. "This gift is for all of you. We have provided all the supplies you shall need for the travels: tents and food."

"Thank you sir," said the group together as they received the heavy luggage and strapped up. The elders nodded and then went back into their hut. Zanatose turned to the group. "Alright everyone, we'll leave first thing tomorrow morning." The group understood why Zanatose wanted to wait one day. Zanatose had just faced off against yet another shadow beast, and he was very pale and tired.

The group said their farewells and all went back to their homes. Once Bill and Zanatose were home, they sat on their beds and talked. "Bill, do you think this is a good idea; what if we run into a big group of those things? Even I can't take on more than one! W... What if something happens to Katie?" asked Zanatose hurriedly.

"Don't worry; I've got your back. And Edwin too," said Bill reassuringly. "Plus Katie is a smart girl, she'll be fine." This eased Zanatose's conscience a little. "Now Zanatose, you can't save anyone from even one beast if you don't get your rest... *hero,*" added Bill with a laugh.

The last line though caught Zanatose's attention, "*hero.*" He thought back to what the elders had said. "*Nah, not me I'm too young anyway,*" he thought to himself as he went into a silent sleep.

CHPT4:
DARK BEGINNINGS

"Alright, everyone has their weapons, food, and clothes ready?" shouted Zanatose to the group at the dawn of the new day. Everyone, but Ethan was there and nodded their heads. "Good, let's go to the northern gate." Zanatose led the tired yawning group northward to an exit gate at the end of their small village.

At the gate was Ethan, waiting for them. "Sorry, I won't come with you, but I give you my advice." Ethan looked at the group and said to them in a serious voice, "Remember to rest often. There are many wolfos and animals out there." Ethan now turned to Zanatose, "And Zanatose, here is a new sword I crafted for you... good luck friend." Ethan handed Zanatose a crimson sword. It was an outstanding hand crafted and grooved sword. "Blazer may not be an elemental sword, but it is still a highly effective sword which can withstand the use of elemental crystals."

"Thank you so much Ethan..." Zanatose paused. He shook hands with Ethan as a token of appreciation. "Farewell friend, for I know your fate will be far more bearable than ours." The group all shook hands with Ethan and said their farewells.

"You're not too bad Ethan," said Bill as the group walked through the gate with a heavy heart. As they walked through, the heavy and wooden gate doors were closed by Ethan. They were now in a dim wooded area leading to a bridge inside of a canyon.

As they were crossing the bridge over the strong river currents, a blue object flew off of a tree and landed right in front of their path. "Halt," said an unusually gentle voice from behind the white hood of the man. He was wearing a rich, blue silk cloak with a white hood. Zanatose immediately took out Blazer and his old dagger.

"For your sake I hope you mean us no trouble. We are a large group led by ME," said Zanatose threateningly. Neither side made a move.

"I mean you no harm..." the man coughed and swayed in place. "I am an elite officer, of Nijad. My name is Brett." Brett removed his hood to reveal his brilliant blue eyes. He had very light skin and was exceptionally tall. "I became lost here for a few days now..." he coughed again. "I really need some...water."

"If you mean no harm, alright, Alexis give Brett some water quick!" commanded Zanatose. Alexis rushed over to Brett and took out a canteen of water from her backpack. Brett drank several gulps then wiped his mouth dry.

"Ah... thank you. May I ask why you are heading in this cursed direction?" asked Brett.

"Our village has been attacked by shadow beasts, I believe you know what we mean by shadow beasts right?" asked Zanatose. He was worried that Brett had never heard of them, but from one look at Brett's face Zanatose knew Brett did know the shadow beasts; he knew them too well.

Brett gave a heavy sigh. "Those... Those things are here? I'm stuck here because there is a whole colony of those things in that cave." He gestured in the direction they were heading. "On my way here they caved in the exit back to Nijad, and now I can't get back alive alone! There are hundreds of those things in there! It's like they're looking for something," said Brett in a single breath. Brett was frustrated by his predicament.

"Now that could pose a problem. We are heading to Nijad," said Zanatose. He and his group seemed concerned. "We are trying to get rid of those things."

"You're going to Nijad?" said Brett in a delighted mood. "That's great! I can't get back alone, but I'm sure if we all go back together it could work. So do we have a deal... um..."

"My name is Zanatose," said Zanatose. Then he turned to the group and pointed them out one by one. "This is Edwin, he's stubborn. This is Bill; he has the Sholkon sword. These two are Alexis and Katie, Katie is a master archer and knows her herbs well." Once Zanatose was finished Brett was about to talk, but Zanatose cut him off. "And yes Brett, you have a deal." Brett grinned broadly and led them into the cave.

While they were walking Bill walked up to Brett and asked, "When we left, our friend said our journey to Nijad would have wolfos, aren't they just a myth?"

"Oh no, wolfos are real. The wolfos are a major issue in Nijad because they get involved with our city's foreign relations with other tribes and races. The wolfos are very agile, and they have huge claws and teeth. They are worse than the shadow beasts in battle. They are led by a wolfo named Fang. We do not know his real name though," said Brett darkly.

"Ethan also mentioned other animals- what other animals?" asked Bill in a high voice.

"He might have meant zombies, they are the undead evil citizens from the era of war, and they're brought back by very dark magic. Fortunately they only come out at night," replied Brett. "Why do you ask these questions? Are there no enemies in your village?" asked Brett.

"There were no enemies for our village up until a few weeks ago," said Bill grimly.

"Come on don't be so glum, Bill!" said Edwin. "We have an entire journey ahead of us to be gloomy about."

Brett laughed once he heard this. "So your village has never been attacked until the dark beast attacked all of you. None of you have battle experience!" said Brett.

"I do!" said Zanatose with a hint of anger. "Ever since I had dark dreams of ill tidings I have started training. I hoped I'd never have to use it though," said Zanatose as he gave a heavy sigh.

Bill seemed slightly suspicious of Brett. "Hey, Brett, you never said why you came this way."

Brett frowned for a moment but then smiled and spoke, "Well, it's a long story. The castle was under attack, and my team and I were chased all the way down here. They launched a huge attack on us in the woods, and we scattered. I ran into the cave... which is now right in front of us!" said Brett. They were all surprised to see they had reached the cave.

They entered the cave apprehensively, not knowing what to expect. The cave had a low ceiling and lots of old mold and assorted bones. Katie gasped at a huge human skeleton in a corner. Zanatose and Brett took the lead and the rest followed very slowly. They walked along the winding path until Brett stopped them.

"Get whatever weapons you have out, and ready," warned Brett. "We have entered their territory." Brett skillfully took out his weapon, a long staff with a sharp blade at the end. He twirled it around his wrist and torso as he took it out. The staff had a golden blade, and smooth silver for the rest. Zanatose drew Blazer, Edwin took out the earth sword, and Bill dropped the Sholkon sword as he tried to twirl it, imitating Brett.

As the sword fell it gave a loud clang that echoed far into the cave. "***Everyone ready!***" yelled Brett who was now very angry at Bill. As soon as Bill picked up his sword they heard a loud, high pitched cry fill the cave, and five shadow beasts appeared.

"We're surrounded," cried Katie. The shadow beasts had made a ring around them. One of the shadow beasts lunged at Katie.

"BACK OFF!" yelled Zanatose as he dashed at it. He rammed the beast hard, and it fell to the ground, writhing like a snake. Zanatose stood over it, and stabbed his sword into the beast and it vanished into dust.

Edwin had also taken one out, but had a few scratches. Bill had taken one quickly with an energy slash, but another from behind took him by surprise, and he was pinned down. The thing opened its mouth to reveal rows of small teeth lining its mouth like a demonic suction cup. It let out a hungry roar.

"*HELP!*" yelled Bill in peril. Brett quickly slashed the beast several times; before it disappeared it had several cut marks. Bill stood up, and dusted himself off, "Thanks."

A tentacle thrashed out from nowhere and hit Bill, sending him flying. The same tentacle swung at Brett. At first he jumped over it, but it came back and tripped him. The shadow beast towered over the fallen warrior. Its head snapped down and Brett stuck his staff in its mouth. He wrestled the beast back until Zanatose gave the beast a hard kick and then a strong slash. "You okay?"

"Yeah, I am. Thanks Zanatose," said Brett. The two shook hands and smiled at each other knowing they would forever help each other to the goal they both understood was up to them. "Nice moves out there."

"Not too bad yourself," said Zanatose.

"Zanatose, you were amazing out there!" yelled Katie. She was beaming with joy. Zanatose turned a little pink until Brett called out.

"Everyone, they'll be back, so let's move on quickly," yelled Brett urgently. The group moved on with urgent steps from then on. After a while of walking in the dim cave they started to get the feeling that they were being watched. "Stay ready, there was a reason I couldn't return alone," Brett said grimly. They all felt like their stomachs did back flips.

Their slow steps echoed in the long tunnels of the cave until they heard several more footsteps. "Is anyone jogging in place?" asked Zanatose. They all stopped, but there was still several footsteps echoing in the cave. They all turned around; there was nothing there... A huge thud and they saw Alexis out cold at Bill's feet. They twirled around to see several dark figures that were too far away to see in the dim light, but now they saw those beasts clearly. "Not again..." moaned Zanatose.

The shadow beasts each double-teamed the warriors. Edwin was quickly pinned down. Brett did several acrobatic moves off the wall and landed behind his attackers. Brett easily sliced both in half. Bill was also pinned down, but he had already taken one out.

Zanatose was facing a demonic duo of shadow beasts. They slowly circled him, growling and screeching. He slashed at one, but the other swung at the sword and it flew out of his hand. He was now unarmed. One beast slammed him down and stood over him and the second turned toward Katie and Alexis. "No," Zanatose growled.

"Zanatose, help!" yelled Katie. Zanatose tried to get up, but the shadow beast pushed him back down. A tentacle flew at Katie, and she ducked.

"That's **it**!" Zanatose was now full of rage. He moved his legs to the beast's chest and pushed it off. Then he sprinted for his sword. A stray tentacle went toward him, but he rolled under it and grabbed his sword. He turned toward Katie; she was backing up into the wall as the beast advanced on her.

He quickly dashed at it and drove his blade into its back. He was stunned to see it did not disappear. It grabbed him and flung him into the wall next to Katie. He felt small droplets of blood leaking out of his head from the impact.

"Zanatose, are you alright?" Katie asked. She was horror stricken to see that even Zanatose fell to the beasts.

"Of course... I don't fail!" Zanatose was burning with hatred for the beasts that made him look weak in front of Katie. He stood up and charged at both shadow beasts, and sliced them in half.

Bill was still pinned down, he was trying to yank off the beast and dodge its bites. Bill already had teeth marks on his shoulder. Zanatose quickly stabbed his sword through the shadow beast, inches from Bill's chest. "Thanks for the help man, but don't cut it so close next time!" said Bill.

As the two got up, several more shadow beasts emerged from their own shadows on the floor. "Is that a good sign, Zanatose?" asked Bill. They were both too afraid to look back even though they felt a heavy, hot breathing on their backs.

"That sign is a sign that means we've got to run!" yelled Brett as he threw off an attacking shadow beast. The group turned and ran forward. Zanatose and Bill were covering the rear. Edwin and Katie were in the front carrying Alexis, while Brett was guarding them.

The group ran and stumbled as fast as they could until Brett saw a pond. "There!" he yelled, pointing to it. The group quickly dived in as several more beasts came from the front. Zanatose stood back to make sure they all dived in, he was about to dive in when a shadow beast hit him across the face and he fell in. The water was freezing and clear. The chill of the water made his cuts and bruises burn. The icy chill of the water woke Alexis. They swam deeper and deeper until they saw an underground tunnel leading upwards. They swam up the tunnel hurriedly; they were all running out of breath and needed air. Edwin started to panic, flailing his arms in an attempt to resurface sooner. Once they resurfaced, they were at a new part of the cave.

The cave's walls were pure crystal. The walls glimmered and sparkled as they walked around, soaking wet. It was like being in a room filled with mirrors. The crystal walls glimmered and reflected a black, crystal, and sinister looking sword. "It's another elemental sword!" Zanatose yelled as he ran at the sword.

"STOP," screamed Alexis. Zanatose did not stop, but the rest froze and stared at her. Zanatose began running even faster for the sword as if any second someone else might take it. He slipped and slid toward it. "Don't touch the sword, it is evil! It is the blade of darkness. It could consume you!" she yelled at him.

"This sword calls out to me!" Zanatose yelled back in a wild rage. "The sword is mine. It wants me, and I need it," he ripped the sword out of the ground. The crystals encasing it shattered into dust. "And that is final." Zanatose felt the fine leather handle of the great sword and swung it around, admiring how the sword glimmered in the light. His pleasure was short lived, cut short by a stabbing pain. Dark electricity came from the sword and shocked Zanatose, engulfing him momentarily.

"Zanatose!" Katie screamed in utter shock. Zanatose swayed in spot, and then fell. He was slightly burned and smoke was fuming from him. His breathing was very slow and deep. He moaned as he forced himself back up.

Bill and Brett quickly ran to his side and helped him up. "Are you okay?" asked Bill in a low whisper. Zanatose simply nodded.

"You're lucky to be alive!" said Brett with a stern look. "This is the most dangerous and powerful elemental sword. Well, the light sword is equally powerful." For a second Brett was caught in his thoughts about the light sword, but shook it off. "Anyway, if this sword didn't want you to wield it you'd be dead! The fact that you survived holding the sword means you were meant to wield this sword."

Zanatose laughed, but his laugh was cut off by even more pain. His arm felt like it was burning. He rolled his traveling cloak's sleeve up to see that there was a small black triangle burned into his wrist. The group was staring at him, but didn't notice his wrist. He quickly rolled his sleeve back down.

Katie was about to walk forward, but he quickly said, "Let's g-get o-out of h-here." He stuttered as he spoke.

Brett led the way onward. Bill and Edwin were close by Zanatose's side since he seemed like he'd fall at any second. Katie was very tense, and so was Alexis. "You sure you're okay Zanatose?" asked Bill as he looked at him.

"OF COURSE!" yelled Zanatose, he felt strangely intemperate. "L-listen, right n-now we need to g-get out of this v-vile place so hurry up B-Brett!"

The group quickened their pace, hoping to see sunlight as soon as possible. Zanatose was oddly disconcerted after he had drawn the sword. The team did not notice because they thought it was the stress of handling those shadow beasts, but Brett was growing slightly suspicious. As they walked throughout the crystal cave they heard their footsteps echo, and stopped now and then to check if they were being followed.

They moved until they came to a crystal wall. "Guess we ought to turn back," said Brett. The entire team moaned in disappointment. It was a complete dead end.

"I don't think so," said Zanatose. Zanatose read the gold carvings in his sword. According to the old writing on the sword's blade, it was named Shadow. He took out Shadow and pointed the blade's end toward the rock. The room turned dark as a big black ball of energy gathered at the end of his blade. He released the energy ball at the wall and it blew up into millions of sparkling bits. The small pieces of crystal danced in the light at the end of the tunnel.

"Nice! Sweet!" yelled the team, except Brett. He was exceedingly anxious.

"*That blade's powers could cause problems; I'll have to watch out for the team.*" Brett thought to himself. He stepped into the light from the outside and turned to the group and said, "Welcome to Nijad!"

The group all stepped into the light and continued forward toward Nijad's castle to meet the princess of legends.

CHPT 5:
AFRAID OF THE DARK?

"Well... finally, we're here..." said Zanatose with a pause.

"Alive!" squeaked Katie as she finished his sentence. She was panting and still completely petrified from all the past events. Alexis was trembling from the horror of the past events. She thought back to her peaceful hut and wondered why she had agreed to come. The only reason she could think of was to look after her best friend, Katie. Fortunately, Brett and Zanatose were both perfectly calm. Bill and Edwin weren't as bad as the girls, but were still a little shaky.

The day was extremely bright and sunny. This was a slight problem for the group, having just left a dark cave. They lowered their heads and covered their eyes as they walked forward. The group kept bumping into each other. "OW! That was my leg man!" said Bill.

"Sorry... OW! Alexis that's my leg you hit!" said Zanatose.

"Look over there!" yelled Bill. He pointed at an enormous purple flower that was three times his size. The flower kept moving, maybe from the breeze. It had a long green stem and was closed at the top which was purple.

"This could be good shade!" Bill said as he ran over to it. Brett took one glance then lowered his head again. He muttered something to himself and as he looked back up in panic, Zanatose had unsheathed both of his swords and was running at the plant. The plant was not a usual plant it was a…

"A MAN-EATING VERONA PLANT!" Brett yelled. He also drew his staff, but decided not to charge in like Zanatose. He was a more cautious fighter.

The Verona plant was eating Bill. He was in its mouth which was lined with small teeth. Zanatose leapt toward it and crossed his swords and chopped it like scissors. The plant gave a disgusting gurgling sound as Bill fell out covered in wet saliva. Zanatose had a strangely violent look in his eyes as he stood straight up and calm.

He put both his swords into their raggedy sheaths. He put out his hand and pulled up Bill. "You okay Bill?" he asked with a laugh. As he nodded everyone broke out in laughter. This was a terrible event, but since it had a happy ending it was humorous to the group and lightened their spirits.

As the group stopped laughing and making fun of the situation Zanatose decided it was about time to continue. "Hey! Brett, which way now?" he asked from Brett. The entire group went silent and listened.

"Well…" Brett seemed a little unsure. "There is a problem in that, the zombies come out at night, and it would be best if we could make it to those woods in the distance before then." He pointed at a far away green patch in the horizon. Everyone squinted and still some of them did not see the woods.

Katie looked concerned and asked, "What are the zombies like?" She asked inquisitively.

"They are people who died back in the era of war, and the people they had killed. They were evil before death, and now their empty shells are used by strange beings even darker than they were," he said gravely. Zanatose gave him an impatient look. "Anyway, I guess we better start moving if we even want to get close to those woods by nightfall." As he started walking in its direction he said, "Oh yeah! And be careful of the wolfos, they're like an unnatural combination of man and wolf. They hunt all over at night, so where ever we are they will be a problem."

"Oh great, so where ever we reach by nightfall we're as good as dead meat," muttered Edwin as he laughed to himself.

"That's a bad way to look at it!" said Zanatose. "We should think of it more as, an all you can eat featuring you." He also laughed at the idea. The group moved on even though they were all afraid of the coming night.

"*I should have done this journey alone. Now I've put all of them in danger*," thought Zanatose. "*I can't let anything happen to them, especially Katie.*"

"Hey, Zanatose, is something on your mind? You seem pensive," said Katie.

Zanatose smiled at her and replied, "Nah, just thinking we should build camp soon." The sun was going down fast and it was now dusk.

Katie looked up at the sky and laughed. "Wow, I didn't notice it was already so late. Guess we should start building the tents before nightfall." Brett turned around sharply.

"That will not help us now; we are still half a day's hike from the woods. We are better off staying awake so we don't die," he looked Zanatose straight in the eyes because he knew what Zanatose was thinking. Zanatose grimaced and looked over at the horizon.

"Quickly, everyone make camp for tonight, I'll stay awake in my tent. If you're in danger give a shout," Zanatose said. Brett opened his mouth, but Zanatose quickly barked, "And they are too tired to fight! Let them sleep, I am more than fit to do guard duty."

"You are making a grave mistake, Zanatose," said Brett as he stared angrily at Zanatose. "The zombies will take one of them unless you can run fast enough to save them all... Are *you* willing to risk that?" Brett asked.

As Zanatose was thinking, Bill stepped between them and said, "Listen I think that's what we should do even if Zanatose didn't bring it up, so stay off his case." Bill was furious that Brett kept nagging at Zanatose.

Alexis was extremely tense, but Katie seemed unconcerned about the situation. Edwin and Bill were setting up camp for the guy's tent while Zanatose and Brett set up the girl's tent. It was long and tedious work as they set the poles from their bags and put the fabric on top, and then hammered down the pins.

The group stretched out a little once they were done, "What a relief! Those things weighed a ton!" said Bill. Brett shook his head as he laughed at them. "We should rustle up some grub don't you think Zanatose?" asked Bill.

Zanatose was standing on a hill and staring at the horizon. He was startled once Bill called him. "W..what? Oh… yeah why not? I'm not hungry though."

"Yeah neither am I," said Katie. She left to meet up with Zanatose. "Come on, don't lie to me Zanatose," she said to him. Then she whispered into his ear, "What's *wrong*?"

Zanatose gave a deep sigh as he turned from the sunset and looked at her. "*She can't know I'm afraid. She thought she could count on me,*" he thought to himself.

Zanatose took a deep breath and made up a story. He was about to talk when Katie said, "I said don't lie to me. So don't make something up," she said.

"Fine, the truth is I'm afraid too. I've acted like I'm sure of everything, but I'm not. I might be more afraid than any of you!" he sighed. Katie did not look alarmed, but was smiling.

"Oh come on Zanatose, lighten up! It's not that bad. We're all fine still," she said.

Zanatose felt slightly reassured. He noticed that all around them was becoming very dark. "Everyone into your tents!" called out Bill.

As Zanatose and Katie walked back to camp Zanatose said, "If you need anything, anything at all just call for me. I'll be there…. and goodnight… *I hope.*" He said under his breath. He could see his breath in the chill night air; this was slightly disconcerting for him, considering how warm the day was; it was almost like an omen of coming doom. He could hear howls echoing throughout the air. Zanatose walked into his dark tent and unpacked his worn out sleeping bag. Brett, Bill, and Edwin's sleeping bags were no better. Especially Brett's which was ripped up. "What happened there?" asked Zanatose as he pointed to Brett's old bag.

Brett shook his head and laughed. "This is what happens when you are spying on the wolfos. I'm lucky that they found me worthless, otherwise I'd be dead."

"Think the girls are fine?" asked Edwin. Zanatose turned uneasily in his bag.

The girls heard a moan and were startled out of their dreams. "What was that!" asked Alexis in a hushed scream. They heard lots of movement and more moans growing nearer.

"It's the wind or something," said Katie reassuringly. "Let's just go to sleep."

"Alright," said Alexis as she shut her eyes tightly. Katie went to sleep as well.

Katie woke up in the middle of the night and yawned. She still heard the moans. "What an eerie night, Alexis," she said as she sat up. "*AAAH!!*" she screamed loudly. Alexis was gone, and a long bloody talon was tearing through the ceiling, making an unwanted sun roof in the night. The thing cut the tent open and Katie screamed louder as she saw a ghostly white figure with long black hair that covered its face. Its skin was decomposing in spots, and its white dress was covered in blood.

As Katie ran away, tree roots grabbed her and tied her hands. There were many more of those things approaching from behind her. They were all ghostly white and covered with blood. The undead staggered as they walked toward her. She screamed again as they drew near. Everything started turning darker than night.

As they drew nearer, a new figure surrounded by a dark light appeared. *"NO! YOU WILL NOT HURT HER!"* roared Zanatose as he jumped forward with both swords. Zanatose seemed strange though; his eyes were wide and completely black, and a dark current of electricity circled him in his rage. He ran at the mass and stabbed two in the back. They both fell and twitched. The rest of the zombies turned around and went toward him. More came up from behind him too, rising up from the ground he stood on.

"Zanatose, NO!" Katie screamed as a black swirling ball of energy destroyed the tree to her right that was holding her. She fell to the ground, on her feet, in an almost cat-like fashion. She stayed where she was, transfixed with fear.

The zombies had surrounded Zanatose, and they stared at him with their cold, dead, and red eyes full of hunger. *"Come on, unless you're afraid,"* said a strange echoing voice. He didn't know where it was coming from, but it sounded evil. *"Come now. You aren't afraid are you?"* They moved in closer.

Zanatose froze; he was shivering and *was* afraid. The voice in his head told him not to remain still, not to fear the fight. Zanatose was stalk still. He could not help it; he stared into their dead eyes and hoped to find some peace. He was too afraid to fight them. As the nearest one raised a long bloody talon and swung down something dark flickered in him; a dark rage that was uncontrollable.

Zanatose did an immediate flip forward and stabbed both swords into the zombie's back. The zombie fell with a thud against the cold grassless ground. Dust rose from beneath it as darkness filled the night. Zanatose brought his swords out from inside the zombie's back and stood up facing the enraged zombies surrounding him. They gave a scream of horror as they flew straight at Zanatose. They glowed with a silver aura in the moon light.

Zanatose now showed absolutely no fear; he had a dark presence in his soul that gave him courage and strength. He flipped in the dark night sky and slashed the zombies one by one. The battle was easy for him until a zombie grabbed his leg and kept him on the ground.

The zombie's grip did not weaken, and others began to pile on top of him. "No! Zanatose!" Katie screamed.

"We can't let his heroics go to waste! We must leave now!" Brett yelled as the group got up and went toward the distant woods. The team went against their will, but they knew they could not help Zanatose even if they wanted to. They ran for their life with their hearts low and a feeling of doom looming over them.

As the group, except Alexis, ran ahead Katie stopped and looked back. She stared at the scene as her eyes streamed with tears then… *"COME BACK! HE'S ALIVE!"* She screamed as she swept her tears off.

The pile suddenly gave a dark purple glow as Zanatose used his dark powers and rose against the weight of the zombies. As he stood, he pushed off the zombies that were still clinging to him. Unfortunately, the zombies did not relent.

More zombies came up from beneath him and surrounded him, but now he had gained control of his dark powers. His legs were clouded by a dark haze as he leapt up as high as the moon and came down, stabbing his sword into the ground. A dark current of electricity came up from the ground; the zombies gave a deafening screech as they fell back into the ground.

The group, led by Katie, ran toward him as he fell, exhausted, to the ground. He rolled onto his back, and his eyes rolled over in his head as he trembled. He could barely move; the transformation and use of the dark energy had drained him. His arm stung badly and he rolled over clutching his burning arm. As he released his hand, he looked at his wrist and saw that the black burn mark on his arm had grown even longer toward his elbow.

Now he could see a snake's head burned into his arm. Its eyes gave a red glint in the moonlight against his pink skin. Zanatose's eyes grew wide. As he stared at it he saw his friends approaching and he pulled down his sleeve hurriedly, hiding the dark mark. He staggered up onto his feet with great anguish.

"Zanatose, are you okay?" asked Bill as he helped Zanatose to his feet. Katie and Brett stood at his side with worrisome eyes.

"I'm alright," coughed Zanatose. He could barely catch his breath after the events. Zanatose still didn't understand what had happened. All he knew is that another part of himself he had been fighting took the better of him, and he had gained near invincible powers. Although, after all of this, his arm stung badly as if on fire, and when he looked at it, he saw the marking of a snake burned into his arm.

"Are you sure you're okay?" asked Edwin as he looked at Zanatose crossly.

Brett turned away and thought to himself, "*So, that is the power of the Dark blade?*"

"Is… is Alexis all right?" asked Zanatose as he almost fell backwards. He looked around at everyone's grim faces. He understood, collapsed to his knees and ruffling his hair with his hands, "No, I thought… she's fine!" he looked up hoping to see them crack a smile.

Brett saw that Zanatose was still in denial so he decided to clear any doubt he had. "She's gone, Zanatose, look around you. Do you see her? You did your best. It's not your fault," he said in a comforting voice.

"We won't let her death be in vain!" yelled Zanatose as

he suddenly got to his feet just to fall back down again. Bill and Edwin rushed over again and helped him up.

"Guess we should rest here for the rest of the night since you're injured, Zanatose," said Bill.

"No, we have already lost one. Now I'm too weak to even fight one more of those things. We have to head for the woods as Brett said," ordered Zanatose. They started their hike to the woods.

CHPT 6:
NIGHT STALKERS

The group carried on slowly and silently, in constant fear of the eerie chaos of a night that was filled with noise. The silence was suddenly broken by a loud, ferocious bird call. The group was greatly startled by this, but continued soon after, once they felt it was safe.

They came upon the woods at last. No one spoke a word because they all understood they must overcome their fears and go through the woods.

The night was cold, silent, and had an occult feeling, as if they were being watched. Their encounter with the undead army demolished all of their hope, joy, and courage. They walked forward as empty shells. The only ones who had any hope of the future were Zanatose, Brett, and Katie. Each of them saw the future differently.

Katie felt there was some hope that the people at the city of Nijad would finish their journey for them. Brett felt they would get help on their journey from Nijad and other cities of righteous men. As for Zanatose, his thoughts of the future did not bring him hope, but a reason to go on. He wanted to finish the quest and keep the rest alive, and he wanted to understand his sword's full potential and its origin. Katie was scared stiff of the current situation, but Zanatose and Brett were hiding their fear the best they could.

Even though they tried to hide their fear, they both

walked very slowly. Zanatose had finally regained enough energy to walk on his own, and Katie leaned on his shoulder to stay close to him. He was the group's hero and guardian in her eyes.

She felt, as did the entire group except Brett, that Zanatose would always be there. He made her feel calm in the perilous night. She made Zanatose confident in his own abilities.

The sky that night was filled with stars and a full moon. It seemed peaceful enough, not a single cloud in the sky. All was quite except for a few owls which startled the group now and then. "Are you sure this leads to Nijad city?" Zanatose whispered to Brett so that Katie couldn't hear.

"Of course, or I hope so at least," said Brett unsurely in the gently moonlit darkness.

The group was starting to doze off from fatigue. Some of the group saw yellow eyes staring at them through the night, but Brett just dismissed this as insanity from lack of sleep. No one in the group could walk straight and Zanatose staggered painfully forward. Katie helped him to walk again. She was exhausted, but she stayed by Zanatose's side to keep him on his feet.

As the night went on, at a drawling pace, there seemed to be more and more interruptions to the silence. The silent night was broken by the constant chorus of crows in the night. "WHAT WAS THAT?" yelled Bill in a panic; Edwin dragged his sword out of its sheath lazily.

"Nothing, you coward," said Zanatose rather harshly. Zanatose was barely awake, but even he knew it was just a crow.

"Easy for you to say; you're barely awake," remarked Bill. Zanatose glared at him, but did nothing since he was so tired. "See," said Bill with pleasure, seeing that he was stronger than Zanatose for once.

"Real nice, Bill. Pick on him when he's weak from his last

fight," said Edwin as he laughed at Bill. "By the way, what exactly did you do in that last fight?" Bill growled at him as they continued on the wood's dark dirt path. Zanatose looked up to see the large canopy of trees above them. Everything was black, and one of the moving twigs was rather hairy.

"*What a weird twig*," thought Zanatose then he saw another hairy twig emerge from the canopy. Zanatose was about to hide in fear, but he noticed Katie was there. "*You saw nothing*," Zanatose thought to himself.

As the group walked on, interrupted now and then by horrific animal sounds like hisses and nearby howls, they saw sticky webs between trees. In the webs they saw the bones and rusted armor of knights and many animals. As Katie gasped in horror, she let go of Zanatose, and he noticed he had gained enough strength to stand.

Ahead, branches clattered and many leaves fell. Through the branches Bill saw many long hairy legs. "I... I saw something up there. It... it's big!" Bill yelled in fear. He looked terrified and so did Zanatose. Zanatose could no longer hide his fear; there were huge spiders in the woods. Zanatose had already known there were spiders in every wooded area, but he was worried the woods were infested by huge, cursed arachnids.

"It's nothing you two 'fraidy ca... AAH!" yelled Brett as he was taken up the tree by a chubby, hungry spider. The spider was fat, drooling, and had eight red eyes that stared hungrily at every one in turn, looking for the next meal he would take away.

Edwin was climbing up the tree when an even larger spider helped him up for dinner. Katie and Bill screamed in panic. Zanatose was terrified from spiders, and was still pretty tired from his last fight, but he thought if he used his sword's powers he could help.

Zanatose took out his sword and concentrated as hard as he could. The sword gave him energy, but it still didn't take hold. The sword's power was slowly soothing his exhausted muscles with its overwhelming power. He was growing nervous as he felt his own strength leaving him and a cold darkness replacing it; it almost felt like death was taking hold of his heart. A spider came down from above him. Katie screamed, and Bill stood petrified as the huge spider dropped itself above Zanatose.

It was the first step for Zanatose, toward his destined path. The dark powers immediately took full hold upon him. He turned pale, his eyes became black beads, and his nails turned into long talons. He quickly back flipped out of the way and slashed the spider with both his talons and sword. Something, unnoticed by the group, with a heavy, raspy breath was behind a tree watching Zanatose.

Zanatose, this time, had supernatural speed. He swiftly jumped branch to branch until he got to the upper canopy where the spiders thought they were safe. He easily ripped through the webbings in his way as he jumped up.

At the top level Brett and Edwin were ensnared in webbing. Zanatose started walking toward them and a spider pounced on him. The spider sank his venomous teeth into his back, but he simply shook off the gigantic spider as if it was a clinging infant. Many more spiders attacked him and he reacted quickly and gave a few of them round house kicks which sent them flying into a distant tree trunk.

As he slowly walked forward, waiting for opposition to feed his temper a group of spiders jumped onto him. He dropped his sword, but his powers still remained. He shredded the spiders to bits with his razor sharp talons. He quickly jumped over the webbing in the way, and slashed Brett and Edwin free. Brett and Edwin were held by a simple string of webbing, dangling them over the tree tops. They fell all the way down and landed with a loud thud onto the ground.

Brett moaned as he rubbed his leg he fell on. "My head,"

moaned Edwin as he held his head. He tried to roll on his landing to avoid too much pain, but he rolled into a tree trunk. His head was bleeding lightly.

Zanatose landed on his feet right in front of them, cat like. They looked at Zanatose with amazement that he could stand. Zanatose soon collapsed to his knees clutching his arm; he was back to normal. Fortunately, no one had noticed the change in the darkness and panic. He did not remove his hand; it burned so badly he wanted to die. He fell onto his side and rolled in pain as he clutched his burning arm.

"Zanatose, what happened to your arm?" asked Katie. She took his hand away and gasped at the long snake she saw; the burn had reached his elbow.

"What is it?" asked Bill. They were all huddled around, but Katie covered his arm with his sleeve.

"It's a terrible bruise," she said. She gave Zanatose a look telling him they are going to have a talk about this.

"Zanatose, you sure you're okay?" asked Edwin. Edwin was very concerned for Zanatose after such a leap.

"Yeah," coughed Zanatose. "I think we." He coughed several more times. "I think we should move on," he said in a strangled voice. He sat up straight, but couldn't stand up so Katie tried to help him up. She tried, but couldn't. She was also too tired to support his weight.

Brett walked over and told her to lead the group forward. "I have a debt to pay to you after that. I think I'll start with carrying you." Brett grabbed onto Zanatose and brought Zanatose to his feet. "Let's go that way," he said to Katie as he pointed toward the north. As they continued on Zanatose regained enough energy to stagger on his own. With a monstrous effort, he slowly bent down to grab his sword.

They walked on small spiders while they continued their travels. They even saw a baby squirrel. "That's so cute!" Katie said in a baby voice as she stopped to look at the little brown squirrel. It quickly scurried right and left as if in a hurry. As she went down to pet it a huge nuzzle and sharp teeth came out of the bushes and swallowed the squirrel whole. Katie gave a high pitched scream and ran back behind Zanatose.

A huge wolfo emerged from behind the bushes. It had a towering figure, and had long, muscular, lanky arms which were armed with sharp claws. It walked on both hind legs up to the group while two more of them burst out of bushes from behind the group. Another one dashed ferociously toward Katie. Zanatose whirled around as the wolfo stopped and gave a menacing laugh. Zanatose drew his dark sword. A strange whirl wind and black gas circled his sword and continued up his arm. Zanatose shuddered, his eyes rolled around, and then he fell unconscious to the ground. A voice mocked him as he fell, "*Is that all it takes for you to fall?*"

The others drew their weapons with a great effort. A wolfo rounded on Katie and walked toward her. Brett leapt toward it, and the wolfo kicked Zanatose's body onto him. Brett hit the ground hard and was left breathless. He wheezed a little, but got up and took Blazer from Zanatose's side and ran at the beast with dual weapons.

The wolfos charged in at the small group. One wolfo easily slapped away Edwin's sword with its huge arms, and slashed at him. Edwin was left with a cut across his chest and he was unconscious shortly after. Brett was using his two swords to fight two wolfos, attacking from opposite sides. One wolfo slapped away Blazer, leaving him with just his staff. He backed up as he twirled his staff like a baton, trying to keep them away.

Bill charged his sword and blasted at a wolfo, which quickly kicked the blast right back at him, knocking him into a tree. The blast was weak due to Bill's exhaustion. The wolfo watched as Bill tried to get up. Brett saw he was distracted and ran at him. Another wolfo immediately leapt out from a nearby bush and rammed Brett against a tree.

The huge wolfo pinned Brett against the tree. The wolfo

got into his face and he could feel the wolfo's hot, heavy breathing as it spoke in a slow growling rasp. "You, you are brave weakling. You and your friend are dangerous. We like tricky meals." It gave a menacing bark and licked its lips.

"We're not to eat so... BACK UP OR ELSE!" Brett yelled as he tried to get free. This only made the wolfo laugh and push him against the tree even harder. The tree had very rough bark, scraping against it was intolerable. The wolfo now looked hungry, and it started squeezing almost playfully against Brett's throat.

Katie helped Bill up, and he slowly went toward Blazer, hoping the wolfos would not see. They were all transfixed with a weak human standing up to all of them. "Your friend is too weak now anyway. We take you to lord; he wanted you," said the wolfo as several more wolfos grabbed onto Brett and carried him off toward the dim light in the east.

"Stop and fight me!" Bill yelled as he leaped at a wolfo holding onto Brett's arm.

Another wolfo from the field pounced onto him and slammed him to the ground. It licked its lips and said in a growl, "Grr. If only we could feast on more. Our master Fang only wanted him," he nodded his head toward the trees they had taken Brett through. It hit Bill with its head and knocked him out. The wolfo pranced after his group.

The wolfos had left with Brett captive. The group's resistance was a joke for their strength. Katie was cradling Zanatose as a hungry stray wolfo was jumping around, acting like it would pounce. It left after a short while to follow its pack like all the rest. Katie noticed they were heading east. Katie was left alone; everyone else lay unconscious. She was deeply troubled by the loss of Brett, and that Zanatose had fallen so easily. He used to be the group's hero, but it seemed he had his weaknesses too.

As Katie was cradling Zanatose's head, she slowly fell asleep too. After a few hours he twitched in his sleep.

"Zanatose!" Katie said, relieved to see she wasn't alone any more. Zanatose gave a soft moan and opened his eyes slowly.

"What happened?" he wheezed. Katie's eyes were full of tears as she told him the story. She whispered how the others tried to help, but failed.

Zanatose and the others regained the ability to stand and walk by sunrise. Zanatose stood up and looked at the entire group with a serious face. "We are going to head east to follow those wolfos and get Brett back," he said as he threw his fist up into the air. He looked at the team and saw they didn't look very enthusiastic. "*WHAT'S WRONG WITH ALL OF YOU!*" he yelled, full of rage. He looked at all of them, but they didn't look back. They were too embarrassed to look up at him.

"We- we were d-defeated," said Bill in a trembling voice. He looked up at Zanatose and said, "Even *you!* Our benevolent leader was defeated by th- the wolfos." He looked down at his feet with embarrassment.

Edwin also looked sorry. His tunic's sleeve was torn off and he had slash marks on his chest. Katie who used to have full faith in Zanatose had also lost some of her hope.

"It's just too much. We didn't ask for this," Edwin said.

"Fine then, you may all come and help until we get to Nijad and then choose if you want to continue. For now Brett needs us so let's go," said Zanatose. And so they started their journey to save Brett from the wolfos.

CHPT 7:
GENERAL WOLF FANG

The group was now out of the woods, and it was midmorning. The sun was shining brightly, and there were remains of old fires scattered on the dirt path. Zanatose was infuriated partly from his team's incompetence and partly from Shadow draining his energy like a fat leech. He did not expect the sword's powers to drain him as if it were trying to eat his soul. It was a horrible feeling that Zanatose could not completely understand.

The group knew he was very angry, and they kept their distance, except for Bill. "I will help you no matter what Zanatose. We're friends and friends are cool like that," said Bill.

"Really?" Zanatose asked mockingly. He had a sinister gleam in his eyes. The team completely failed the one time he was not there to bail them out. "You guys need a babysitter! You're not warriors *yet*," he said. He made it seem like he had confidence in them becoming warriors eventually by adding "yet."

"Come on, Zanatose! We were all tired from being awake. Even you failed!" Bill argued trying to make himself seem innocent.

"Bill! I was the only one who stepped forward to fight off all those zombies and spiders. Without help from either you or Edwin," he said with finality. "This will also be the

53

same. I will save Brett on my own, not that you could help even if you tried." Bill looked furious; he was about to talk, but Zanatose was quicker. "If you come, you'll just become another person I would have to save."

Zanatose said everything in a cold, unnatural voice. At the end of the conversation his teeth were chattering and he looked cold. Katie took notice and walked with him. "Zanatose, what's going on?" she asked him. She didn't look angry, but concerned. Zanatose looked at her blankly and was turning red.

"*What should I tell her? I don't want her to know that I feel like this whole journey is going to end with all of their deaths,*" he thought.

Katie looked at him and said, "I want the truth about your sword and that snake marking on your arm."

Zanatose was about to talk, but another part of him wanted to tear her to shreds for no apparent reason. He turned pale for a second, but his conscience took over again and he was back to normal. Katie seemed calm; she knew he would never attack her. Zanatose shook his head under the morning sun. His dark black hair glimmered in the sunlight. He closed his eyes and decided it was time to tell someone about the dark powers of his sword. Maybe then he can learn to tame the sword and withstand its mysterious powers.

"Here's the story, Kate," he said grimly. They were behind Edwin and Bill, walking only a little slower as they talked so that the two would not hear them. "When I picked up the sword, it shocked me and left a start to a snake's tail burned onto my wrist. After that the sword has morphed me more and more into a dark warrior of some kind. It almost made me go mad when you asked me about the sword. Sometimes I wonder who's in charge- me or the darkness in the sword. Who could have been mad enough to use a sword like this in such a dark war," he said as he looked down at his sword. He nervously toyed with its sheath.

He looked very gloomy and he slowly turned his head up to see what Katie had to say. To his pleasant surprise he saw her smile at him. "Well, that's not too bad, right?" she gave a little giggle. Zanatose looked at her as if she was crazy. "Maybe you didn't notice, but you told me that the sword tried to make you attack me... you stopped it!" she said gleefully. "Don't you see, Zanatose? You are not evil, so the sword could never fully consume you. For you it is safe as long as you have your friends and your own inner strength. This sword chose you because you can control it."

She looked at him cheerfully. He didn't care much for what she said, but he felt comforted that she was not outraged or afraid of him. Zanatose felt that the situation was nowhere near that simple; he had felt the power of that sword, and it was not something to be controlled by anyone except by the greatest hero, or the greatest villain.

He gave a heavy sigh and looked up at her. Her blonde hair was dazzlingly beautifully in the sun light. Her beauty grasped his attention for a moment too long and he stumbled on some black rocks. He fell, but broke his fall with his hands. Zanatose stood back up with Katie's help.

"You okay?" she asked. He nodded as he looked down to see what he tripped on. He saw a ring of black smoldered rocks. It seemed like there was a fire there relatively recently. He wondered whether or not wolfos would need a fire, but concluded that if these were not left by wolfos, they were left by something worse like a traveling army. The last thing the ragged group could handle was a trained army.

As Zanatose looked ahead to Bill and Edwin, he saw many more remains of fires scattered across the plain, grass field. Bill also stumbled on a cluster of blackened rocks. Katie and Zanatose ran toward them. "Hey guys, wait! It looks like a lot of people were here," Zanatose said to them.

"Yeah, people... or wolfos," Edwin said grimly as he looked down at the ring.

"Either way, we'll find out the hard way," said Bill. "Let's keep moving. I hope we're not too late to save Brett."

"That's right, Bill. Let's move guys," said Zanatose confidently. Zanatose was still angry at them, but he just did not care at the time. He thought that there might be trouble up ahead, so he needed to try and stay calm and keep his anger at bay. As they moved forward, they saw holes for tents in the ground too. The group was becoming increasingly uneasy. The possibility that some foe was up ahead was growing, and the foe had very large numbers.

"Zanatose, you think we can stand up to all those wolfos a second time without Brett?" asked Edwin. Edwin asked this in fear of Zanatose's reaction, he still seemed very unapproachable.

"Definitely," said Zanatose with a wink. "You have something this time you didn't have before. You've got me this time," said Zanatose. Zanatose's spirits jumped up when he saw Katie laugh at his haughty remarks. Some joy in the group helped him, out and he was not as angry anymore.

The day was sunny and not as hot as the day before. Since it was not as hot, Zanatose he could finally see the land's beauty. The sun lit up the many oak trees, and gave life to the various fragrant flowers along the way. There was a calming breeze in the air that drove away all of the group's fears. The sun got into their eyes but it was still better than yesterday. *"At least it's not as hot as yesterday,"* Zanatose thought.

They walked on forward for a whole of two hours until about noon. Zanatose decided they were walking for too long and should rest a bit. "Guys!" he yelled to get their attention. "I think we should stop for a bit to eat, and drink some water."

"About time," Edwin whispered to Bill. They decided to stop and make a fire at a spot which already had been used before.

"That's funny; it's still warm," Bill said as he laid down some fire wood.

Edwin came back with a hand full of wood and placed it on top. Zanatose lit the fire with some rocks he had packed. Once he was done, he placed the rocks back into his old bag. "Bill, don't worry. It's warm, meaning the things that were here already had left and are kind of nearby, so it's good that we stopped," said Zanatose calmly as he stuck a flattened chicken leg on a stick to cook over the fire.

"I guess you're right," Bill said as he also found some meat in his bag to cook.

"Of course I'm right," said Zanatose. "Where's Katie?" he asked with urgency. "I just remembered she hasn't come back yet."

"Is that her?" asked Edwin as he pointed to a running figure. It was Katie and when she reached them she was out of breath, but still gasped in enough air to speak.

"There... the... there's a huge army back there!" she screamed as hundreds of men on huge horses came over the hill. They all wore identical golden armor chest plates and had red shields with a large, golden lion emblazoned on them. Their horses called out loudly and threw back their heads viciously as the whole group came to an abrupt halt.

From behind the lines a heavily muscled man on a giant horse rode to them with a magnificent golden blade in his hands. Zanatose drew both Blazer and Shadow instinctively, seeing a man that large with such a sword awoke an immediate response of panic in him. He stood ready for the enemy's charge, but it never came. The man on the horse pulled on the reigns and the horse stopped before Zanatose. Edwin and Bill were behind Zanatose. Katie was even further back behind Edwin and Bill.

The man had thick black hair, a strong jaw, and his shield bore the symbol of a lion. He spoke clearly and officially. "My name is General Jonathan Gateman. What is your business here wanderers?" he asked. General Jonathan Gateman's armor looked like he had seen many battles, but his sword was still fine and unaltered. His armor's shoulders looked like they had been hammered back into the appropriate shape far too often.

Zanatose looked at Jonathan's large muscular build and back at the huge army on the hill and decided not to be too violent. He cleared his throat and looked at his team; they looked just as worried as he was. They had all drawn their weapons except Katie who did not have a weapon.

He looked back up into Jonathan's stiff, brown eyes. He could not see if Jonathan was happy or ready to kill him, but he decided to answer the question. He gave a small bow and said, "My name is Zanatose. I'm the leader of this group."

He gestured toward his group and continued with his response. "Recently in our village, we were attacked by shadow creatures, so we decided to go on a quest to stop the shadow beasts. Unfortunately along the way, we ran into the wolfos, and they kidnapped my friend Brett. We are heading this way in search of the wolfos to get him back," Zanatose said. He waited and held onto his weapons tightly and was ready to fight in case Jonathan was against them. He could see kindness in Jonathan's eyes, but such a large and well-armed army does not ride around to aid travelers.

Jonathan smiled at him. "Good, we can use you and your team. We are assaulting the wolfos as well because they raided our peace partner, the city of Nijad. We are hoping to stop the wolfos before they attack our grand home, Theragorn City. You may come with us as long as you fight the wolfos and not us," Jonathan said. "As a matter of fact I happen to know Brett. He's a good friend of mine. He's an elite guard at Nijad castle right?" Zanatose and the group nodded vigorously. They finally felt a little bit more at ease since an entire army was on their side. "Well then, what are we waiting for? It is time to move men, MARCH!" Jonathan yelled to his army.

Jonathan rode on his horse and led the army and Zanatose toward where their intelligence reported the wolfos meeting point to be. As they rode onward, Jonathan asked Zanatose about what the wolfos had said when they attacked them. "I'm not sure; you should ask Bill or Katie. I was um… out of commission."

During his brief pause, Zanatose noticed one of the stranger soldiers with long black hair staring at him. The soldier had conniving snake eyes. "Who is he?" Zanatose asked as he pointed to the soldier. The man looked like he was tainted by some kind of dark magic.

"Oh him? He's my sharpest soldier. His name is Gray. He's the one that scouted out the whereabouts of the wolfos," Jonathan said proudly. They rode up to Bill together and Jonathan asked him the same question that he had asked Zanatose.

"Well, the wolfos said its master, Fang, wanted Brett and said Zanatose was too weak at the time," said Bill.

"Why would they want to take Brett?" Zanatose asked Jonathan.

"I'm not sure," Jonathan said unsurely. "Unless Brett's just bait… it's a trap," Jonathan murmured to himself. "We must be careful," he said to Zanatose. Zanatose nodded in agreement. "I'll ask it from my top man, Gray. GRAY, COME HERE!" Jonathan yelled. The strange man heeded the command but came leisurely with little interest.

Now that Zanatose saw him close up, he saw that Gray seemed exhausted. He looked very healthy and strong, but he looked tired just like Zanatose after he used the dark sword too many times. "My friend here says the treacherous General Fang has taken their friend Brett for no apparent reason. Do you understand where Fang is going with this strange ploy?" asked Jonathan.

Gray looked down at Zanatose and smiled at him under dark eyes. The question seemed to bring a smirk to his cruel face. Gray spoke in a low rumbling voice similar to the wolfos. "General Fang is an evil warrior of great power, but I do not see purpose in all of his actions. Perhaps he was just a little hungry," he sneered at Zanatose.

Zanatose was about to talk, but one of Jonathan's soldiers came running and made an announcement. "The wolfos are here!" he yelled and pointed to the woods.

To their horror, they saw every tree branch lined with the hungry wolfos army like vultures lined up to feast upon their prey. The sun gleamed and revealed the beautiful white fur coats of the wolfos. Zanatose turned to look at Gray, but saw Gray draw a dark staff similar to his sword. Gray ran into the woods and Zanatose followed, knowing something was askew.

Jonathan turned on his horse and bellowed out commands to his army. "EVERY ONE READY!" all the men turned toward the wolfos and drew their weapons. Edwin and Bill stood as body guards for Katie. "ATTACK!" and all the men went forward to fight the wolfos.

It was not a fair fight at all. Each wolfo could easily dispose of a number of soldiers. Bill used his blade's power to assist the soldiers without leaving Katie's side. Both Bill and Edwin knew if another one of their team was lost, Zanatose would kill them both, personally. Jonathan was an expert fighter; he rode by the wolfos and with brute strength easily slashed them through the chest with his huge golden sword. His men were not half as fortunate.

Zanatose ran through trees and crashed through even more branches and bushes. Gray led the way to a small clearing where Brett was tied to a tree. "BRETT!" Zanatose yelled. "What have you done to him?" asked Zanatose with a threatening glare. He skidded against the dirt, coming to an abrupt halt before Gray and Brett.

"So now you know my secret," said Gray with a smile. He took out weapon of choice, a sinister looking bisento. The bisento was a unique weapon with a threatening, gold dagger at the end of an ivory staff. "I am General Wolf Fang!" said Wolf as he transformed into a larger version of Zanatose's transformations.

Zanatose in reply drew his sword. "So you're Fang? I expected you to be a wolfo," said Zanatose.

"From the stories my wolfos said of you, I expected you to be bigger. You're shorter than your friends. I hope looks are deceiving," said Fang.

"Why did you take Brett?" asked Zanatose as he tightened his grip on Shadow and looked around to make sure they were alone.

Fang was still smiling as he replied, "To bring a mighty warrior of great power to my side against the shadows."

"I would never join you! Now let go of Brett or else!" Zanatose yelled. He again tightened his grip on his sword; he knew that Fang was probably more effective with the dark powers than he was.

"Why don't you just join me? We can lead the wolfos army and defeat the shadows together! It is our sacred powers that have chosen such a path for us," Fang said. He looked on at Zanatose who seemed unsure. "You are young; you don't see that we are not evil."

"But Brett said…" Fang immediately cut him off and spoke.

"They call us evil because we're different, but we deserve the same respect as everyone else. To be a good leader, you must understand the difference between good and evil for yourself. Good and evil are mere opinions." Zanatose stood pondering what he believed makes a decision either right or wrong.

"If we're fighting for the same cause, then how could I see him as evil? Was I too quick to judge? Isn't he simply taking

another rout that I'm just too afraid to take?," wondered Zanatose to himself.

"Join us Zanatose or face the consequences," concluded Fang. Fang had begun to feel impatient with Zanatose's uncertainty and was curious as to the limits of Zanatose's power.

"Never," said Zanatose as he stood erect, ready to fight.

"You are a fool to oppose me Zanatose!" Fang rushed at Zanatose with incredible speed. Fang's swift and heavy steps scattered the leaves around him, making him seem like a crazed demon.

Zanatose blocked with his sword, but could barely resist falling. He was amazed by the power Fang possessed. The fight was a hopeless resistance on Zanatose's behalf, but he just couldn't give up. Whether or not Fang was right did not matter to him; he only wanted to save Brett.

Zanatose pushed off Fang's blade and slashed back with all of his force. Fang blocked, and they stood pushing against each others' weapons. Fang used his dark powers and gave a strong push that sent Zanatose stumbling backwards.

"You can't win Zanatose," Fang said as Zanatose stood up painfully and ran at him again. Fang stuck out his staff and gave an energy blast. The blast was a huge, sparkling sphere of dark matter. "Use your own powers and maybe this fight will be even."

"Here I come!" Zanatose yelled. He began to remember Alexis's death, the spiders, the wolfos, and finally the pathetic sight of Brett tied to a tree. He could no longer endure all of the pain. His life had turned into a hell within days, and he was not about to let any more lives be lost. His rage took control, and he turned pale, his eyes grew wide, and he grew talons for hands. Zanatose felt a surge of adrenaline pulse through his body; he felt like a caged dog let loose. He used his dark power and rammed through Fang's blast and against Fang's chest.

Fang snickered with a stiff breathe. He could feel the darkness coursing through Zanatose. Fang was impressed by this show of strength, and he gave a left hook with his free hand that collided harshly against Zanatose's jaw. Zanatose let out an inhuman growl and returned the blow with a clenched fist against Fang's abdomen. The impact did not hurt Zanatose, but it added fuel to the fire in his heart.

Now the fight was raised to intense levels. They thrashed and slashed at each other as fast as their dark powers would let them. The two leviathans gave energy blasts back and forth; they ruined sections of the forest in this way. The orbs of pure energy shredded the trees, creating a hail storm of splinters.

At last they clashed in a stale mate until Fang gave Zanatose a back kick in the lower abdomen, making him keel over. "Very good for an amateur," said Fang with a smirk of delight on his face. "If you join my ranks, you would learn more of the dark powers I know and together we could rule *this* world and vanquish the darkness."

"Why don't *we* finish this now?" said Zanatose through gritted teeth. He was back to normal; he drew Blazer and threw it at the rope holding Brett. The sword cut through the rope and Brett fell to his knees awkwardly, and got back up, drawing his staff as he passed Blazer back to Zanatose.

"We'll defeat you together Fang!" Brett yelled. Zanatose had both swords ready and Brett had a slight limp, but was ready. "Now come on unless you're scared." Brett had a look of pure hatred for Fang. The look was only skin deep. Brett was not a bitter man, although he could kill for the right cause, he could not hate for any cause.

Fang laughed at them, "What a pathetic attempt. You really think you two can beat the commander of the wolfos?" laughed Fang.

"No, I believe *we* can defeat you together," said Jonathan as he joined the ranks with Zanatose and Brett.

Fang's grin vanished, but he was still very haughty. "Alright, it shouldn't be too difficult to defeat all of you." He took out a glistening black crystal which he jammed into the base of his bisento. The bisento was surrounded by a dark aura of energy from the crystal's power. "This is where the real fun begins," Fang laughed demonically.

Fang turned into his dark form again, and he used his dark powers to jump behind them in a matter of seconds. The team turned and tried to fight him. Brett was quickly elbowed in the face by Fang; the impact caused his lip to bleed as he crashed into a nearby tree, grazing his shoulder against the bark.

Zanatose tried to slash Fang with both swords coming down, but Fang blocked that with his bisento. Jonathan tried to drive his sword into him like a lance. Fang kicked Jonathan's sword out of his hands and pushed Zanatose aside with his free arm. Jonathan ran to grab his sword and saw Fang going for it too. Jonathan jumped for the sword, but just like a bad dream, Fang was there above the sword before him with his foot resting on it.

Fang looked down at Jonathan with a dark grin. "So this is where it ends for you General? How pitiful; kneeling before my feat as I slaughter you," he said, laughing at Jonathan. He raised his bisento and stabbed down at him.

"No!" Zanatose yelled. He was furious at Fang for kidnapping Brett and his dark powers took over again. Dark electricity came out of his sword and rammed Fang through a tree. The tree gave a loud crack as it split in two, covering the entire area with wood chips.

Jonathan was shocked for a moment until he remembered where he was and grabbed his sword, running back to Zanatose's side. The second half of the tree fell with an earth-shaking crash.

Brett was hurt badly and could not get up, so he sat under

a tree, leaning on its trunk. "Where'd Fang go?" he asked. He surveyed the area hurriedly, but saw no movement.

Zanatose walked slowly to where the fallen tree was with both swords ready to stab down at anything there. Once he looked over the trunk, he saw that there was nothing. "He's gotten away," he said disappointedly. Zanatose placed his swords back into their sheaths as he walked over to Brett and tried to help him up.

"Bravo! Bravo my new friend," Jonathan said to Zanatose with applause. "I hope you plan to keep fighting by my side. You were magnificent against General Wolf Fang," Jonathan said cheerfully.

Zanatose looked up at him from under Brett's weight with a chuckle. He felt honored to be offered to fight in an army. "I'm sorry, but as I told you I have a bigger, more dangerous journey to attend too. I couldn't stay and enroll in your army if I wanted to," Zanatose said.

"I understand," said Jonathan as he nodded with disappointment.

Brett was very grim because he knew they were going to be stalked by the wolfos throughout their journey. Fortunately one of Jonathan's battle-worn men pranced into the scene with joyous news. "SIR!" he yelled out of breath. He stopped before Jonathan and took a deep breath. "I bring you marvelous news!"

"Go on, out with it man!" Jonathan yelled.

"The wolfos are retreating and moving back north to where they came from," he said with great pride.

"Yes," Brett and Zanatose hissed as they patted each other gently on the back.

"That is marvelous news indeed. You are dismissed soldier and tell all the others we're going home at last. The *hunt* has ended for now," Jonathan said cheerfully. He turned to Zanatose and Brett; "Thank you, both of you.

And especially you Zanatose; you saved my life and that is something I will not forget *hero.*"

The three of them staggered back to camp and both Zanatose and Jonathan helped Brett there. They went through the deserted woods and received many scratches from the thorn bushes in their way. Within minutes they reached the camp once more. Everyone there was covered with wounds, but they were cheerful as they ate heaps of food in jubilant celebration.

From the crowd, Katie, Bill, and Edwin ran to greet them. "Zanatose, Brett you guys are alive!" Katie yelped in joy. "We were here holding off the wolfos army while you guys had a one on one with Fang. What was he like?" she asked.

Brett looked at her grimly and said, "He is an elite fighter who could have taken all of our lives if Zanatose didn't use his sword's powers." Zanatose blushed with embarrassment and turned to talk with Bill.

"Get this, Gray was Fang in disguise!" Zanatose said to Bill. Bill was stunned.

"You'd never have guessed from the way he gave an evil smile or laughed in joy when we said Brett was kidnapped. Never," said Edwin sarcastically. They all laughed.

At this point it was early evening. The festivities seemed like they would go on into the next day. As the group was talking together, Jonathan came over with two large glasses filled to the brim with fine red wine. "Come on old chap, join in on some of the fun!" he said with a red face as he elbowed Brett in the rib.

Unfortunately Brett was in bad shape, the playful tap gave him extreme pain and he fell clutching his ribs. Jonathan chuckled and yelled for a medical soldier. As he nodded to the soldier, the soldier, who was bald and thin, pointed to himself in confusion. "Yes you, come over here!"

demanded Jonathan, his light-hearted mood vanished for a moment and revealed a darker side of the General.

"Aye, aye general Gateman," the soldier squeaked in fear of being in trouble.

"Don't look so sour. I just want you to fix up this poor kid," he said as he pointed to Brett on the ground.

The little man wiped off his brow in relief as he bent down to inspect Brett. He poked Brett here and there as Brett moaned in agony. "Oh this is nothing too bad, just a minor fall. I'll just wrap it up a bit, and he'll be fine in a day or two General Gateman." Once he finished, he stood up, saluted Jonathan, and walked Brett to a nearby tent to wrap his injured ribs.

"He is taken care of, back to the festivities," Jonathan said cheerfully.

"Agreed, we need some down time Zanatose, no use in being all serious at a party," said Bill.

"We are not too serious!" Edwin said sarcastically. "Serious is, we come to this party with an army and say goodbye to anything with legs." The group laughed except for Zanatose.

"No," said Bill as he shook his head. "That would make us party poopers. Serious is, we get rid of all their wine because without that, they can't party." He pointed to Jonathan who was red in the face, carrying two glasses, empty glasses.

Zanatose still wasn't laughing, and he had a blank stare. He gazed into the surrounding darkness with a pensive look. "You okay Zanatose?" Katie asked.

"What!?" said Zanatose with panic. "Oh it's you, what a relief."

Katie looked concerned. "Hey you guys go and party!" she said to the rest of the group. Once they left in joy to join in on the festival, Katie turned to Zanatose. "What's wrong now?" she asked almost with an air of impatience.

"Nothing, why would anything be wrong?" he was trying to act innocent.

"Oh come on, I've known you for too long, you can't trick me."

"Fine but it's not good news…"

"…Obviously!"

"Fang wanted me to join sides with him and be second in command."

"That's not a problem just say…"

"… But he brought something to my mind. He said Good and evil are opinions."

"Yeah, so? We already know he's evil."

"He also said…"

"Enough! You listen too much to that guy. Don't worry about what he said. He's just trying to trick you into joining him," she said, trying to ease his mind. This didn't ease his mind though. She was not in the mood to talk, but he needed someone to talk to. He could see the fires of hell rising about him, and he did not know what to do.

CHPT 8:
EVIL OR GOOD?

A dark cloaked figure who is it?
Is it friend or foe?
Be it thy savior or a fiend in disguise?
You ask one he say it foe!
You ask another he say it friend!
Few shadows are seen before they fall, is this
another shadow or your very beacon of hope?

The sun was setting and falling, lazily, under the horizon.
The sun had a breathe taking orange hue as it fell below
the grassy hills in the horizon. An army of hundreds of men
clad in red and yellow armor made their way across this land
with a small group of teenagers walking in the front with the
large and valiant General Gateman.

"Should we make camp General Gateman?" asked Brett.
His wounds had been wrapped up and he felt well enough
to walk again.

"Alright, it is getting close to nightfall. Men set up camp!"
he ordered. Within minutes they had set up camp and a jolly
fire was crackling warmly. They were all full from the food
and drinks of the party, so instead of eating, they polished
their swords and repaired their battle worn armor.

Everyone grouped around the various fires and told
old battle stories. Jonathan, Bill, Brett, Edwin, Katie, and
Zanatose huddled together around one big fire inside
Jonathan's tent.

Everyone was staring at Jonathan in awe as he told them an action-packed battle story. "There I was alone with an enormous ten foot shadow beast towering above me!" Jonathan said in a dramatic voice as he waved his hands around.

"What'd you do sir?" asked one of Jonathan's smaller soldiers. Jonathan turned to him and smiled. The soldier was new to the battle field and had not heard his great General's legends yet.

"I took out my legendary sword of Theragorn," he said as he drew his sword and waved it in the air. "I sliced and diced the thing. It was as easy as one, two, and three until I saw that he had friends." He paused and put on a look of fear as he continued. "There they were; thousands of the hugest shadow beasts this side of the world. It seemed like I was a goner before I even became a General."

"This was when I was younger," he said to the confused faces in the crowd. "Well, now back to the story. Where was I?" Jonathan asked.

"The part where you single handedly take out thousands of shadow beast," Zanatose yawned as he spoke. "You know, your great victory over an army, even though you can't beat Fang without my help." Zanatose laughed at Jonathan's farfetched story. Also, he still had some kind of bent up hostility in his system, as if the dark sword still had some kind of power over him in his normal state.

Jonathan was out-raged by the comments and replied with a forced sense of calm in his voice. "I didn't take them all out single handedly at all, quite the contrary actually. Let me finish the story. Well, there I was alone against an army. I was about to run, but another huge army came from the hills. This army was the army of the great majestic beasts of legend. They were and still are the greatest warriors of all time and their leader was armed with a great mythical sword. This army stormed in on their own four feet and many only used their claws as they ripped the shadow beasts to bits."

Zanatose was puzzled by the last part of the description, as were the rest of the General's crew. "Wait, did you say the soldiers had claws? Last time I checked people don't have claws," he said.

Jonathan laughed at how naive Zanatose and his team were. "These are legendary warriors. They are not human, they are more like wolfos. They are the Hayvan."

"Hayvan?" Bill asked bewildered.

"Hayvan are the land of Nijad's most powerful race. They are part lion, part human, and are a wondrous sight to behold. Very few men have seen them," said Jonathan with great pride.

"Amazing, I hope we get to see them in our journey," said Katie.

"You very well may see them in your journey to stop the shadow beasts," said Jonathan. "Now, who will tell the next story?" he asked cheerfully.

"I will," said Zanatose. That night he told Jonathan and his men the story of how they arrived where they are now, and of the terrible loss of Alexis to the savage zombies. After the story, they decided to go to sleep. Jonathan set up a number of his men as sentries, watching their position. The ground was very rough, but they laid out their sleeping bags and tried their best to go to sleep. They had an uneasy feeling as they tried to sleep in the middle of the quite, eerie night. The moon shined far above them with a menacing red glow.

Early in the morning, as the sun was dim and had just begun rising; a sentry blew the alarm horn. The horn gave a very loud and high-pitched screech that could have awoken the dead from their eternal slumber. The sentry that blew the horn had a huge partner with a loud booming voice who was yelling at the top of his lungs to the army.

"Katie No!" Zanatose yelled as he woke up with a start. He had a terrible nightmare where Katie had fallen into an icy lake in a clearing, and he dove in, but the water turned into ice and Katie was locked in the water. He turned to check on Katie; Zanatose felt great relief as he turned around and saw that he was just dreaming. The chill that had over taken his body resided back into the depths of his mind, a self-made pain.

She was awake and staring at the huge soldier yelling. His yelling woke up the rest of his crew and Jonathan. Jonathan wore a very serious and fearful face. Jonathan looked like he was the one with the nightmare; Jonathan's hair was even messier in the morning than in the day. He abruptly stood up and grabbed Zanatose's arm tightly and yanked him up with himself. The whole army stood up to listen to the call.

"What's wrong?" Zanatose asked in panic. Jonathan silently nodded toward the loud soldier.

"Everyone, attention!" the man yelled in his deep voice. "We could not see in the night, but now we can see that the city of Nijad is under attack by the shadows!" Everyone looked beyond the hill in unison and saw, by the dawn's light, a magnificent flag of green, blue, and red: the flag of Nijad city. The flag had the cross on it, a moon, and a star. The flag symbolized the unity of man's soul: good and evil, moon and star. The pure blue color was for inspiration, the red for courage, and the green was for generosity and prosperity.

The entire army got up and mounted their horses as they raced into Nijad as fast as they could. To this army of conquerors, Nijad was one of the last pure safe havens of man. Nijad city was not a conquering city but a city of peace and holy grace. The city gleamed as a pure sanctuary of divinity under the dark sky.

The charge was the most ghastly sight ever seen. Hundreds of soldiers were rushing past in a panic, utter chaos toward a glorious castle which was fading from sight.

In the battle below, there were many dead corpses and random shadows moving quick as lightening as countless men fell to the ground without just cause.

As the men rushed past him, Zanatose stood in the middle of the stampede glued to the spot with dread in his heart, his face was white as chalk as he fearfully watched the shadows at work. He could not comprehend the horrors he was watching. Edwin, Bill, Brett, and Katie went to his side as they drew their weapons. They patted him on the back and Brett said, "Zanatose I know you can overcome this, if any of us are meant to overcome this hell, it's you and the rest of us. You're not alone. Together we will survive this and we will stop these monsters."

"Yeah!" Bill, Edwin, and Katie yelled with forced battle cries. Zanatose slowly nodded his head and drew both Blazer and Shadow without much thought.

"Let's do this," he said as he gave a vicious nod and led his men down the hill into the sadistic battle.

As they went down the hill, Edwin threw his bow and arrows to Katie so she could use them for combat. Back at home they played archery games together, and Katie always had the highest score. She grabbed them and went to work immediately. Edwin drew the earth sword with a look of purpose.

Bill and Edwin stopped at the foot of the hill, and fought side by side. They were brutally pummeled by several shadow beasts as they tried to slay the vile villains. Brett and Jonathan headed into a huge mass of the beasts and fought bravely back to back with each other. Katie was still using the arrows and Zanatose was trying to protect her as they moved further into the maelstrom.

Countless shadow beasts leapt at him, Zanatose blocked with his twin swords and slashed back. Every time he had to block for Katie, he felt more and more rage against the shadow beasts. His arm was burning and the snake was growing even longer and the voice in his head pleaded with him that it could help.

The battle seemed absolutely hopeless. Men would drop like flies and the dark beasts were barely taking any causalities. The masses of shadows surrounding Zanatose and Katie constantly increased, as if they were drawn to the darkness plaguing his heart. The voice in Zanatose's head turned from one pleading to help him into a dark ranting, throbbing against his skull. Zanatose released his restraint and morphed once more into his dark form. He was fuming with rage as he fought back with a lack of control.

Every man fought against the shadows with all the strength they had, but their forces had already been depleted by the last battle. Even the brave and loyal soldiers of Nijad, clad in their fine emerald and ruby armor, could not last much longer.

Katie had run out of arrows to cast, Brett and Jonathan were getting tired, and Bill and Edwin were in over their heads with countless shadows surrounding them. Zanatose was fighting like a starved wolf, but he too was getting smashed down to the ground with an earth shattering impact as he charged the seas of shadows.

As a shadow beast tried to pounce at Katie, Zanatose flew into the air and punched the beast back into the earth. Zanatose landed on his toes and quickly made a 360 turn, sweeping his swords around him. Twenty tentacles flew into his back and another ten hit him from above, slamming him into the ground, partly buried under the earth by the impact.

As all hope was fading, they heard echoing howls on the hill. The howls froze the blood in their veins. Even the shadow beasts stopped to see what it was. It was the figure of General Wolf Fang and his entire wolfos army. Fang was standing there holding his bisento as the wind blew through his long hair. Under the ominous sky, the men watched as

Fang transformed into the beast he really was. Fang, with his army, joined the battle against the shadows. They stormed down the hill looking like a huge wall of rabid wolves, biting and growling like hellhounds.

The men were weary of the idea of fighting alongside of the wolfos. They knew better than to make an enemy of them in such a situation though. With the wolfos' help the fight once again had some glimmer of hope. It was amazing how much power the wolfos had. In this fight, the men saw that in all battles before now, the wolfos were barely trying.

The wolfos flexed their muscles to their full extent as they ripped the shadows to shreds. It was a terrifying sight. The slobbering beasts tore huge shadow beasts apart with their claws beside an army of men with blood-stained hair and armor, stained by their fallen comrades. The wolfos all had a hungry glare whenever they looked at the men, but it seemed they were commanded to leave the soldiers alone.

A stray tentacle smacked Edwin in the head with a bone crushing impact, and he fell to the battle floor. The shadow beast who delivered the hit stood high and tall over his body. Bill ran at it in vain, slammed to the ground with a single blow. It raised its tentacles and was about to eradicate Edwin until Zanatose suddenly jumped into the scene and back kicked it to the ground.

"And stay down!" Zanatose yelled as the shadow beast vanished into dust. Many more shadow beasts circled Zanatose. He was a normal human at the time and he braced himself to defend against the beasts. There was a black cloud all around him, filled with staring hollow eyes, as he thought to himself, "*This can't be the end of me. This journey can't end without me, I have to fight!*"

Zanatose decided to give the first blow. As he leapt at the cloud of unworldly beings, he heard a strange voice in his head. "*You need my powers. Let me take over.*" Zanatose listened to the mysterious voice and his arm burned agonizingly as he morphed into his dark self. He snarled with pain and anger as the changes came over his weakened body.

"Now the fun begins," he said as he looked at his powerful arms and twin blades.

He jumped onto one beast and gave it a vicious thrashing while hundreds of tentacles flew at him. They rained down on him like a wintery hail, and he fell to his knees.

The shadow beasts rounded on him, and they stared at him with their heartless eyes. Every breathe they took made everything darker and foggier for Zanatose as he laid there at their mercy. He was out of breathe and out of ideas. He saw the faces of his friends flash through his mind as he lost all his hope. He looked up at the beasts. "If I die it will be to save them," he said as he mustered up all his energy and stood once more.

"Leave them to me," said Fang. From the tree, Fang sliced two with his staff as he jumped down. He landed cat like on his feet. He stood up tall and swept his hair out of his snake like eyes.

"What, and let you have all the fun?" laughed Zanatose. The two of them fought off the beasts back to back like partners. Zanatose's pain vanished as he allowed the sword's powers to control him.

Soon the shadows disappeared without a trace. "Mysterious," said Brett as he thought to himself. The wolfos had left as well, back up the hill, except for Fang who was still by Zanatose.

The afternoon sun shined superbly on Fang's gold armor as they stood there together as friends and not enemies. Fang was truly the *savior* of the armies of men this time. "Have you decided to join me yet Zanatose? I have shown you where I stand. Now, what is your opinion of us Zanatose?" Fang asked as he gasped for air after the fight, Fang seemed very serious as he asked this question.

Zanatose seemed unsure, but he was being swayed none the less. As he gazed up into Fang's eyes, Fang returned the gaze with a glare. "Zanatose, good and evil are perspectives. Soon you will realize that, but until then farewell," Fang left unnoticed by all except Zanatose.

Jonathan and Brett ran over to Zanatose. "Wasn't it insane? Humans fighting alongside wolfos against the shadow beasts!" said Brett excitedly.

"The wolfos saving humans? What's next? The eternal fires of hell turning into the eternal ice ring of hell?" asked Edwin.

"Wonder why they left us alone just like last time *again*," said Jonathan.

"No idea," lied Zanatose. He quickly looked away from Brett's gaze and at the huge wooden draw bridge being lowered from Nijad. Zanatose and his group stepped onto the draw bridge as they walked down into the city of Nijad. "Good luck General Gateman!" Zanatose yelled.

"It was an honor," said Jonathan as he and his army mounted their horses and left to their own city.

"We finally made it. That was a dull trip. Now we have no stories to tell," said Edwin in a sarcastic voice. Zanatose chuckled at Edwin's cynical sarcasm.

"We're here at last," sighed Katie.

As they crossed the draw bridge they looked back at the corpses of the few dead wolfos and unimaginable number of heroic soldiers. "What a terrible loss of men," said Brett as he shook his head in grimace.

"... *And wolfos*," thought Zanatose.

CHPT 9:
PRINCESS OF LEGENDS

Zanatose had thoughts of Wolf Fang's aid swirling in his head. He thought back to Fang's words, "*Good and Evil are only a perspective.*" Zanatose now decided to believe some of what Fang had said. "The *past evils of the wolfos were before his time anyway,*" he thought to himself.

The group entered the marvelous, vast city of Nijad. It was a beautiful and overwhelmingly large city full of many joyous people. It had several market places full of strange and exotic goods. The city was made of stunning polished marble. The sun beamed down fabulously into the crowded city square. There were groups of people scattered about mingling together.

Brett took notice of the fine brand new tunics in a nearby stand. The tunics were rich with vibrant colors. Bill was very interested in cooking and was a superb chef. He was overjoyed by the many skillful chefs he saw there with their many seasonings. He loved all of those extraordinary foods and spices.

Katie was amazed by the striking silk dresses. They had lots of scintillating colors and were made of fine silks. Zanatose was looking at the different swords, shields, and other weaponry they sold there with great curiosity. There were huge mallets and even arrows that whistled to attract attention.

Everyone, except Edwin, was exploring the city's many commodities. Edwin waited, but grew tired quickly and decided to rush the group along. "Come on, to the castle!" he yelled to the rest.

Everyone raised their heads and got back together. Brett cleared his throat and then spoke very formally, "Alright everyone this way to the castle." The group was distraught to leave the market, but went along any way.

As they went up the steps to a large metal gate a stern looking man in the Nijad uniform walked up to them threateningly. The tall man stopped them and yelled out, "You have no clearance to pass, leave now or face the consequences."

"And what if we don't?" laughed Zanatose as he walked up to him with Shadow in his hand. He felt the battle was a joke. As Zanatose raised his sword Brett panicked.

"No, he's a friend Zanatose; he was just joking!" Brett yelled.

"Sorry sir, no hard feelings?" asked Zanatose with embarrassment.

"No that's fine, sorry I startled you." The man walked over to Brett and patted him on the back. Then he smiled and talked excitedly. "Brett and I go way back, as far back as the training academy. We used to both be normal gate guards together."

"Yeah, how could I forget?" Brett sighed. He laughed as he recalled some old memories. "We used to always joust against each other in the grand tournament." They both laughed as Brett turned to the group. "This is my old friend Macbeth. We were the top two in all the grand tournaments. We always used to lose to… Wolf Fang. Wolf, Macbeth, and I used to be old friends until the shadow beasts returned a year ago to Nijad. Fang left to find a way to stop the shadows from rising."

"Don't dwell in the past," Macbeth said. Macbeth was

a full grown man, and had brown hair with a five o'clock shadow. Zanatose thought he saw jealousy in Macbeth's eyes as he stared at Brett, but maybe it was just a trick of the mind. "Now, I hear it's very important that you see the princess so off we go." Macbeth walked over to a switch and pulled it and the gate slowly rose up.

They walked through the gate and saw on the other side the marvelous palace grounds, a breath taking garden full of colorful exotic plants. It had tall trees and under the trees were benches and little fountains. The bright sun in the background added a heavenly touch to the setting.

"We'll go talk to the gate guards," said Macbeth as he gestured to Brett to follow him. The gate guards stood still as statues at the other end, they were very large and bulky. They were also armed with huge maces.

"Friendly fellows don't you think?" asked Edwin.

"Yeah just don't say I have to go talk to them," said Zanatose as he eyed them apprehensively.

As Macbeth and Brett approached the gate guards the gate guards relaxed a little, seeing two allies coming. The two big headed guards grinned at each other as they saw them. The one with a heavy beard announced in a gruff voice, "Welcome back Brett, what took you so long?" he laughed. The laugh sounded more like a bark. "One moment you're off to the market the next we're out looking for you." The guard acted like he was looking into the distance with great drama.

Brett smiled at his friend's joke. "I was attacked by shadow beasts on my route. I was forced to go to this village, what's its name?" Brett thought for a moment then remembered, "Oh yeah, Sholkon village. There I found some odd friends who were strong enough to help me through the cave and back here after a long journey."

"That's quite a tale old friend. We should discuss it with

the *princess*," said Macbeth. Macbeth was trying to remind Brett that they had a job to do.

Brett took the hint with disappointment. "Right... May we enter the princess' garden to talk to her?" asked Brett.

"Sure, of course *you* can... Raise the gate," the bearded guard murmured to his partner. The partner quickly complied and went to the door to take out his keys.

He fumbled around with a large ring of keys until he reached the gold key which he put into the large oak door's key hole. They heard a loud clank as the doors opened slowly.

"Thank you," said Macbeth to the guard as he walked into a flawless white marble corridor.

"Come on guys let's go!" Brett yelled to the rest of the team, waiting for his command.

Zanatose nodded to Bill and they set off into the castle. The group entered the castle, it was beautiful beyond words.

The white walls were plastered with many dazzling works of art and stories of heroes. As they walked down the many corridors Zanatose noticed an art work of a hero holding a dark blade, but it was at least twice the size of the one he had. Then another painting of the absolute darkest church he had ever seen. Lightening above it, black inside, and it was surrounded by fire, or something else. Edwin didn't let Zanatose get a closer look at this sadistic piece of art. As Zanatose slowed down, Edwin rushed forward and pushed him forward. Soon they saw an opening to another private garden.

By a vibrant patch of flowers stood the princess, dressed in a stunning white and blue silk dress. She had beautiful long blonde hair and sky blue eyes. Macbeth and Brett bowed as she turned around. Zanatose took notice of their actions and bowed too, he gestured with his hands that the rest should bow too.

She had a very solemn and gentle voice as she spoke. "Welcome to Nijad castle. I am very glad you have arrived Zanatose," she said merrily as she saw Zanatose.

Zanatose was stunned, "How do you know my name?"

"I've seen you in my dreams. You were the bringer of light against the darkness. Darkness stood at your feet though. Strange, I don't see any darkness in you," she smiled contently. She didn't seem completely convinced though.

What she had said reminded him of his own dream. "I also had that dream, but I didn't notice the darkness."

"Show her your elemental sword Zanatose," whispered Bill. "That might be the darkness or something."

Zanatose agreed and told the princess about it. "Princess…"

She cut him off. "Please, call me Elizabeth."

"Elizabeth, maybe we should show you what elemental swords we have so far." Zanatose, Bill, and Edwin took out their elemental swords.

"Alright very nice, you have already collected two and a half of the swords," announced Elizabeth. She was impressed they even had one. "Edwin has half of the earth sword, Bill has the sword of inner strength, and Zanatose!" she gasped as she saw his sword. "So there is darkness," she muttered as she stared at the sword, anxiously.

Zanatose was disappointed to see that his sword was so troublesome. "It has helped us in dire times and I can control it," he said confidently to the princess. He knew he was lying about the latter part.

The princess sighed and said, "The last wielder of the sword had killed the holder of the sword of light. I hope the same dark deed does not await you." Zanatose felt insulted that she thought *he* could fall to the darkness.

"I will not fall to the darkness, I am not the last guy," said Zanatose.

"Zanatose don't worry, I don't think you will fall either; I was just warning you," she said calmly, he could still see the doubt in her eyes. "It's strange that you -the one I thought was the chosen one -wield a dark blade," she pondered a little.

"It doesn't matter what blade he has, but how he uses it matters," said Katie in his defense.

"You're right," said Elizabeth. "I just hope Fang doesn't try to sway him," she said looking down gloomily. Katie and Zanatose looked at each other in alarm. "You know Fang can sense every time you transform to your dark form. For some reason he also has dark powers, but we don't know why."

"Is it his staff?" asked Bill.

"It could be, but then again it could be something else. Something that has the same dark principles as Zanatose's sword," Elizabeth said.

"Elizabeth, don't worry about Fang. He will be the least of our worries. I can handle him," Zanatose said firmly.

"As can we," said Bill as he and Edwin stepped forward.

"Thanks guys, see we're ready as a team." Zanatose was very satisfied with his team's support.

"It'll take more than all of you to stop the darkness," said Elizabeth.

"She's right it'll take us too," said Brett as he and Macbeth also stepped forward.

"What I was about to say is, it will take all the elemental weapons. Dear me, Fang will have a number of you to contend with won't he?" Elizabeth laughed her gentle laugh that calmed Zanatose's nerves.

"By element weapons, you mean swords right?" asked Edwin.

"Yes, but also elemental amulets and crystals exist too. Your second sword was built to hold elemental jewels Zanatose. You all have a long journey ahead of you," she said.

"So, Ethan did help when he gave me Blazer," Zanatose muttered to himself. Then he remembered what the elders said. "What do the elemental swords unlock?" he blurted out.

Elizabeth looked up at him and thought for a moment. "It unlocks new powers in the hero or heroes' swords. But most importantly it opens a path into the darkness so you can defeat the shadows' leader and lock the path between the two worlds. The first elemental heroes dared not venture into the unknown darkness, so they sealed the entrance from the other world with an elemental seal," she said.

"What's the story behind those vile shadow beasts?" asked Bill.

"They are called the tarik. All the other races call them by that name. The tarik were caused to enter our world back in the time of Ares," said Elizabeth.

"We keep hearing about that time period, what happened back then?" asked Zanatose.

Elizabeth shook her head grievously. "It was a long time ago. So long ago that law didn't even exist yet. It was a time of war, and hatred. Since it was so long a time and so many awful things happened during this period, it was called the time of Ares. There was absolutely no peace between any two cities. Created from all the hatred and violence, was born an even greater evil. This unsurpassed evil was the tarik."

"We're strong! Can't we just fight them with a strong army?" Zanatose asked. He thought back to Fang's suggestion.

"No human army can withstand the tarik! Don't you remember the battle you had just fought in?" said Macbeth with anger. The visions of mass death still plagued his head like a recurring nightmare.

"A wolfos army might," Zanatose muttered to himself.

"Anyway," said Elizabeth, seeming a little worried. She continued the story. "This new evil was so powerful that, after a few years of fighting, the civilizations joined together and began to unite."

"So all the civilizations had fought against the tarik on their own and failed?" asked Zanatose.

Elizabeth was about to speak, but Brett replied sooner. "Not quite. The wolfos and a few others only defended themselves rather than to attack on their own, like we did here in Nijad. Perhaps they were wiser than men back in that time."

"Perhaps," agreed Elizabeth. "Well where was I? Oh right!" she remembered the story again. "As our cities were torn to bits we had finally decided to join forces against the tarik. After a while we noticed they came from strange vortexes. We predicted they came from another realm or something of that nature. In the mean time the kings of the cities decided to craft magical swords. They used their most valued metals and built amazing swords of beauty and power. The priests placed blessings upon the swords and the blessings gave the swords magical powers."

"So every elemental item has its own power?" asked Bill.

"That's right, and the dark and light swords are the most intriguing. Their formation was not by human hands and their powers include killing the holder if they are not destined or worthy to wield them," said Macbeth.

"*What?!*" gasped Katie. She stared at Zanatose with great worry.

"Don't worry, I'm still alive aren't I?" he said.

"He's right, and you know some blades need special crystals to make them work, like Edwin's," said Macbeth.

"How do you know so much? That knowledge belongs to our high priests and royalty," said Brett suspiciously.

"When I first had my visions I told him in case something should happen to me since you weren't near at the time," said Elizabeth. Brett nodded and Elizabeth continued the story.

"The magical swords reunited us onto one front. Now we fought as one, but the shadows were still too strong. Only the kings with sacred swords stood a chance. After a short while the kings were killed and the heroes of each city stepped up to the challenge. Each hero had their own elemental power which they used their sword for. Wolfos for darkness, cheetahs for wind and they also have the blade of light. Those are the ones I can remember best," she said.

"My blade is craftsmanship of the wolfos?" Zanatose asked stunned by the truth.

"Yes, or at least that's what we suspect. We haven't thought of any other alternative. The dark sword is still a mystery to us, answered Macbeth. "Now go on with the story princess."

"Alright," she said as she continued. "The tarik, against these heroes whom could control the elements themselves with the elemental blades, stood no chance..." She was immediately broken off.

"We can control the elements with these blades?" asked Bill.

"That's their purpose, you didn't know that?" asked Brett.

"So I can control the earth?" asked Edwin.

"Not exactly how you'd imagine, but basically yes," laughed Brett. He could not imagine the odd antics Edwin would do if he was given so much power.

"Back to the story?" asked Elizabeth. Everyone nodded and she continued again. "After a great battle the tarik retreated to their own world while others hid. The heroes followed them to where they entered to our realm. They found a vortex into oblivion. The heroes were not willing to enter it, but now we know it's the only way to win this war, you must enter the vortex to see where it leads."

"What? You mean you don't even know where the vortex of *oblivion* is, or if it'll even help! You expect us to risk our lives on the old heroes' legend?" asked Zanatose. He was outraged that they were willing to gamble their lives on a guess.

"Do you have a better idea?" asked Elizabeth.

"Y…" Katie elbowed him in the rib painfully. He looked at her and she shook her head disapprovingly. Zanatose sighed and said, "No, no I don't."

"Exactly, we need the swords to unlock the temple's elemental seal, built to contain the vortex," Elizabeth said. "And I warn you now. Their realm has been visited only once by a single man named General Bronx, and he has never returned. Their realm is heard to be like ours only darker." Everyone looked puzzled at what she meant. "I'm not sure what that means either. There could be more tarik I guess."

"Great, so now which way do we go?" asked Zanatose. He was frustrated with the size of the mission. It no longer seemed like a matter of days or months, but a matter of years before the threat of the tarik was even dented by their efforts. Seeing the last battle, he didn't believe people could survive that long. Through the years to pass, cities will fall and men will die by the thousands, all in the effort to simply survive.

"So many ways, but all will have one final ending," said Macbeth. He had a blank stare, he was obviously thinking of something else.

"He's right, there are many places all of you need to go," Elizabeth said. "But I suggest you head to Theragorn city first, where General Gateman came from. After that you should head to see the cheetah race. They are very protective, fast, and above all dangerous!"

"They're fast and dangerous? I like the cheetahs," laughed Brett.

"Do not under estimate foreign races, and especially not the cheetahs!" said Elizabeth in an alarmed voice.

"I could care less about some wild cats, the wolfos are far

more powerful," said Zanatose impatiently. "I'd like to hear more about this General Bronx guy. How did he get through the vortex if we need all the elemental weapons?"

"As if I knew, all I've heard is that he suddenly left the city with three other men. No one knows which way he went. He saw something in the castle and realized that he had seen it in a dream. He just left after that," replied Elizabeth.

"Thank you princess, and farewell," said Zanatose as they all bowed. He led them out of the castle to start their true journey, the rest of the group soon followed.

"Good luck heroes and farewell," said the princess as they left. The group left the castle grounds and went to Nijad city market to buy their supplies for the journey. The princess watched them leave anxiously. She knew more than she would tell them.

CHPT 10:
MYSTERIES OF THE JOURNEY

Nijad market was huge. To gather all their supplies for the journey they split up into small groups. Macbeth would join them in Theragorn city later in a couple days; apparently, he was rather busy at the time. Bill and Edwin went together to gather foods and spices. Katie went to buy clothes. Brett and Zanatose went to buy new bags to hold the supplies.

The market was full of appealing and appalling goods brought from distant places. There were tasty looking exotic foods which turned out to be poison. You had to be careful with what you bought in the market. The market turned out to be helpful but dangerous if you didn't pay close attention.

The many spices and random foods confused Bill. There were so many things he wanted to buy, but he had never used most of them. One odd pepper he had bought had a dark blue powder, it smelled horrific. The pepper turned out to be delicious as he tried a food with it in the dish, Edwin had expected it to be poison.

Zanatose bought several sleeping bags and back packs that were very strong and light. The bags had a light brown tint. They all met at the town square, heavily crowded with loads of people. The tunics Katie had bought were a soft and beautiful silk. The food bought by Bill and Edwin was plentiful and promised by Bill to be delectable.

Now that they had their supplies the group started off toward Theragorn city in the east. Once they left the safe haven of Nijad city and continued toward Theragorn city on a dirt trail they realized that the darkness was closing in on them.   "Great it's nightfall on the road. We definitely need a sentry to guard the tents at night this time," said Edwin.

"I agree. We could take turns," suggested Zanatose.

"What a relief," said Katie. Zanatose laughed with a bitter taste in his mouth. The awful memory of that night came back to him again; the bloody corpses staggering toward him, the spiders drooling over him, and the wolfos who kidnapped Brett.

As they traveled, the trail died away and they began to hike without a road under their feet. "I hope we don't go the wrong way," Zanatose whispered to Brett.

"You don't have to worry about that. I think I know the way," said Brett calmly.

About a hundred yards in front of them was a very thick jungle. It had gigantic oak trees, and strong red wood trees. The forest was so thick that they could not see what was on the other side of the forest. "I'm sure the city is just through those woods," said Brett.

"You're *sure* or you *think*?" asked Zanatose.

"Um…" Brett stalled a few seconds and then it began to rain. It rained heavily and suddenly as if the sky was torn open by a wretched hand.

"Run into the woods!" Brett yelled. Everyone ran into the woods as fast as they could to get out of the sudden down pour. Only inches behind them crashed down a bolt of lightning that shook the earth with rage.

"What a sudden storm! Good thing we were so close to these woods," said Bill.

"Yeah we're still all wet though!" said Edwin. Edwin noticed that everyone was staring with awe in the opposite direction "What is it? Is it another lightning bolt trying to tear our heads off" he asked from Zanatose.

Zanatose grabbed his head and turned it to where everyone else was looking. He saw a dark figure against the darkness. It was slowly approaching from in between two trees. "What is it?" asked Edwin again, this time with apprehension.

"I'm going to find out," replied both Zanatose and Brett at once as they both drew their weapons. The two walked up side by side silently and slowly, trying not to break any branches, as they approached the unknown enemy.

They stopped a few feet away from it and gasped from who they saw. "Alexis?" yelped Zanatose. He could hardly believe his eyes. "You're alive?"

Alexis had blank eyes, and was breathing heavily. She looked up at Zanatose and Brett with blank eyes and nodded slowly. The others tried to see what was happening. Zanatose decided to tell them the good news. "It's Alexis everyone, she's alive!" he yelled.

"No way!" yelled Katie as she ran to her old friend. "You're alive!" she said with utter joy. She noticed that Alexis didn't look so well. "You alright?" asked Katie. Alexis wordlessly nodded again. She seemed vexed by an unseen presence.

"How did you... what happened?" Zanatose blurted out. They had all been sure she was unquestionably dead.

Alexis took a big breath and cleared her throat. "That doesn't matter. You all need to know how to get to Theragorn city. You must travel through the old village up ahead," she said in a croaky voice. The voice didn't sound like what they remembered of her voice.

"Really?" asked Brett. He had never known there was a village in this direction.

Zanatose had other things on his mind, like whether or

not *Alexis* did actually survive the attack, and how she knew they were going to Theragorn city. He decided to keep this to himself so the others wouldn't feel alarmed.

Katie, who had been best friends with Alexis, doubted if Alexis was well. Katie kept looking at Alexis crossly as they continued the journey to this *village* Alexis talked about.

Brett was the best leader of everyone present, in Zanatose's perspective, so he decided to inform Brett of his suspicions. Zanatose walked close to Brett's side and whispered in his ear so that Alexis could not possibly hear. "Don't you find it odd that she knows where we're going, or that she knows of a village you never knew was there? I don't think it all adds up."

"I think you're just too suspicious of her. You raise a good point, but maybe she's just been in a rough spot. I couldn't imagine what she's been through to survive a zombie attack," Brett said sympathetically. Zanatose gave him a look of disbelief. Brett sighed. "I'll keep a watch on her."

"What do you know about this place we're visiting?" asked Bill.

Zanatose and Brett were engrossed to hear what Alexis had to say. "Any strange tales of this place?" asked Brett. He was sure if he heard the story he might recognize the place.

She looked at him with her blank eyes, drops of rain coming down through the leaves of trees from above. She spoke in her croaky voice. "There is an old tale of the village which speaks of doom. It is said those who are unwise or over confident come to the village and fall into oblivion," she actually laughed at this while the rest gasped.

Zanatose and Brett were both sure this was some kind of a trap now and kept their hands on their weapons at all times. "What is wrong with the village?" asked Zanatose as he tried to act friendly, feigning a smile.

"There was a witch there who placed a curse upon the village. An odd plague was the curse... A very odd plague," she laughed again but her eyes had no joy. Her eyes were still as blank as before. "The town's leader drowned the poor witch and she was never *seen* again. The town's leader survived and now she waits for vengeance upon their ancestors."

"What a wonderful story! Just makes you want to visit this place on vacation over summer," joked Edwin.

"No, this is serious," Katie looked very nervous as she said this. She was tense and pale. "Zanatose, Brett, everyone be ready." She commanded them to be prepared, but for what? She never said and they didn't ask, but the urgency in her voice told them enough.

All the men drew their swords and Zanatose walked over to Katie. "Don't worry Kate. No matter what happens I will keep you safe," Zanatose whispered into her ear. "But why does this place spook you out so much?" he asked.

"Family secret," she replied.

"We're almost there," Alexis said in a dead voice. The rain was still coming and they had just exited the forest. They could barely see through the rain and black darkness. It was an eerie night. They all expected something, but for a half hour nothing happened.

"Are we there yet?" Zanatose asked. Alexis shook her head. As the night went on a fog emerged and thickened until they could barely see. Alexis led the way and she was slowly disappearing into the fog. They could hear all kinds of animals in the night, but could not see even one source to all the noise.

"Creepy," muttered Bill. Zanatose nodded. Even though Zanatose had his sword of darkness, Shadow, he still feared the mystery of the dark. The dark night and all its strange animals, calling to the mischievous moon, were starting to take a toll on his mind, unsettling his nerves.

"How much further left to go?" asked Zanatose from Alexis.

"Hey, where'd she go!" yelled Bill in panic. He was the closest one to her, and as far as he could see, she vanished.

"She's right there. She's sitting down, see," said Zanatose as he pointed out a vague human figure against the fog. They closed in on it and grabbed the man by the shoulder.

Katie screamed and the rest jumped back. It was the remains of a dead body. Its skeletal face was grimy from the decays of time and its eyes were hollow. They could see claw marks against its cheek. "I guess we're here," squeaked Edwin.

They all stood transfixed, silently trying to muster up their courage again. A crow called out against the stillness, and dove at them. They all ran from the menacing bird, covering their heads. In their panic, they tripped on debris from the ruined village. Edwin fell hard onto his face and cut his lip. Katie was falling, but grabbed someone's arm.

"Thanks," she muttered, almost to herself. She raised her head to see who it was, expecting Brett or Zanatose. It was another dead body. She held in her scream until she saw a snake slither onto its arm and toward her. The snake reminded her of the she was trying to escape. "Let's leave!" she screamed in a terrified voice.

"Definitely, but first show us which way to go. I can't see anything in this fog and rain. Can you?" asked Brett. His head was dashing in every direction.

"Not a thing. It's like trying to see through a marble wall," Zanatose replied. He looked around at the group and realized a few were missing. "Alexis is missing and so is Edwin." Panic was settling into him like the fog that was shrouding his world.

They looked around and felt around for the two. No one felt or saw either one of them. Only Bill, Zanatose, Brett, and Katie were left. "Alexis! Edwin!" Bill called out. They heard footsteps and hard breathing approaching.

"We want to find them, but we don't want something

else to find us. Don't yell!" hissed Zanatose. He took out Shadow and stood, prepared for whatever was approaching. They waited for impending doom, unable to see, unable to understand the secrets of the darkness. Each thought to his or her past, and regrets. Their minds swarmed with confusion and confliction until they blinked and saw the dreadful state they were in. Thunder and lightning illuminated their surroundings long enough for them to see it was Edwin running from a bubbling lake, the surface glowed with the pale moon's reflection. Brett thought the moon looked ill, as if it was watching the world and was sickened by what it saw.

"Edwin!" Bill yelled with relief, seeing that his childhood friend was still alive. Edwin was not all that they saw from the flash of lightening. Zanatose noticed some movement from the water, millions of dead clammy hands grabbing sodden land from within the lake. The rows of hands looked like a white fog rising up from the water. Then there was darkness.

"Oh sh…" Zanatose's voice was cut off by the lake water spraying up like a spring. They were soaked by the lake's water and the rain. Again, the lightning hit the ground close to the group, it shook the surroundings, and it showed them a horrific sight.

Hundreds of zombies were chained to the lake grounds and they were moaning and reaching out at them from a long distance. The chains seemed ancient and rusted. The undead had cold heartless eyes, and were hideously deformed from decay and signs of cannibalism.

Katie broke down and started crying. Zanatose stood transfixed, white in the face, not believing what his eyes were seeing. "You have got to be kidding me. This can't be real," he muttered to himself.

It went dark again and they heard the unearthly moans of the zombies and the strain of old metal chains. "At least they're chained up," said Bill trying to see a bright side. Zanatose did not care about the chains, he felt like running, but still could not move. He'd had nightmares about zombies killing him in his dreams for years. Now he was face to face with a horde of them.

"*Zombies, that's nothing,*" said a dark voice in his head. "*We'll tear them to shreds real easy, just like last time.*"

They still heard the rain hit the ground and the lightning, but there was another sound too. It sounded like branches being broken off a large tree. Bill jumped at the sound and so did Zanatose, who finally woke up from his trance and drew Blazer as well as Shadow. "What was that sound?" asked Bill.

"Nothing, I'm sure," said Brett. He was starting to lose his cool. He was looking around in dread but could not recognize where they were because of the darkness and the fog. They all knew the sound was not nothing, but something.

"Which way now?" Bill asked. Brett shrugged, but Zanatose replied for him.

"Take out your weapons and stand ready. I can sense some kind of dark presence," said Zanatose as he tried to see beyond the fog. He felt very uneasy.

Zanatose could sense a dark presence lurking in the night somewhere, but that presence did not feel the slightest bit human. He turned round and round, but he could not see anything no matter how hard he strained his eyes. "I know you're out there. Stop hiding!" Zanatose growled to himself.

"I figure we should… WHAT WAS THAT SOUND?" screamed Katie. They started hearing sounds of wet feet slapping the old road, approaching against the rain and thunder.

"It's nothing, just calm down," said Brett as he trembled. Brett knew just as well as everyone else that he was lying.

They were all soaked to the skin by the heavy rain. Another strike of lightning came and they felt relieved, they could see for a moment, but that relief vanished when they saw what the sounds came from.

The zombies had broken their chains and were limping toward the group, giving their bone chilling moans of pain- the pain of living without a soul. Zanatose's legs buckled, yet another force within him kept him from collapsing. Katie hid behind Brett as the group drew their weapons. They were compelled to courage by their instinct to survive.

"Maybe if we stand perfectly still, they won't see us," suggested Bill.

"Oh yeah, if we're still, they won't see us even though they saw us from the lake in this rain. Great thinking there, Bill," said Edwin in anger. "Now what the hell are we going to do? You have any more bright ideas Bill?"

"Enough bickering! Now get ready to fight for your lives," yelled Brett. He took command, noticing Zanatose's apparent inability to move. "And Zanatose, wake up, we need you!"

Zanatose shook his head and nodded. "You're right. What are a few zombies?" laughed Zanatose. Zanatose had decided that it was best if he allowed his new instincts to take over for this part, he could barely stand. Zanatose felt insignificant in the eyes of so many zombies and the inexplicable dark presence. The lingering presence of absolute darkness gave him a chill that not even a thousand zombies would be capable of. It was a tainted presence, a presence of something that does not belong in this world.

"You think we can take them?" Katie asked from Brett.

Brett looked very doubtful and worried. "I don't know if we even stand a chance against this many," he said. The first hand hit Edwin hard in the face and that was their signal to start fighting. No one could see their target in the darkness. They slashed as hard as they could and hit the zombies. The zombies hit them back through the bombardment of swords, unyielding to the cuts in their flesh.

They fought valiantly, but their efforts were futile. As more zombies fell, even more came, stumbling over the fallen bodies, standing again despite their lost limbs. The zombies would stand back up with their hanging body parts and twitch convulsively as they approached the group. The rain mixed with blood as it dripped to the ground. The group backed up again and again until they backed into a wall. "This is the end for us. I am proud to die alongside such fine warriors," said Brett.

"Don't say that," cried Katie. She could feel wet tears dripping down her cheek, taking a sharp intake of breath, she began to lose hope.

Zanatose nodded. "She's right, Brett, this isn't over until *I* say so. You think I can lose to such pathetic creatures?! No, I will *not lose!*" Zanatose was working himself into a fit of rage. There had never been a challenge he could not face and he was not about to fall now. His life had meaning for the first time. If he died, if Katie died, that meaning would be lost. He had saved Katie from zombies before, he had saved Brett and Edwin from spiders, his village from the tarik, and now he was determined to save them all from the zombies, no matter how many there were, no matter what the cost to him.

"Zanatose, don't," Katie pleaded in a low whimper.

"I must, I can't let it end like this. I promised you that you'd be okay. I plan to keep that promise. Our backs are against the wall, but that has never stopped us before," he said with a bold look in his eyes. He was hurting all over from the clawing of the zombies, but he knew what he had to do. He had to succumb to the power of Shadow and save Katie.

He morphed into his dark form and used his anger to alleviate the pain. He shuddered from all his angst and felt the darkness consuming him. He forgot all his fears, he forgot his pain, and he forgot everything but Katie, the one thing allowing him sanity and strength. He charged out ahead, slashing with both swords, using his powers to send the zombies flying back. Every time a claw slashed out at him, he jumped up and gave them an aerial attack. Every set of nails that tore into his skin fueled his rage, his power.

Although Zanatose was fighting off many zombies, the rest still had to fight their hearts out, contending with hell's servants. Bill was handling the pain the best, but even he was starting to fail. Brett sliced through his advisories and pushed them back with his staff. Edwin had dropped his sword when a claw struck him in his shoulder, grasping it and digging into his skin.

"Edwin, no!" Bill yelled. He grabbed Edwin's sword and fought with both swords. He pushed the zombies away from Edwin. A zombie strained itself to get one last bite. Bill swung his sword through its neck like a guillotine. "Alright, everyone, follow me," yelled Bill over the rain and flailing arms and chomping mouths. He slowly made a route through a weak point in the zombies created by Zanatose's ballistic assault. Brett tried his best to protect Katie as he followed Bill. Sharp claws dug into their sides as they ran blindly after Bill.

Zanatose was losing himself to his rage more than he had anticipated. He could no longer distinguish the difference between a building and a zombie in his struggle to keep conscience control over himself. He was destroying the entire village and the zombies with dark blasts and his own brute strength. He kept erratically ramming into the old, decrepit buildings in his confusion. Eventually, he could no longer withstand his dark form. Every last drop of energy was drained and he fell to the ground. He crash landed with tremendous force and left a crater in the village's dirt road. The zombies sensed his weakness and piled on top of him.

They bowed their heads down to feed upon the lost carcass and renew the blood in their bodies.

"This is the end, I'm sure," said Edwin as he staggered along. Edwin had lost hope upon entering the village, seeing it as a place of no return. He held his wound tightly, and his head low.

"Not yet!" Bill yelled through gritted teeth. He was slashing at the zombies with both his and Edwin's swords. He was surprised at how heavy two swords were compared with one, or maybe he was just too tired. His arms burned every time he had to push off a zombie that was leaning on his swords. The blood, stained mouths of the zombies tried to clamp onto anything in reach.

Brett fought by Bill's side, and his spirit had found its vigor beside Katie. Brett chopped off one zombie's arm, but the zombie felt nothing and kept coming. He did not stop, and he did not lose a glimmer of hope, he fought on. Brett's drive did not fade in the blackest night because he fought with compassion in his heart.

Zanatose's charge did support them for a time, but now he was out of commission, perhaps indefinitely. He had made his choice when he divided from the group, hoping to be some kind of God sent hero. His arrogance was his downfall; he was young, inexperienced, but powerful. He believed his power could allow him to overcome anything. As he opened his eyes to the multitude of deformed faces, to the hue of blood and rain, his thoughts went immediately to Katie. Those gentle rose buds, parting as she spoke, the eyes sparkling in the sun, and her hair, giving light to his days. He took a breath and he exhaled his arrogance, and his anger.

"I can't let her die. She needs me, I… need her, I lo… I love her!" bellowed Zanatose as he stood up from under the weight and the pain of the zombies' sharp claws. He could see clearly, his heart was under his control, Shadow could not even penetrate him. Once the first zombie grabbed him, preparing to bite down, Zanatose elbowed it in the face. Even more zombies staggered toward him, surrounding him, and grabbing him. He closed his eyes and pushed with all of his remaining strength and hope as he tried to run to the other side of the crowd. Pairs of arms grabbed onto him and he struggled free of a few until heaps more clasped onto him. He still kept trying to stand, but the zombies pushed him down against the floor, trying to pin him down.

He pushed with all his heart, rising to his feet, but his body gave way and he collapsed face first into the dirt floor and went unconscious. Seconds later, dark blasts rained down from above and created large craters as the zombies fled to the lake once more. They all narrowly missed Zanatose and the others.

After the hail of dark blasts, everyone was dumbfounded to see Wolf Fang from the top of a roof. He was thoroughly soaked from the rain just like everyone else, his hair pasted onto his forehead. He jumped down and landed beside Zanatose. He scolded the group, "Your leader is here *alone and unconscious*. He needed your help." The group came up. Katie helped Brett back to his feet. Brett, just like Bill and Edwin, was exhausted and covered in scratches. The group walked over to Fang, and Zanatose's unconscious body. For the first time they saw Fang rattled.

"He could have died," Fang hissed at them. The group was confused, why would Fang care about Zanatose's life?

CHPT 11:
TIES THAT BIND

Zanatose woke up. There was a dreamlike fog everywhere. He was all alone in the cursed village. He recollected what had happened up until now and thought. He finally remembered the zombie fight. "Katie! Bill! Bre…" he stopped his yelling, having heard footsteps. He whirled around and there was no one there. "Where is everyone?" he whispered to himself.

There was a hollow breeze that echoed through the abandoned alleyways. He searched the alleyways slowly and quietly. He walked very cautiously, and was afraid that at any second he might have to fight again. He examined the peeling sides of the poor, aged structures. He walked down another dark alley and saw an odd hooded figure, but he could not make out any features against the darkness. It shifted off to the side, soundlessly, down another alley. Zanatose hurriedly followed. As he rounded a corner he heard a terrible scratching noise against a wall. He slowly looked toward the sound, with difficulty. He peered through the fog and saw that it was a zombie scratching at the brick wall like a miserable dog at a door. It had blank eyes, a half open mouth leaking black, viscous blood, and half of a leg. Its nerves hung loosely out of the tears in the leg.

"Oh great, you're still here," he said, as he drew Shadow. He noticed that Blazer was by his waist somehow. As he drew nearer to attack the miserable corpse, the zombie turned into Alexis and he stopped. "What… wait- you're not Alexis… are you?" Zanatose was perplexed and he started to back away.

Alexis turned to look at him with her blank eyes, and now that he thought of it, her lifeless eyes. She shook her head slowly. "Just call me Alexis for now," she said in a dreary voice, and a smile slowly spread across her face.

"Where are they?!" Zanatose yelled as he tried to swing at her with Shadow. Some force pulled down his sword and lodged it into the ground. He tried to lift it back up, but it would not budge, it was kept there by a mysterious force.

"They're safe… for the most part. Zanatose, I am here to warn you," she said. Her voice stayed the same, a lifeless monotone.

Zanatose was still struggling to take his sword out of the ground. "I knew from the moment when we saw you in those woods that you weren't the normal Alexis. I should have never followed you to this forsaken village. You're the one from the story who was drowned aren't you?" asked Zanatose. He had put his suspicions together.

She nodded and Zanatose shuddered, turning pale, and his eyes turned into beads for a moment. "No… not now…" he moaned as he fell over trying to resist the metamorphosis into his dark form. Alexis gave a cruel menacing cackle which was just as brief as his transformation.

"So you are the one," she said in a dreamy voice.

He looked up, losing his prior stability, and said, "If you mean the one who will bring an end to you, then you're right," he said coldly. "Where is everyone?" he demanded of her again.

"Oh … them, that doesn't matter right now," she said calmly.

"Yes… they… DO!" he lost control and turned into an

even larger dark warrior than any time before. The dam containing his rage burst.

He was larger than normal. His veins bulged out of his muscular arms and he looked like a vicious demon. His eyes had lost any trace of humanity and were consumed by a heated darkness. He pounced at Alexis like a lion on its prey. His claws simply went through her as if she wasn't there. "Are you a..."

She cut him off midsentence. "I am here to warn you. Now don't be rude, and listen." Once she finished, she forced him to human form and pushed him down onto the rock floor. He growled like a dog and tried to get up, but it was useless.

"Let me go!" he yelled. He turned pale again despite her powers.

"Temper, temper, Zanatose," she laughed at his feeble attempts. "The girl, Katie, her ancestors are not from Sholkon village. This is strange for most in the village except for you and her." She said this as if it were a commonly known fact.

"I'm not from Sholkon village?" he asked slowly. He had never known this about himself or Katie. He had never known his parents, and the mystery always gnawed away at him from the inside.

"Of course not," she stared blankly at him as she continued. "Her ancestors tie back to this village –if you haven't figured that out yet. Her ancestors were among the few who survived and were conceited warriors who refused death under any circumstance –like you. Even if it meant to kill another, they would do it," she said this all in the same emotionless voice.

"So her ancestors, are they the ones who killed you?" Zanatose had finally put two and two together. She nodded slowly.

"They figured out that the curse was mine and they

drowned me for having some fun. I'm a specter now. Nothing more than a ghost, but I will find my vengeance upon her," her words were all empty, lifeless. "Hero, Zanatose, I ask you to stay out of my way. My bone to pick is not with you."

"Not a chance! If you want to get to her, you'll have to get through me," declared Zanatose. "This curse you placed, I still don't understand what it did."

"It gave the village's people eternal life. What a magnificent visionary I was. Katie's ancestors tied the cursed people into the lake with my body and hoped no one would be harmed by us," she said.

"You mean those things will keep coming?" asked Zanatose. The thought of zombies that would never give up petrified him.

"Yes, they will keep coming until dawn. And they will exist until I get my revenge. A complete village of people is my army for my retribution. Well, it's more than just this village after so many years," she said.

"Too bad, you will never get to harm her!" he yelled. He turned into his dark form and stood against her restraint. "Let us leave or else!"

"Or else what? You can't harm me, weakling," she said in a cold voice.

"Let's see about that," he sent a barrage of dark blasts toward her through the fog with his dark powers. Once he was done and the smoke cleared he saw that she was unharmed by any of it. He finally understood that he was only dreaming.

"My warning is simple, stay out of my way, *hero*. Heed my warning or her fate also awaits you," she said against the thickening fog.

"I'm not a hero, yet, but I still won't let you harm her!" he yelled. The fog thickened and she disappeared. Everything went black.

"Zanatose you okay?" asked Bill. He stood over him looking down at his body with concern.

"Please be alright Zanatose. I'm sorry you had to be dragged into this," cried Katie.

Zanatose started to move his hands and he tried to open his eyes. He found it near impossible to open his eyes. He was exhausted and felt pain everywhere. "What happened?" he asked in a hoarse voice. He looked around at his friends, all staring down at him and saw everyone was still alright. He also saw Fang absolutely beaming at the sight of him.

"So, you're glad that I saved you?" Fang laughed. The thoughts of what had happened rushed into Zanatose's head again.

Alexis leading them here, zombies in the lake, and then the rest was a blur ending with a dream. The dream flooded back into his memory and he remembered everything. He sat bolt upright as he remembered the dream. "The dream, Alexis possessed, she's here to get her revenge on you, Katie," he blurted it all out at once.

"We know, but it's strange that you know," said Edwin. While Zanatose was out cold Katie had explained it all to them.

"Why did you come here?" asked Brett. He did not like Fang at all and never had.

"I have my reasons," Fang replied as he smiled at Zanatose.

"Who is she anyway? She just said to call her Alexis," remarked Zanatose.

"She is an old sprite named Abigail," said Fang. "I once fought against her, but I found fighting her is useless."

Zanatose was still hurt and struggled to stand. He was breathing heavily and with difficulty. "Do you need some water?" asked Brett. Zanatose nodded and Brett took out a flask of water from his bag. The water was warm, but it did the job. He felt the great relief of water against his dry throat and felt his strength coming back.

"So you know I'm not from Sholkon then?" asked Katie.

After a gulp of water Zanatose took a breath and said, "Neither am I."

"None of you knew that?" asked Fang from all the shocked faces.

"And you know where I'm from?" asked Zanatose sarcastically.

"Yes, but I won't tell you *yet*," Fang said mysteriously. Fang heard a hollow breeze and looked behind them into an empty alley. "She's back."

"Oh joy," Zanatose was happy to get a chance to fight Abigail in the flesh. He dragged Shadow and Blazer off the ground from where they had fallen when he went unconscious. He rolled his neck a little bit and prepared to fight.

Sure enough, in that alley was a ghostly figure, Alexis. Alexis's hair was down, covering her face. She staggered side to side toward them, and slowly turned increasingly pale. It was still dark so they could barely see her full body as she approached. She almost seemed like an eerie head approaching through the darkness and rain. She stopped in front of them and raised her head. It was rotting away; the eyes were crusted over and her jaw was visible through a hole in her cheek. She gave a loud scream and jumped onto Zanatose.

Zanatose fell under the weight from his exhaustion. She started scratching him with her sharp nails. The others were about to help, but Zanatose said otherwise. "She's mine!"

Fang was pleased by his reaction for some odd reason. Zanatose kicked her off and she landed on her feet. "Did my servants give you a scare, Zanatose?" she asked. Abigail turned into Zanatose and back kicked him into a wall. "Are you afraid yet?"

He was smashed through a decaying, hard brick wall and felt like his back was about to snap. Zanatose stood back up and dusted off the debris. "You wish," he said as he picked up his swords. "I'm going to finish your reign over these people. You can't defeat me and neither can your army."

"I don't plan to defeat you. I plan to kill you all!" she said in the form of Zanatose.

"Abigail, you old fool! My wolfos army reported something of true evil here, but I thought they meant something worth my time. Do you honestly think you stand a chance against the wolfos?" Fang laughed at her.

"I also felt an odd darkness in this area," she said. Zanatose shortly recalled the odd presence he had felt earlier. "No matter how many you are, I will destroy you all with my army," Abigail turned into a transparent ghost and dove at them like a hawk.

"I got her," yelled Zanatose as he dark blasted her out of the sky. His dark energy blast went through her and she disappeared. The fog slowly thickened again. They heard the sounds of a large bird flapping in the distant night sky.

"Zanatose, please don't leave me again," Katie pleaded.

"I won't leave you this time," he said. He turned to Fang. "Fang, this is up to us. We must lead everyone to safety." Fang nodded in agreement.

"Yes, of course," his eyes glimmered in the dark. "Quickly, this way," Fang led them down an alleyway.

"Stop!" yelled Brett as he raised his staff. "Why are we following the enemy?" Everyone stopped and turned to look at him.

"We're following him under *my* command. That should be enough for you," Zanatose replied with authority.

"Thank you, Zanatose. Now, let's keep going," Fang

commanded. The group felt uneasy about following Fang, but followed nonetheless, having no other options.

Everyone followed Fang except Brett. "Let's go," said Bill. He did not feel comfortable following Fang but he trusted Zanatose, and it was their only hope for getting out of the village alive.

"No, he is the enemy. I don't know why Zanatose trusts him so much, though," Brett said as he glared at Zanatose with distrust.

"He has helped us many times. I don't see any reason to doubt him. Now, either come or contend with this village alone," said Zanatose coldly.

"He took me hostage to bait you!" Brett yelled in rage. He paused to recall the day he was captured and a thought occurred to him. "He baited you to talk. What did you two talk about?" he asked skeptically.

"Nothing of your interest," said Fang menacingly. At this, Brett swung at Fang and Zanatose blocked with Blazer and pushed Shadow against Brett's throat. "That was unnecessary," remarked Fang in a calm voice.

"Sorry," said Zanatose as he lowered his weapons and backed away.

"So, that's how it is?" asked Brett with disgust as he massaged his neck.

"I was just protecting our only hope at getting out of here," said Zanatose.

"Then what am I?" asked Brett.

"We shouldn't be attacking Fang," said Zanatose. "He has proven to be a great ally. Nijad fears the wolfos, but for our journey we will use their aid."

Brett turned to Fang. "I still don't trust you Fang, this changes nothing." He turned back toward the group. "Fine, I'll follow," Brett said as he joined the group again. "I would hate for my men to see me following your command." Sneered Brett, Fang laughed at him.

"Katie, what were your parents like, did they talk about this place?" asked Zanatose. He was trying to get out of the tense moment when the group almost fell apart.

"Well, my parents did tell me old stories about this place. I guess they weren't kidding," she said grimly. "They talked a lot about my ancestors who lived here. My family members were respected warriors and part of the council. Their wisdom was greatly respected among the villagers. They worked up a big reputation and some of the village was jealous. They talked about a strange girl before, in their stories. I guess that girl is Abigail. She was the village's only witch. She used her magic often; everyone grew to resent her for it. After years, her magic turned malicious. First, causing a few deaths, next she resurrected corpses and disturbed funerals. Her magic later escalated to this curse," concluded Katie, with a mournful tone.

"Abigail's got some issues!" said Edwin. "And I don't mean ha, ha issues, I mean deep issues!"

"I think a brain dead zombie would have caught onto that," said Bill. The thought of placing such a curse on a village scared the group and made them think about what she might do next.

Suddenly, they heard a loud call and they all jumped except Fang. "It's just a crow," Fang said, as if he had expected the crow to be there. He looked up at the foggy night sky, seeing his scouting crow, and laughed. "That scared you?" he asked Zanatose.

The night was still, silent, and tranquil as they walked on through the dark deserted alleys. The rain had finally declined and was down to a light drizzle. The fog was still dreadfully thick and at every alleyway the heroes turned into, they expected some kind of trap. No one was at ease except Fang.

As Bill walked cautiously at the back, a dead zombie's hand burst out of the ground and grabbed his ankle tightly.

It started pulling him down. "Wow, what the hell!" he yelled as he sliced it off. He quickly got back up with panic and sprained his ankle in the process.

More hands burst out of the ground and even more zombies came out of the houses. The hands grabbed the earth and pulled themselves out. Their already filthy bodies were covered in black mud. The army of zombies slowly limped toward them with glazed, senseless eyes, mere puppets of a specter.

The zombies staggered toward them slowly, with their arms outstretched. The zombies had old stains on their ragged clothes and skin. Their eyes were blood shot, if at all present. "Quickly, into that building," commanded Fang. He pointed to a building around the alley. "Run!"

The group of heroes ran as fast as they could behind Fang. As they ran from the pursuing zombies, Katie stumbled and fell on a piece of debris. "Katie, I'm coming!" yelled Zanatose. Zanatose turned around and started running toward her, toward their pursuers.

"No, keep going, Zanatose. I'm the one they want," she yelled back. He did not listen though. He helped her to her feet and took out Shadow. He slashed at a few of the zombies to move faraway enough to give himself and Katie a chance to run into the building everyone else was in.

The two of them burst through the threshold and Zanatose instinctively slammed the wooden door shut. He looked around for something to barricade the door with and found a wooden block. He grabbed it and tossed it into its hinges. It acted as a lock for the time being. Everyone sighed with relief and Zanatose leaned on the door, breathing heavily from the sprint and nerve racking terror.

"Good, now we're safe," he said, relieved of the zombies. The entire group was breathing hard from the dash and absolute fear. He closed his eyes and almost instantly started to drift off to sleep. He was calm until he felt a hard impact against the door he was leaning on. "Ahh!!" yelled Zanatose. He woke up from his daze with a jolt of fear. Zanatose quickly jumped away from the door and drew his two swords. Everyone held their breath in hopes that the zombies would not hear them and just leave.

"Maybe they left," suggested Bill hopefully. He was not in the mood to run anymore. His sprang ankle burned like fire every time he stepped down. They listened closely and started to hear the zombies scratching at all sides of the building. The zombies still persisted by ramming the door. With every impact the building shook.

"What do we do Zanatose?" asked Edwin. He was scared stiff. "Those things won't leave us alone!"

Zanatose stood stalk still. He was completely clueless about what to do next, and this was what scared him the most. He had never been so indecisive in times of need. "I don't know," he said slowly. Everyone was distressed by his reply, except Fang. He still seemed calm, and prepared.

"I know what must be done," said Fang, grimly. Everyone looked back at him and listened as if they were listening to a priest giving a last sermon. "We must open the door and blast straight ahead. They have no other way in." Then a bolt of lightning hit the alleyway near their window. It illuminated the building long enough for them to see there were actually many doors all around them. Some of the doors were open too, revealing the renewed rainfall.

As they looked around they saw broken windows in which the zombies' hands were reaching in from. "That's really not good!" yelled Edwin. They all took out their weapons. Fang grabbed an antique vase on a pedestal and threw it at the zombies reaching in. It smashed against their hands and made them fall back. Then the hands reached back in, with shards of pottery wedged into their hands, and persisted.

Zanatose felt a strange presence nearing him. The

presence was unlike anything else he had ever felt. The dark presence numbed his mind, body, and soul. His eyes could barely focus, his body ached in pain, and he fell to his knees. The dark presence was not human, was not even from his realm of being. He could feel the dark presence engulfing him. His body slowly arched forward unwillingly under the power of the dark presence. The entire group was oblivious to the occurrence, each obsessed with their own survival.

"You!? You will defeat me and my kind? HA haa haaa! I could crush you right where you stand, cowering in fear. What a hero you are! Do you fear the darkness this much? Stand up you pathetic worm. You have to survive to meet me in person," said a cryptic voice that surrounded Zanatose from all sides.

"Then let me go!" whispered Zanatose with rage. He raised his neck against the pressing force upon him. He raised his head to see the very same shadow upon the wall as in his dream, an odd, hooded figure. It was not really there though; it was only a shadow on the wall, without a source.

A terrible feeling arose in Zanatose's stomach as he looked at the shadow. That hooded figure was the dark presence he had sensed, that Abigail sensed, and so did the wolfos. Zanatose cautiously stood up, never letting the shadow on the wall leave his eyes. "What- no-who are you?" asked Zanatose.

The shadow did not reply; it simply disappeared. Zanatose stared at the wall until a loud bang against the door woke him up.

THE DOORS RATTLED AND THE WINDOWS SHATTERED.
SHADOWS CREPT IN THROUGH THE CRACKS
AND CONSUMED ALL THAT MATTERED.

THE SHADOWS CRUSHED THE HOPE
THE COURAGE
AND THE SOULS OF THEM ALL,

FEAR FROZE THE SOUL TO ICE, MADE SOLID BY THEIR FEAR.
THE ICE WAS SHATTERED BY A SHALLOW KNOCK.
KNOCKING ALL TOO NEAR TO WHAT WAS DEAR.

DOOM KNOCKED UPON THEIR DOORS.
WHAT WILL WE DO AS OUR OWN DOOM KNOCKS?
WILL WE ANSWER THE CALL, OR TRY
FASTENING THE LOCKS?
WILL WE REMEMBER OLD SCARS, OR WILL
WE REMEMBER ALL THAT WE HELD DEAR?
WILL WE FIGHT, OR WILL WE GIVE INTO FEAR?

THERE RESTS ONLY ONE CHOICE.
ANSWER DOOM'S SHALLOW KNOCKS OF DEATH,
AND REPLY IT WITH OUR COURAGE AND OUR HOPES.

CHPT 12:
DOOM'S KNOCKS

The doors broke open with a loud snap as the wood split. The zombies fell in through the doors. The windows shattered and allowed even more zombies to climb in. Edwin laughed nervously. "Um... Zanatose... got an um... plan?" he asked, as the zombies closed in on them.

"Not quite," said Zanatose. He was trembling and he felt weak from the encounter with the ethereal, dark presence. The dark transformations had made the burn on his arm grow, and now it looked almost like a dark snake. "You got a plan, right, Fang?" he asked as he rubbed his arm.

"We can only do one thing since, as you can see we can't run," Fang said calmly. "You know what we must do, Zanatose," said Fang. Fang took out a strange black crystal and placed it into his staff. Almost immediately after, a surge of dark energy surrounded him and he turned into a dark warrior.

Fang now had wide black eyes, claws, and pale skin. He quickly rammed a large group of the zombies back out the door. Zanatose was still trembling and started to breathe heavily. He was completely exhausted. *I have to help them but I can't move... Maybe I could use the dark powers to heal somehow,* thought Zanatose.

Zanatose tightened his grip on his swords. Zanatose was still standing at the same spot. He was trembling from head to toe as he tried to stand. A zombie raised its gruesome hand and slashed down at him. Fang quickly reacted on Zanatose's behalf, he pounced on the zombie and pinned it against the ground. Zanatose tried to turn into his dark form. Instead of transforming he felt a sharp pain against his arm; it was the snake burn. He winced from the pain and fell to his knees against the hardwood floor. His knees almost felt like they'd shatter. He raised his head to look around at his friends.

Everything was going to chaos. Bill and Edwin were pinned against a wall. They swung their swords heavily with exhaustion. They hacked the approaching zombies to pieces, but many got close enough to dig their claws into Bill and Edwin. By another dark corner of the house Zanatose saw Katie shooting at the zombies with her arrows as Brett pushed against a small clutter of zombies with his staff. He held out his staff and the zombies would just pile against it and he'd have to keep them back until Katie shot every one of them off.

The zombies saw Zanatose lying on the ground and started to approach him. "*So is this how it ends? No, not yet,*" he thought. "*I can feel another presence, but it's not as dark as the last one. It has a power that few possess, maybe it can save us.*"

Zanatose heard footsteps from somewhere above. He started to look up and then there was a blinding flash like lightening. He closed his eyes painfully and when he opened them again he saw that all the zombies were frozen in place. "What are you doing here?" asked a grim voice from atop the stair case. The heroes looked up at the stairs and as did Fang after turning back to normal. They saw a pale, thin man with sleek brown hair, black robes, and dark eyes.

"We're trying... to get out... of this place!" gasped Zanatose. Zanatose was still on his knees from exhaustion. "Can... you help?"

"I came here, pursuing some sort of unearthly anomaly, but I haven't found it. I have seen enough. I would be content to leave this place," he said stiffly. They could tell from his face that the stranger did not think they could escape.

Brett looked him up and down as the stranger descended the stairs and did not recognize where the black robes were from. "What's your name, where are you from?" Brett asked with suspicion.

"My name is Anton and I'm from the region called Hades… perhaps you've heard of it." Anton said.

"Not really," replied Brett. He grew increasingly suspicious of Anton.

"I have," said Fang.

Zanatose stood up with painfully and slowly walked over to Fang. He nudged Fang with his elbow and whispered into his ear, "Do you trust him?" The dark robes reminded him uncomfortably of the dark presence, but he knew the two were not related.

"He is from Hades and just because of that he should not be trusted, but I think we should let him lead us out before we judge him," Fang concluded.

Zanatose nodded then turned to Anton. "Alright, Anton, lead the way friend," he said. The last person they trusted was Alexis and she turned out to be possessed, Zanatose knew he was not the same. He believed that past Anton's gruesome exterior was a compassionate champion in the making.

They took a back exit from the old house which led them down another dark alley. The alley had a disgusting odor from the drenched buildings. The night was still silent except for Zanatose's rigid breathing. He still did not feel too well, and he had Fang helping him to walk.

"This way, through here," said Anton as he pointed to a closed, rusted gate.

"I'll deal with that, unless you'd like to Zanatose," said Bill with a chuckle as he looked at Zanatose's pale face.

"Oh no, I'm fine, go right ahead!" said Zanatose. He chuckled a little too. Even if he wanted to, he knew he could not break that metal gate. For him standing was hard enough.

"Sometime today, Bill," said Fang. He wanted to leave as soon as possible.

Bill took a deep breath then stepped back and ran at the gate. He rammed it with all his force. The gate gave a loud rattling noise and then fell off its hinges. Bill rubbed his shoulder and grinned at the fallen gate with pride.

"There you go," said Bill. Everyone walked through following Anton. It was still too dark to see well. Everyone followed Anton's dark figure closely so they would not get lost.

"You okay, Zanatose?" asked Katie in a low whisper. Zanatose was still trembling and paler than usual.

Fang tried to listen to their conversation. "The sword drains my energy every time I use it," said Zanatose. "That fight against the zombies in the beginning was too much. I shouldn't have used the sword's power for that long, and look at my arm!" He rolled up his right hand's sleeve to show a long snake burned into his skin.

Katie ran her fingers tenderly across his arm. She noticed it was etched into his skin like a tattoo. "You should tell Brett. He might be able to help," she said.

"No, only Fang can help me. I'm sure he knows more than Brett about these dark powers," said Zanatose.

Fang smiled as he listened in on their conversation. "You shouldn't trust him so much, Zanatose. You should put your faith in us, your friends." She was starting to get worried that Zanatose would join Fang after all. "We can help," she said reassuringly.

"There's the exit," said Anton as he pointed forward at some wall or gate. They could not see far enough through the darkness.

"You won't leave so easily!" screamed Abigail. She was right in front of the exit. Lightning hit the ground again and showed them the largest army they had ever seen standing behind her.

Abigail's presence triggered something in Zanatose and he morphed into his dark form again. He grunted and choked under the pain of the sudden transformation. "Get out of our way!" he yelled in a distorted voice, a blend between his voice and the dark voice in his head. He took out both swords and blasted the ground with Shadow.

The explosion against the ground propelled him at Abigail. He slashed at her with Blazer. Abigail dodged, but her zombies weren't as lucky. Once he landed he shredded a large group of them with Shadow and Blazer.

He slashed at one zombie and a large group disappeared. "You're using magic to hide your loss of slaves?" laughed Fang. "You're weaker than I thought." Fang took out his staff and ran at the zombies and started using his dark attacks on them just as Zanatose was.

Zanatose was jumping right and left into huge clusters of them and using his dark powers to shred them to bits. He used his newly enhanced speed in a lethal combination with his dual blades. He began to notice that if he concentrated hard enough, the darkness of the sword did not drain his energy as much and actually gave him more energy.

Katie took out her bow and arrows and shot them at the zombies as they approached with perfect marksmanship. She did not waste a single arrow; each one flew straight through the skull. Edwin, Brett, Anton, and Bill fought in a tight circle around her. They took out anything that got too close. Bill stopped fighting every few seconds to concentrate and make his sword glow to add more light and power.

Zanatose was tired of fighting weak zombies and jumped at Abigail. He thought he had her by surprise, but he was wrong.

Hammed Akbaryeh

"You think I'm stupid?" she laughed as she changed into a mirror image of him. She kicked him aside into a large cluster of zombies. "Let's get this over with already," she said impatiently as many huge trolls rose from the river. They were the size of a small building. "Take care of them," she commanded.

Zanatose got up with anger and started growling like a dog. Zanatose quickly jump kicked a troll and used his dark powers on a few that he decided he'll fight. Fang was doing the same exact thing. The trolls were massive, ugly, wrinkly, and reeked of fish. The trolls had green eyes and pointed ears as well as rotting fangs. Their demonic faces were set into a snarl.

Anton had a long, black staff made of wood that he was using for battle. With it he could cast spells. Anton kept muttering incantations and blasting fireballs with his staff at the trolls and burned them to ashes. Katie shot them as Edwin, Bill, and Brett fought them at close range.

A troll swung its hands down at Brett and he rolled out of the way, then he grabbed onto its arm. It swung its arms savagely trying to get him off. Brett had a strong hold and let go above its head. He jumped down and stabbed his staff into its thick skull. He heard a disgusting sound as the skull broke and allowed the staff to pass its hard surface.

Numerous more were rising from the lake, and Anton took notice of this. Meanwhile, supplementary zombies were rising out of the ground. Abigail laughed at a distance as she felt her revenge coming closer by the second. Zanatose was now far from weak and he was fighting side by side with Fang, surrounded by trolls and zombies.

They used their dark powers together to take care of the zombies. Zanatose would quickly slice and dice anything that got close and Fang was given the time to blast the trolls with dark blasts. The blasts would blow away the trolls' faces, spraying the ground with blood.

"I'll try to block up the river. It might help to stop the trolls from coming," said Anton in a doubtful voice. It was his magic against a dead witch's. He could not tell who would win.

"Everyone, surround Anton!" commanded Brett. Everyone except Fang and Zanatose surrounded Anton and tried to defend him as he worked out his spell.

Anton muttered strange words under his breath as he moved his hands in different patterns. "Come on, Anton, hurry up the magic act!" yelled Edwin as he rolled out of the way of a falling troll, blinded by arrows.

Bill charged his blade and blasted a troll's shin. It fell to its knees and Bill shoved his sword into its forehead. Brett used acrobatic moves to dodge the trolls. He rolled under one and attacked it from behind, then grabbed onto the next one's arm.

After a few minutes, Anton was done and he produced a white beam of light that froze the lake into ice. "Nice magic act, right?" he asked from Edwin with pride. This stopped the trolls from coming out of the lake, but the zombies were already out of the lake, as were a few trolls. "Now run to the exit!"

They all ran blindly through the darkness to the rusted gate as fast their exhausted bodies would carry them.

They rammed zombies down on their way, and fought a few trolls too. Each of them had to jump out of the way of the falling trolls, shaking the floor like a collapsing building. They were feet away from the gate when boulders fell right in front of the gate, blocking it.

"NO… NO!!!" screamed Abigail. "It's too close! I won't let you go!" she looked like she was going mad. "Get her Now! **Now**!" she screamed at the zombies.

Everyone looked at Anton for a solution. "Don't look at me! I'm not strong enough to move those rocks," he said grimly as the zombies rushed in on them. The zombies seemed to be stronger than normal and within a few blows had thrown Edwin and Bill out of their way. Abigail's rage fueled the zombies' strength.

"Get back, you monsters!" growled Brett as he swung his staff at as many zombies as he could. He could only take out a few on his own until one of the zombies grabbed his staff. "Let it go!" he yelled as he tried to pull back his staff. The zombie tightened its grip and spun him around, throwing him out of the way.

"Zanatose, help!" screamed Katie as the zombies grabbed her and dragged her toward Abigail.

Zanatose turned away from the zombies he was fighting and saw that she was in peril. He ran to her side like lightening, fueled by his empowered form. There was a strange dark gleam in his eyes. A current of dark energy pulsed around his body, but he was still in control.

He controlled the current of dark energy so that it threw the zombies off Katie. It looked like he was blasting the zombie off with lightening. "Thanks Zanatose," Katie said with relief. She was immensely relieved to be free, as was Zanatose.

Zanatose was thoroughly exhausted and he turned back to his human form and collapsed. He rolled up his sleeve nervously, but to his relief he saw the snake did not grow much further up his arm. He blinked once and could not open his eyes again.

About a minute later he opened his eyes again. Zanatose looked up and saw that Abigail and her zombies were gone. He also saw the sun starting to rise. It brought back a spark of hope in him to see the sunrise. It gave him hope that even through the darkest hours there will be a light at the very end. Zanatose stood up and spoke with some difficulty. "We have won our first battle, first true battle. This is a sign of hope that we can see this quest to the end."

Everyone felt they had accomplished something through

surviving that night. "Good thing that's finally over," said Brett.

"That's something we can all agree on," said Edwin. Everyone in the group felt exhausted and could barely raise their hands. They all wanted to move onto Theragorn city and hopefully get some rest.

"Now let's move on, but which way?" asked Katie.

"That way!" said Anton as he pointed into the sunrise. "We have to go that way to Theragorn city."

"I hope we never have to see Abigail again," said Katie.

Everyone nodded in agreement. "Oh don't worry. That's not the last of her. Don't forget that she's a ghost," said Fang.

"Even ghosts can be defeated. And I will be there when she tries to strike again," said Zanatose.

Fang was not listening to Zanatose. He was staring into the sunrise instead. Fang was thinking about something. "What's wrong?" asked Zanatose.

"You still have much to learn about your dark powers. They drain too much energy from you," replied Fang with disappointment.

"Thank you for helping us in this dire moment," said Brett. "But keep in mind that this doesn't make us friends. I will forever keep a watching eye upon you," he said coldly.

"As will I," said Fang as a crow with beady eyes flew above them.

Fang rammed the gate once and it rattled open. "For this moment in time, we were allies. Goodbye," said Fang as he jumped onto a jet black horse waiting for him on the other side. Fang rode off into the distant sunrise. He grew harder and harder to see as he rode away.

The group now had a new addition to their team. This addition was very strange, powerful, and incredibly knowledgeable. Zanatose explained their purpose to him and he understood and decided to help as well. "I've seen the sacred temple you're talking about," said Anton. Everyone looked hopefully at him to hear where it was.

"Really?" asked Brett in astonishment. He had never known anyone who had seen the sacred temple.

"I've seen it in a picture. It was so long ago I've forgotten what it looked like. It's probably in some castle. The painting is, not the temple," said Anton.

"Great, so no one knows where the temple is," said Edwin. The group was slightly disappointed. They were all hoping that Anton would know everything about how to get to the sacred temple since no one else they have met knew.

"Well, we better start moving everyone," said Zanatose. He yawned then said, "You lead the way, Brett." The group was very tired, especially Zanatose. Zanatose had still not recovered from the long battle. He was still limping and shaking from holding up his own weight.

Bill was also badly hurt from the battle. He had a few scratches and wounds, he was not as bad as Zanatose, but he was still exhausted. Edwin was badly thrashed in the battle and he had many wounds. Edwin, though, was not very tired. Brett was limping just like Zanatose. Brett had fought too many zombies on his own when he tried to protect Katie.

"You don't look too good, Zanatose," said Bill as they were slowly following Brett.

"Neither do you," said Zanatose as he looked at Bill.

"It's awful having to carry these bags on our backs!" complained Katie.

"Yeah, it's killing my back! When are we going to stop and make camp?" asked Edwin. The sun was rising higher as the time went on. They drew closer to a river which Brett told them they were heading for.

"Soon as we reach the river we can set camp and rest for a while till we recover," said Brett while he took deep breathes to talk. They were going up a steep hill and Zanatose stepped on a big rock that he did not see. The rock gave way and he fell backwards down the hill.

"Zanatose!" yelled Bill as he tried to grab onto Zanatose. Bill missed Zanatose narrowly and so did Edwin. "Look out!" warned Bill to Zanatose. Zanatose stopped rolling and started sliding on his back down the tall hill instead. Zanatose could feel his skin peeling away as he slid down the hill against his arm, looking down below he saw that he was about to fall off the hill onto the ground far below.

Zanatose grabbed a loose tree root and an odd rock. He hung there staring at the rock. He was perplexed by it. For some reason he was obsessed with it. As he looked at it closer he saw it was a magnificent, black crystal.

"Zanatose, you okay?" yelled Brett from the top of the hill. "Don't worry guys. He's probably fine," said Brett. Everyone was worried about Zanatose, dangling from a single tree root.

"I'm fine!" Zanatose yelled up to them. He hid the crystal in his bag and grabbed onto the root with both hands. He began to pull himself up with just his arms. Once he finally reached flat ground he stood up, his right leg gave away and he fell back down painfully. He looked at his leg and saw that the fall he had grazed the side of his leg. "I need some help standing back up!" he yelled.

"I'm coming, Zanatose!" yelled Bill. Bill started to go down the hill cautiously. He stumbled on a few rocks, but regained his balanced from a tree branch or boulder. He helped Zanatose up to his feet and Zanatose held onto him for support.

"Ahh... my leg burns!" said Zanatose as he limped up the hill.

"Just a little further," said Bill as they finally reached the top of the hill.

"Zanatose, are you okay?" asked Brett.

"Yeah, except for my leg," said Zanatose as he showed them his bleeding leg.

"I could fix that up," said Katie.

"Good, but save it until we reach the river," said Brett. "Let's keep moving." The group started to move on toward the river. The sun was now high in the clear blue sky and birds sung in the distance. The terrain was made up of grass, rocks, and trees.

Zanatose decided to show the others what he had found. He reached into his bag and took out the crystal. "Bill, hold on a sec," he said.

"Alright, but why?" asked Bill as he stopped dragging Zanatose forward. Zanatose showed him the crystal. "What is that?"

"I don't know, but I think Anton might." Zanatose turned to Anton and tapped him on the shoulder. Anton turned around and seemed a little aggravated to be disturbed. "Do you know what this is?" he asked Anton.

"Is that what you tripped on?" asked Brett. Zanatose nodded and Edwin laughed.

"You fell on that little thing?" laughed Edwin.

"Well, do you know what this is?" asked Zanatose again from Anton. He brought it toward Anton and he backed away quickly.

"Keep it away from me!" he said. "It's a dark crystal," his face was even grimmer than usual. "That thing has a large concentration of dark energy. It could kill anyone who is not use to using dark energy." Everyone's eyes grew wide.

"A small shred of dust from that crystal and you could poison and kill anyone," concluded Anton in his grim voice.

Zanatose's hand was starting to sting a little from holding it. He placed it back into his bag, no longer willing to bear the pain. "So, it's that dangerous?" Zanatose asked.

"Yes, it's deadly," said Anton. "Dark crystals were

studied by our high priests. It is incredibly deadly, but to someone who can control it the dark crystals can give you unimaginable power."

"That's amazing, and I have one," said Zanatose joyously. The group carried on thinking about the dark crystals' powers as they followed Brett to the river.

"The crystals seem too powerful to be manmade," interjected Katie.

"They're not manmade. They may not even be from this realm of existence," replied Anton.

The truth worried Zanatose, but Brett was most apprehensive of all. *"He's acquiring every dark weapon in existence and he's supposed to be the Chosen One... There's something wrong here and I'll figure it out,"* thought Brett silently.

They traveled on toward the river without any hardships. Their only hardship was their own exhaustion. Bill had to carry Zanatose and this slowed them down significantly. They traveled the distance of ten miles to the river in an entire day rather than a few hours. They had finally reached the woods with the river in it. Bill started hearing rustling in the bushes.

"The wolfos don't collect the dark crystals, do they?" asked Bill quietly.

"No, they don't, but there are creatures that treasure dark crystals," said Anton. Anton went quiet and so did everyone else as they walked on.

Katie heard another rustle in the bushes. She broke the silence and asked Anton a question about the crystals. "You said there are things that want the dark crystals. What wants the crystals?"

Anton paused then replied. "A few things do. For example, the tarik do. So do the Roctinian raptors. The Roctinian raptors have many nests. Unfortunately if you wish to open the sacred temple's doors you'll need their dark crystals."

"What do they want the crystals for?" asked Katie as she saw Zanatose had become interested in the conversation.

"The tarik want it for their leader which no one has ever seen. But the raptors have no reason to want the crystals. I don't really understand why *they* want the crystals," said Anton.

"Great, another thing added onto the to-do list, I'll just put it down next to the army of wolfos and zombies," said Edwin. Then he started rambling on about how their journey was becoming too difficult. "At this point, we need an army to get to that temple."

"Enough Edwin!" shouted Zanatose more sharply than usual. Everyone stopped dragging themselves forward and listened. "Edwin, if this is becoming too difficult for you, then leave! Otherwise be quiet and continue on with us."

"Sorry," mumbled Edwin. Edwin felt embarrassed as they walked onwards in silence. Brett soon decided on a fit place to set up camp and he gave everyone a job. He asked Bill and Edwin to get fire wood, and everyone else started to set up the tents. The forest had many old trees which that had plenty of green leaves. It was easy to find fire wood since there was broken tree branches everywhere on the ground, but there were lots of thorns too. They had to make sure they did not set up the tent too close to the thorns.

"So, what are you making today?" asked Brett.

"I think I'll make a nice steak for everyone," said Bill. Anton lit the fire with his magic and Bill started rummaging through his bag for his spices and meat. "What do you guys think?" he asked.

"You read my mind, Bill," said Zanatose happily. Zanatose was lying down and relaxing a little in the shade of a tree. Bill soon made an excellent steak for the group, and they all ate it on wooden plates. Once they were done they decided to go to sleep, and recover from their exhaustion.

CHPT 13:
DARK FORCES

Zanatose fell asleep, but he had an unsettling dream about himself becoming some kind of dark lord. He saw himself wielding two dark blades. He was attacking the city of Nijad and he was fighting all his friends. He woke up with a start. He was covered in cold sweat and his heart was beating quickly. He sat bolt upright to see where he was. His leg immediately stung, he saw that he was inside of his tent. He decided to get up and take a walk. He took his sword, Shadow, and the crystal.

He used his sword as a cane to ease the pressure off his leg as he walked out of his small tent. He saw that Katie was also awake, sitting down on the grassy hill, staring at the red moon in the dark sky.

The group all slept soundly in their own separate tents, except for Zanatose and Katie. Zanatose walked over to Katie in the dark and tapped her on the shoulder. "Hey Kate," whispered Zanatose. "I couldn't sleep either."

"Yeah, neither could I," replied Katie. She yawned and stretched out a bit, lying down on the grass. "Is your leg still hurting you?" she asked.

"Yeah, it still hurts," said Zanatose. "Think you can wrap it up a bit, please?"

"Sure, it's something to pass the time," she said as she went back into her tent and came out with her bag. She took out some bottles and bandages to clean and wrap his leg. "This won't take long."

"Thanks, Kate," said Zanatose as she started to dab some of the fluids in the bottles onto a cloth. She begun cleaning the cut with the damp rag, and it stung a bit. She started wrapping up his leg where he had the wound with some cloth. "What kept you awake?" asked Zanatose. "For me it was a nightmare."

"I just couldn't sleep that's all. I just can't get over what's happened in such a short time," Katie said.

She started to sniffle and hold back her tears. Zanatose understood why she was so sad. She had lost her best friend. It would be like him losing Bill. "I'm sorry about what happened to her. I wish I could've saved her, but there was nothing anyone could have done," Zanatose said, trying to lift her spirits.

She kept wrapping up his leg silently. "I'm sorry about what happened in the village," said Katie. "I'm so sorry that I dragged you into this mess."

"Katie, don't worry about that. Abigail is the least of our worries," said Zanatose. "In a day we'll be at the doors of Theragorn city and we'll be safe for a time."

She looked up at him slowly with reddening eyes. "We both know it's not that simple. A day hasn't passed that we haven't been attacked by some thing," she said desolately. She had finished wrapping up his leg and she sat back on the grass. The moon was high in the sky and there were countless, bright stars. The two laid back and stared at the stars for a time with an extensive river stretching out before them. One fork went toward a mountain, one toward a city, and another into an ocean. They both had different things on their minds. One thought where was he being led? The other thought about her grim past and even grimmer future.

Katie turned to Zanatose and asked him, "Do you think we can beat the tarik?"

Zanatose sighed and thought for a few seconds. Then he nodded his head. "There are times when I'm confused, and afraid. That's when I don't know, but here, with *you*, I really think *we* could make it."

"Zanatose, what are you trying to say?" she asked with a bright look in her eyes. "Hey, wait… Zanatose do you hear something?" she asked. There was a small rustle in the bushes nearby.

"I hear it, but I doubt that it's anything," he said reassuringly. He was preparing to finally tell her how he felt about her. He wanted to tell her that all his life, he could attribute his achievements to his pursuit of her; he wanted to tell her that he would do anything for her; he wanted to tell her everything in his bleeding heart.

She still looked doubtful as she stared at the bush, ignoring the longing look in Zanatose's eyes. "I'll check it out," he said. He struggled to his feet and dragged his sword along with him.

Zanatose pushed the bush's leaves aside to peer inside. He saw something long and thin moving on the ground like a snake of some kind. "That's strange," he muttered to himself. He reached in, but the thing moved quickly and whipped him in the face. He fell backwards and came to a stop at Katie's feet. She helped him back up to his feet.

"What was that?" she asked him. He shrugged and the thing in the bush gave a high pitched screech like a bird call. This seemed to be some kind of signal judging by the number of them that jumped out of the bushes. A handful of Roctinian raptors emerged from the bushes and trees around them.

The tall raptors stood on two legs, with massive claws, and an extra big toe claw on each foot. The menacing raptors had red gleaming eyes that glittered like tiny rubies against the dark sky. They looked from Katie to Zanatose then back again, each raptor was synchronized perfectly. They would use different sounds like clicks and screeches to communicate with each other.

Katie gasped and jumped back away from them. Zanatose struggled to stand up with the aid of his sword, but it did not work too well. One of the raptors in chest armor stepped forward. Zanatose guessed that it must be their leader. It gave a series of grunts and whistles. Then a few raptors approached Zanatose and Katie and sniffed them down.

"Don't worry Kate, it'll be alright. I promise," whispered Zanatose into Katie's ear. A raptor raised its hand and was about to slash Katie. Zanatose used his sword as a balance as he kicked the raptor back.

The raptors all gave low growls, and the leader approached Zanatose. It towered above Zanatose. The thing had malicious eyes filled with hunger, but not for flesh. This raptor looked like it was seeking something. Zanatose looked up at the raptor's powerful jaws. The raptor's scales resembled the same dark green as the bushes it had jumped out of.

"Come and get me. Unless you're afraid," taunted Zanatose. He wasn't sure if the raptor understood him. He stood ready, leaning against his sword, for the raptor to pounce on him.

"Zanatose, even you can't take that thing," cried Katie as she held on tightly to him. "You can't stop their leader *alone*," said Katie. She was going to take Zanatose's sword to use it in her desperation, but Zanatose slid it away.

"Katie it has dark energy just like the…" Zanatose had a moment of realization as he remembered the dark crystal. "The crystal! It'll give me enough dark energy to fight their leader," Zanatose exclaimed excitedly.

Zanatose took out the crystal from his pocket. The raptors stared at it in awe as he used its powers to morph into a larger dark warrior. He had changed into a true beast from using both the sword and crystal's powers. He was bigger, and resembled a wolfo more than usual. He clenched the sword in one hand, and held onto the crystal tightly in the other. Katie was horror-stricken by his transformation.

Zanatose braced himself for battle with the Roctinian raptor's leader. The raptor sprang at him and attacked with its hind legs. Zanatose rammed the raptor back. The raptor's claw had grazed his shoulder and made him drop his sword.

Zanatose brought out his hand claws like a cat. He slashed at the raptor. The raptor dodged left and right, and then head butted Zanatose in the chest. Zanatose lost his breath for a moment. The raptor quickly rounded on him and tried to bite his arm. Zanatose whipped around and slashed the Roctinian raptor across the face. He left a gash on the raptor's face, across its left eye.

The raptors became enraged, and were about to pounce on Zanatose, but their leader commanded them otherwise. The leader nodded toward Zanatose then pointed its head the opposite direction and the raptors left. The leader kept staring and snarling at the crystal as he backed away slowly.

Once the raptors were far away, Zanatose turned back to normal and collapsed to the ground. The crystal rolled out of his hand. "You just can't catch a break Zanatose," said Katie sadly as she shook her head. "You're probably in so much pain." She saw that he had a fresh wound on his shoulder. Katie moved toward the dark crystal, as she reached down for it, Zanatose moved his hand over it.

"That thing is the reason I'm in this state," he said weakly. He stored it back into his pocket. "If that's what it does to the one chosen to wield it, imagine what it would do to anyone else." His arm burned, but he ignored the pain and regarded it as a battle scar. Katie helped him up and back to the tents. Zanatose picked up his sword on their way back to the tents.

"Good night, and thank you for everything," said Zanatose to Katie as she left his tent for some sleep.

It was now almost sunrise; the two were exhausted and slept in the following day. Later in the day, once Katie and Zanatose woke up for a late breakfast, Katie told Brett about the raptors.

"That's a cause for concern," said Brett disappointedly. "Bill, come here." Bill came to Brett; he was still tired, and he was a little cranky that he had to do something.

"What is it?" asked Bill irritably.

"You and me will be leading a scouting mission in those woods for any traces of the Roctinian raptors Zanatose and Katie fought last night," said Brett.

"Zanatose is alive so aren't the raptors long gone?" laughed Bill. "There's absolutely no one Zanatose can't take out." Zanatose hung his head down in disappointment.

"He's right, I should have taken care of them last night," he muttered.

"In your state?" laughed Brett. "Well... let's go Bill," said Brett as he waved his hand to Bill to follow him. "See you guys later." Bill waved his farewells too as they went into the woods.

Once the two had disappeared into the thick jungle Zanatose told his story to Anton and Edwin. "There I was with just my sword, Shadow and the crystal. I could barely stand without the sword and then I used the crystal's awesome power. The raptor thirsted for blood as he charged at me. It sliced me with its vicious claws," said Zanatose dramatically as he slapped his own arm. "I thought it was all over, but then I stabbed my sword into its guts and vanquished the horrendous beast!" said Zanatose proudly. He had extended the truth, but the others did not need to know that. The raptors' leader was actually still alive. He told his over-dramatized story over some soggy bread and cheese at breakfast.

"Wow, even I'm impressed Zanatose. I have never met any of the pack leaders of the Roctinian raptors," said Anton. Anton was staring blankly at the jungle which Brett and Bill had gone into. "You think they'll find anything?"

"Probably not," said Katie hopefully.

Zanatose thought about this a little bit. He knew he hadn't defeated all of the raptors so they may plan to attack again. A gut instinct in him told him he was right. "I think they will be back for revenge," said Zanatose.

"I'll take care of them this time," said Edwin. "You guys just sit back and relax."

Zanatose shook his head at Edwin, and his bold statement. "These raptors are very powerful and intelligent," said Zanatose. Zanatose rolled up his sleeve to show them the cut he had from the raptor's claws. He rolled up the sleeve of the arm that did not have the snake scar. "I fought just one with my dark powers and look what I got. Plus, these things can talk to each other."

"They can't be worse than the wolfos or tarik," said Edwin carelessly.

"I think they maybe stronger than the tarik," said Zanatose grimly. He shook his head slowly and talked about the raptors. "You should've seen them. They moved in such a uniform fashion. The leader would give commands, and they would follow in less than a second, no hesitation."

"Zanatose are you actually intimidated by them?" asked Edwin. Zanatose shook his head and Edwin laughed. "You're actually afraid of them!"

"He is not," said Katie forcefully. "Leave him alone. He's been through enough lately," she said.

Edwin, chuckled, but left Zanatose alone for the rest of the day nonetheless. The remainder of the group relaxed for a few hours as they waited for the scouting crew to return.

Toward midday Bill and Brett were running back to the camp as fast as they could, covered in sweat and full of fear. They stopped in the middle of the camp, they were out of breath. They gasped for air as everyone surrounded them. Katie seemed concerned and so was Zanatose. "What happened?" asked Zanatose.

"There is an army of raptors out there and they have some kind of *dark* artifact. We think the raptors may be recovering something powerful," blurted out Brett. "You have to see that thing to believe it!"

"Everyone, pack up!" commanded Zanatose. "Once we finish packing, you guys have to lead us to the Roctinian raptors." Everyone in the group started to pack up their tents as fast as they could. They stuffed everything crudely back into their bags. Zanatose decided to keep his swords and the crystal near hand so he could use them all together if necessary.

The group finished packing in a matter of minutes. "Let's go," commanded Brett. Brett and Bill led the group through the thick jungle. They pointed out deadly plants along the way. There were many colorful trees everywhere overhead, but no time to admire their many shades of red, orange, and green. As the team rushed forward, Edwin would try to admire the hues of red, but would soon stumble into a sharp thicket of thorns.

After a short walk and a lot of painful thorns, they came to a clearing where they saw countless Roctinian raptors trying to transport some kind of odd artifact. It had strange carvings from some far away time on it. It was an ancient sword that time had tried to conceal, or at least it looked ancient. The raptors had been digging it up restlessly it seemed. The sword had a resemblance to Zanatose's sword, Shadow.

They watched the raptors circling the area and they noticed on the other side the raptors were circling a far-reaching perimeter. "That's odd. If they went off so far on that side how come they haven't seen us?" asked Edwin.

Zanatose shrugged, but he felt uneasy. He pushed his leg into the dirt and was content, feeling no pain there. That day had given him enough time to heal his leg, although his shoulder was still in some pain.

The group was patiently lying under the bushes, watching the raptors go about their work. Zanatose thought to himself that maybe the raptors were not as smart as they seemed, they were not even found yet. The group was waiting for the opportune moment to strike until they heard a loud sound that was a mix of a bird call and a very loud bark. They all stood up and instinctively stabbed their weapons behind them, into the same raptor, at once. The raptor gave a low growl and fell motionless.

"I think they know we're here," said Bill.

"We might as well have announced our entrance," Edwin muttered bitterly.

All of the raptors stopped towing the artifact, dropping their ropes, and all of their beady eyes were on the small band of heroes. The raptors gave little clicking noises that seemed to mean "Wait for the command," because none of the raptors attacked until their leader came up and gave a loud, bellowing bark.

Malice glinted in the leader's eyes when he looked at Zanatose. The beast's long snout opened wide and displayed its rows of sharp teeth as it gave loud howling barks of rage. The raptors all attacked as if compelled by indomitable spirits. The sea of frenzied raptors clustered around the group with protruding claws and snouts. Katie was blocked by Zanatose, but another raptor pounced onto him. The beast forced Blazer and Shadow out of his grasp with a whip of its tail. He tried to reach for his swords, but the raptor kept whipping his hand painfully away.

Katie carefully made her way behind a tree and took out an arrow from her quiver. She took a deep breath pressed her bow back and shot her arrow through the skull of a

Roctinian raptor. Bill, Edwin, and Brett fought against the raptors in a back to back triangle. They were attacked by waves of the viscous monsters. Edwin fell off his feet after a few tackles. Bill saw his friend fall, and felt a sudden surge of panic creep through his body. Death was near him and all that he held dear. He controlled his panic, knowing that yielding to it now may be the last mistake of his life. He focused on his sword and charged it up so he could fight like a real hero.

Brett's staff broke under the weight of the claws and jaws jumping onto and snapping on through with razor sharp teeth. The metal staff split like a tree branch against the strength of the raptors' greedy snouts. Anton rolled, jumped, and side-stepped the maelstrom of teeth and claws as he used his powers to incinerate and freeze the raptors. He wore a grin as he watched the raptors pounce at him, miss, and burn. The strength of the raptors insignificant compared to Anton's occult power and speed. He was no stranger to war and death; he was an expert combatant with a dark past stained with blood.

Zanatose kicked the raptor off and reached out for both of his swords. He used Shadow to stab the raptor in the back. The Roctinian raptors' leader suddenly jumped at its fatigued prey. Zanatose tried to block with Blazer, but his sword flew out of his weak grasp and dropped at Brett's feet.

Brett pushed a raptor off and grabbed Blazer out of desperation. He swung the sword across his chest, slicing through his aggressor's abdomen. Brett felt his sword trapped against a bone as he tore it out, unleashing a stream of red blood. The blood reminded him of the first man he had ever killed, a dirty peasant boy who had a knife between his teeth. The boy was coming of age, and was part of the wrong crowd. The ruffian slew a rope over the garden wall and tried to climb over, Brett caught sight of him and told him to cease and desist. The boy dropped down and came at

Brett with the knife. Seconds later, blood was running down the assailant's shirt from a puncture in his chest.

The other men in the group could barely hang on any longer. Edwin was on the ground and struggling with a raptor that was on top of him, its powerful jaws clamped shut inches from his sweaty face. With every snap his heart would drop. Bill was becoming too tired to fight. The strain of pushing off raptors and swinging his sword was exhausting him. Zanatose was in another one-on-one showdown with their leader and a few of the raptors.

The Roctinian raptors' leader rammed Zanatose to the ground with its hard head. Zanatose felt a sharp object jut into his side as he fell. He had fallen on the strange artifact; the inscriptions seemed oddly familiar to him. *"I wonder if my crystal will awaken the sword's dark powers?"* thought Zanatose. He took out his crystal and placed into one of the several craters on the sword's handle.

The faded color of the sword was gone and it was now magnificent, renewed with life, awakened by darkness. It had a dark blue sapphire blade, and its handle was decorated with rubies. He stood up and a strange, incredibly painful, surge pulsed through him from the new sword. It stunned him for a moment, but he quickly shook it off. His survival was the sign of the sword's recognition of him as its new master. He began to hear whispers in his ear, but they were not coherent to him.

He used the two dark blades, allowing their power to course through his body. The raptors' leader pounced and on instinct he gave it a round-house-kick in the face. The disgruntled beast crashed into a tree, and slithered out of sight. Zanatose used his dark powers on the raptors; he directed two currents of dark lightening. It sent them flying through several trees, scattering woodchips into the sky. Zanatose's new power was a terror to behold. The savagery in his eyes matched that of the terrible monsters he fought, and his sanity was starting to bend.

The raptors stopped concentrating on the group and only attacked Zanatose. Edwin released a broken sigh as the raptor left him alone; tears were starting in the corners of his eyes. For a few short moments, Zanatose was fending off all the raptors, then there were too many and he was trembling and losing control. The extra dark sword was burning his hand like a boiling pot, and his grip was slipping. Zanatose could feel the influence of the two swords, but he resisted its full control with what was left of his mind. He felt the sword burn him, and he heard the whispers in his ears. His inner turmoil slowed his mind and movements. A slash caught him in his arm and he blanked out from all of the pain.

"We're coming Zanatose!" yelled Brett as he rushed into the flurry of claws and fangs. Bill used an energy blast to shoot a few off. Katie also came out of hiding and helped Zanatose with her bow and arrows. Anton created a bright flash of light with his magic, blinding them momentarily. The raptors' leader was on top of a tree, giving a loud booming call that forced the heroes to cover their ears. It was another retreat order. The raptors gave up the fight.

"Zanatose, you okay!?" asked Brett as he tugged Zanatose back to his feet.

"I don't know…" said Zanatose. He was still shaking. He placed Shadow and the new sword into his two sheaths. "The artifact they wanted is some kind of dark sword which needs the crystal for power." Each sword tugged at Zanatose, trying to conquer his mind. He could not resist the power, but he feared being conquered by the influence of the two swords.

"How strange… the prophecy of our doom is unfolding," said Anton grimly.

"What?" Bill was annoyed by Anton's pessimistic view points.

"Never mind that, we should start moving toward Theragorn before it starts raining again," said Brett.

The group moved on. The day became continually cloudier until it started to rain. They ran with the haste of a humming bird through the jungle to the nearest cave for cover. It was a dark, moldy cave. There was very little smooth rock to sit on; it had jagged rocks hanging from the ceiling and protruding from the ground. "Well, we're not too wet at least," said Edwin. Their tunics were covered with specks of rain. They got into the cave minutes after the rain started.

Anton built them a fire which Bill, Edwin, and Katie sat around. Brett and Zanatose sat together in a corner near the entrance. "Do you think there's another crystal nearby? Maybe that's why it's raining," suggested Brett. His mind was elsewhere as he stared through the rain toward some invisible beacon, calling him from the distance.

Zanatose closed his eyes and focused his mind. He sensed something light, not dark. "If it's a crystal it's not a dark crystal," remarked Zanatose. "How did you sense it?"

"I don't know… I just can feel it somewhere in the distance, calling to me," said Brett. Zanatose found Brett's behavior strange, but he disregarded it.

The group did not stay in the cave for long. The rain stopped after a short hour. "Guys, the rain has stopped," yelled Katie.

"Then let's go," said Anton. They all stood up and dusted rubble off of their tunics before following Anton out of the cave.

"Zanatose, I think those raptors were the worst of the things we've met on our journey," said Bill. "Good thing we're just a day's hike from Theragorn city."

"Finally we're almost at our first destination," said Zanatose. This was the first time he noticed they were finally nearing the promised city of aid. So much had happened that he felt like years had passed.

First, they met the wolfos who beat them easily. Then, they met General Jonathan who hopefully will help with their journey. Next, they met General Wolf Fang. He was said to be evil, but he had helped them so far.

Then worst of all, they met Abigail and lost Alexis, but gained Anton. Zanatose still could not ignore that dark cloaked figure he saw in the broken down village. It was the first time that he had felt a truly dark presence; it had no mercy or compassion in its heart. Now, they met the Roctinian raptors and the dark artifact.

The most important part to Zanatose was the fact that the snake burn on his arm was becoming longer every time the darkness took more control over him. He knew that after he had used the new sword the snake had extended. He was thinking, "*What will happen to me soon? Will the darkness take over?*"

**In the darkest hour, there is always a
ray of hope. Never give up in it.**

PART 2:

Parting of the ways

CHPT 14:
THERAGORN CITY ASSAULT.

The group had finally caught sight of the great Theragorn city; it was truly the stronghold of Nijad. They were at a clearing and they saw tall skyscrapers, and a few castles. They were all worried once they saw smoke coming from the center of the majestic, safe haven.

"What do you think that smoke is from?" asked Bill.

Brett shrugged and so did Anton. Zanatose stepped in front of the group and started marching toward Theragorn city. "Whatever it is, it can't be good, so let's get moving," said Zanatose.

They marched through the huge city's gates. Oddly enough there were absolutely no guards on duty for the gate. The city had an even larger market place than Nijad city. Rather than little stands they had big bazaars with roofs. They saw tall buildings on either side of them as they walked through the seemingly deserted city.

"Where are all the people? I thought this place was supposed to be famous," said Edwin. He was disappointed at their first glimpse of the city.

They looked around at the many tall buildings made of stone and they found nothing in them. They tried looking inside, but the shutters were all closed. It seemed like the city had been evacuated or put on lockdown. They passed many blocks of houses until they were at an intersection of the streets.

"Looks like trouble. The soldiers are out," said Zanatose. They saw a large group of Theragorn's soldiers. They recognized a few from the battle to save Brett. They also saw the leader, General Gateman. "General! What's going on?" asked Zanatose.

Jonathan turned around from his notes and saw Zanatose and his team approaching. The General seemed lost in his thoughts. He seemed relieved to see them, the authority started to return to his face. "Well, you guys aren't the reinforcements we needed, but you'll do. Theragorn city is under siege and we're planning a two pronged attack on the beasts that have killed our king," explained Jonathan. "Can I count on your assistance in my hour of need?"

The group looked at each other then they all looked at Zanatose. Zanatose sighed, nodding his head. "If it's for the good of this city, then of course we'll help," he replied.

Jonathan smiled and said, "I knew I could count on all of you. Thanks for coming in a niche of time."

"Great, another battle," said Edwin dejectedly. "Can't we ever catch a break?"

"It is our duty as servers of justice!" replied Brett proudly. Bill, Zanatose, and Edwin laughed at him. Anton shook his head with amusement.

Zanatose ignored them and asked Jonathan, "What's the plan? We can't just charge in there and hope to overpower them," said Zanatose. "What are we even facing anyway?"

"We're facing the wolfos," said Jonathan as he looked over his battle plan on a piece of brown paper. He traced some of the lines with his finger and shook his head. "I just hope this plan works. The wolfos are such an awful nuisance!" he roared in frustration.

Zanatose was surprised that the wolfos had time to attack Theragorn city, and kill the king just two days after their leader helped them out of a haunted village. "You still haven't told us the plan," remarked Bill.

Jonathan had forgotten that the group was not part of his city's army and they did not know the plan. "Oh right, the plan," said Jonathan. He was starting to seem a little tense. "It may or may not work, but we're hitting the wolfos from two sides. We're sending one battalion in, a smaller one, to the city square, and another will come in as a back up in a few minutes. We're hoping the backup, led by me, can surprise them."

"Wait, if you lead the backup, then who leads the main charge?" asked Zanatose. He felt he already knew the answer and he was not too happy about it.

"I was hoping that I take three quarters of the army and you lead the rest Zanatose," Jonathan shook his head and coughed. "No, I meant *General* Zanatose."

Zanatose laughed at his sudden promotion, but was proud none the less. "What do you think the wolfos are after?" asked Zanatose. He hoped it was not an elemental item, because that was why they had come.

"They came for our elemental shield. Once we get rid of them you guys can have it," said Jonathan. Brett was about to talk, but Jonathan quickly cut him off. "Enough chit chat lets execute this plan before it's too late," he said urgently.

Jonathan turned to his men and commanded most of them to go with him. "Alright you all follow me." Jonathan turned to Zanatose and asked, "Zanatose, may I take a few of your crew along with me?" he asked. Zanatose nodded; Jonathan pointed out Brett, Katie, Anton and Edwin. "Alright follow me! We'll station at the eastern front of the city." Jonathan walked off leading his men toward the eastern wing of the city.

This left Zanatose with Bill and a small battalion to go and charge at the wolfos head on. "Alright follow me!"

commanded Zanatose. He headed straight toward the heart of the city. "You think we stand a chance?" asked Zanatose.

"You've got me and a quarter of the greatest army. Why not?" replied Bill. His voice was not firm with confidence, but they had no other choice than to lead the charge.

As the army marched onward, they saw movements up on the rooftops, but they could not catch a good glimpse of what it was. Zanatose and Bill were surprised to notice that there was no damage to the houses they passed by in the desolate city. "Well this has been easy enough so far," remarked Zanatose. He was relieved that they were still alive after venturing so far into the city.

"Sir, watch out!" cried out a soldiers suddenly. One of the soldiers closer to Zanatose jumped in between Zanatose and a wolfo which had tried to jump onto him from the roof tops.

The soldier fell under the weight of the wolfo and struggled against it until Zanatose's sword came down through the wolfo's skull and almost through the soldier. Zanatose kicked the wolfo's motionless, maimed body off the soldier and helped him up. "Thank you," said Zanatose. He felt conflicted over the wolfo's death; it was different from killing a tarik, or a zombie.

"Thank you sir," croaked the soldier. They looked up at the roof tops and saw nothing. Then they continued to a fountain in the middle of a small plaza that Zanatose guessed was the city square.

Bill tapped Zanatose on the shoulder and they all stopped. "What is it?" asked Zanatose.

"L… look up," whispered Bill. Zanatose looked at Bill, first noticing his eyes. His eyes' pupils had shrunk with fear. Zanatose looked up and saw that the wolfos army was lined up around the roof tops surrounding them. "Everyone, get ready to fight!" commanded Zanatose. A loud sound of swords being unsheathed echoed through the small plaza.

Every man in the army took out their weapon and Zanatose took out only Shadow, fearing his new sword's power over him.

The wolfos growled menacingly from the roof tops. As the archers tightened their arrows against their bows the wolfos let out mad barks. Wolf Fang appeared from behind a group of wolfos. He looked very pleased to see Theragorn city's army. "So you think so few of you can defeat me?" he asked with a laugh. Zanatose saw the soldiers around him starting to tremble in fear, loosening their grips on their arrows. "Tear them to shreds," he commanded to his wolfos.

The wolfos jumped down and started to sprint at them. "What are you waiting for!? **Attack Now!**" yelled Zanatose with such vigor that he spit as he spoke; his voice echoed through the city's square. The men quickly ran at the wolfos onslaught with their spear men and swordsmen in front. The archers stayed back and fired as fast as they could before the wolfos overcame the front line, galloping through the wall of men.

Fang also joined the fight, running straight for Zanatose. Zanatose's back was turned and Fang was about to ram him down. Zanatose was busy fighting a cluster of wolfos with his sword Shadow, slashing two through the throat and elbowing another against its nose. Bill was fighting back to back with him; he saw Fang coming. Bill went to fight Fang alone, without hesitation running forward.

Bill and Fang stopped in front of each other in the middle of the epic battle. Men and wolfos were dropping on every side of them, but neither one was moved by this. "This time you'll have to pass by me!" roared Bill. He had enough of Fang taking on his friends. It was time for his revenge.

Fang was infuriated that Bill stood in his way. "Stand aside, weakling," said Fang through gritted teeth. "Or face worse than any army can give," he threatened.

"Come and get me," said Bill. Fang rushed at him and rammed Bill hard in the gut. Bill almost fell, but used his sword to stay up. He stood up and gasped for air. "Is that all you've got?"

"I warned you!" yelled Fang as he went in to strike again.

This time Bill was ready and he blocked Fang's staff with his sword. This only infuriated Fang further. Fang gave quick stabs to him in every direction. Bill struggled to keep up. Bill stabbed his sword at Fang. Fang dodged and hit Bill in the face with the end of his bisento. Bill fell unconscious. "Next time you won't be so lucky," said Fang to Bill's unconscious body.

Zanatose was surrounded by a cluster of wolfos and his men were starting to fail. "*Where is Jonathan?*" he thought to himself. He drew his second dark sword out of desperation and fought off the wolfos. The wolfos kept ramming him, but he stayed up, unwilling to give up after all he had endured. He slashed the wolfos with both swords, using one sword to block the claws of the wolfos and another to strike at the wolfos.

A wolfo rammed against Zanatose and he lost his balance, falling. "No, I will not fall. Not like this!" he roared. "For Theragorn city!" he yelled as he threw the wolfo's immense weight off him. Many soldiers heard him and repeated what he said, boosting their morale. The soldiers fought harder than ever before, just as unwilling to die as Zanatose. He rose back to his feet and was staring Fang straight in the eyes. "Oh great," he moaned as he raised his weapons. He was panting from the effort of wielding the two swords. His left arm hung lower than his right, still burdened by the pain of a Roctinian raptor's scorn.

"I've dispatched your friend," said Fang as he pointed at Bill lying on the ground. "You cannot expect to get all the elemental items against us."

"You're right," admitted Zanatose. "That's why I'm going to take you out now!" Zanatose ran at him with both swords and slashed at Fang with all his might.

Level headed, he ducked and weaved away from the blows. "Join me Zanatose. Together we will conquer this world and rid it of any evil," said Fang.

"I trusted you, and this is what you do? I actually thought you were right till I saw this. You killed an innocent king!" yelled Zanatose, slowly feeling the burning fire of rage come to life within him.

"I am here to collect the elemental item. I had no idea that the king has died. It was not my doing. Something of those sorts' sounds like a power struggle between two hungry men," said Fang. "I want to rid the world of the darkness." Zanatose stabbed at him with Shadow, Fang blocked and kicked him in the gut. Just like Bill, he refused to fall. "You're just like your friend. You're both arrogant enough to think you can challenge my strength."

"I am power," said Zanatose as he succumbed to the temptations of the dark voices in his head. He used a dark energy current to strike at Fang alongside his twin blades. Fang attempted to dodge until Zanatose's sword tore through his shoulder. Fang stopped and blocked the barrage of blows with his staff. Zanatose pounded his swords like hammers, down, against Fang's staff. Each blow sent him closer to the ground.

"You are bound by your restraint; you are too weak to release yourself," laughed Fang as he hit Zanatose across the face with the end of his staff. "If you join me, I will show you how to release yourself from those chains and become truly powerful. We could rid the world of darkness!"

The two stopped fighting and Zanatose considered the offer. He began to realize the corruption around him. *"Perhaps Fang is the victim in all of this,"* he thought to himself. "Will I have to harm my friends?" asked Zanatose. He raised his swords, awaiting the answer.

"No, unless they try to harm you," replied Fang. Zanatose turned back to normal and thought that perhaps Fang was right. In the background, Bill had woken up again and he fought his way through the wolfos toward Zanatose and Fang.

The wolfos dashed at him from every direction as he fell under their weight time and time again. Every time, he pushed himself back up and threw off the wolfos. One wolfo fell into the fountain and it broke, revealing a shield with a lion's face emblazed on the front.

"The shield," Bill murmured to himself. He ran toward it, believing that attaining the shield could somehow save him and Zanatose from death. The wolfos became crazed at the sight of the shield, and tried to ram him down. He ducked a few of them and dodged some other wolfos' heavy bodies. Another dashed at him straight on and an archer shot a lucky arrow through its skull.

Bill reached the fountain's remains and took the shield. "This'll do the job," he said, blocking an oncoming wolfo with his shield and then slicing its neck. The warm blood poured out along with the wolfo's last breath. "Now for Fang," he said; Bill turned and ran toward Fang, thinking only of his friend's safety.

"So will you join the wolfos?" asked Fang. The wolfos had made a defensive circle around Zanatose and Fang to keep everyone out. Zanatose looked up and saw Bill coming. A wolfo quickly tackled him.

"No!" yelled Zanatose, referring to Bill's condition. He raised his weapons again and ran to help Bill, but Fang was in the way.

"What!? No!?" Fang looked outraged by Zanatose's reply. He stabbed down at Zanatose. Zanatose blocked and tried to attack back. Fang dodged and kicked Zanatose to the ground. Zanatose's swords flew out of his hands. "Then you shall die," growled Fang. He placed the blade of his staff against Zanatose's throat.

Jonathan came leading his men into action at last. "Everyone attack!" Jonathan roared over the heated battle. His men caught the wolfos off guard.

"Everyone retreat!" commanded Fang. He looked back at Zanatose. Zanatose tried to get away and he rolled to the side, but Fang still stabbed down at him. Fang stabbed him in his rib.

Zanatose groaned with pain and by the time he turned over and looked up, Fang and the wolfos were gone. "Zanatose, are you okay?" asked Bill. Bill was covered in claw marks and had a few deeper wounds, but nothing serious.

Brett, Edwin, Katie, Anton, and Jonathan all had circled Zanatose and they looked down at him with concern. This was because Zanatose had many deep wounds from his battles and the gash he received from Fang was bleeding heavily. "Zanatose, you didn't face off against Fang again, did you?" asked Brett.

Zanatose slowly nodded his head. His whole body was stinging from all of his wounds. Many of the wolfos had stabbed their fangs and claws into him in the battle. "Someone, take him to the hospital," commanded Jonathan from his men.

"Aye, sir!" said a small group of men which rushed over with a stretcher and took Zanatose off to the hospital. As they lifted Zanatose up onto the stretcher they brushed their hands against one of his wounds and it upset him, he gave a loud groan before he went unconscious.

Zanatose was standing right next to Fang at the crater of a volcano. This was no normal volcano though. It had bridges of indestructible metal and tall structures. In the center of the volcano was a gigantic temple with its double doors thrown open to reveal a fire burning inside of it. "Go and embrace your destiny," he said.

Fang handed Zanatose both Shadow and the ancient dark blade, and Zanatose headed across the bridge to enter the fire. He could hear his heavy steps echo throughout the crater. He felt immense power in his every step. He was near the temple when Brett appeared. Brett looked at Zanatose with murder in his eyes.

Zanatose looked at himself and he saw Fang instead.

"*NO!*" yelled Zanatose as he woke up from his nightmare covered in cold sweat. He gasped for breath as he recalled the awful dream. He tried to get up for a walk, but a burning wound on his side reminded him that he was injured.

He looked around through the darkness of the night. He could barely recognize anything, but he did see rows of beds with injured soldiers from the battle. "I'm still in Theragorn... good," he murmured as he went back to sleep on his bed.

He woke up the next morning from the hushed whispers of many people. "What's all the commotion?" he asked in a croaky morning voice. He slowly opened his eyes to see a crowd of kids around his bed. "......... hi," he said. Zanatose was surprised to see so many people. He looked around and saw that the place was made of polished white rocks and that his swords were at the side of his bed. A little boy was reaching for them.

"Nice swords, sir," he said admiringly.

Zanatose quickly stopped the child's hand. "No one is permitted to touch my swords," he said in a stern voice.

The boy back away slowly while the rest thrust out pieces of parchment toward Zanatose. They kept asking for his autograph and "was Fang really as strong as they say he is?"

Zanatose had to undergo this torture for an hour until

his friends came in and got rid of the children. "Nice kids," said Jonathan. "So how are you feeling?"

"I guess I'm alright except for that cut in my side," replied Zanatose. He was uncomfortable with Jonathan, suspecting Jonathan may have him assassinated next if he stays too long. "How long till I can travel again?" he asked.

Jonathan and the others looked around at each other grimly. Zanatose guessed that they had already spoken with the doctor. "After one month of rest," said Jonathan. Zanatose was out raged. Jonathan tried to shed light onto the situation. "Well, in that time, I will be able to prepare an army to help us on the quest," he said. "I've been promoted to king." Not even a mask could hide his delight. The others had already heard, and were very pleased, lacking Zanatose's knowledge of Fang's innocence.

"And tomorrow we have received word that Macbeth will be here," said Brett.

"No," said Zanatose irritably. "I will not stay here for more than another day. We will wait for Macbeth, but no longer."

"You can barely move!" protested Brett. "It is unwise to travel in your state."

Zanatose and Brett both looked irately at each other. Jonathan interrupted them and tried to relieve their tension. "I could provide horses instead," he said.

"Thank you," said Zanatose. "Well, in that case, we're off tomorrow. Why did so many people know I fought against Fang?"

"The battle was announced to the entire city," said Jonathan. "My people like to be well informed," he said with a tone of irritation.

"I suppose we should let Zanatose rest," said Katie. Katie seemed the most worried about Zanatose's condition. The rest of the group had little concern, expecting him to get better in a month.

Everyone left, and Zanatose went to sleep. He had many dreams and they were all very grim, tying back to that strange place in the volcano. When he woke up for dinner he could not remember any of them. He just remembered the pain he felt in those dreams.

It was close to nightfall, and a doctor in white robes came to Zanatose and placed his dinner on his side table. "It smells good," said Zanatose as he sniffed in the fumes of the strange food. "I have never seen this plate before. What is it?"

The doctor laughed cheerfully. "Then this will be a great surprise to you. It is the prized dish of Theragorn city," said the doctor. Zanatose looked wearily at the odd plate. "Don't worry, you'll like it."

The doctor left to take care of the other injured soldiers of Theragorn city. The odd dish had strangely colored rice with little red beads in it. Zanatose took a spoonful and loved it. The red bead things were a little sour. After he ate the flavorsome dish, he went back to sleep to prepare for the adventure that lied ahead for tomorrow.

CHPT 15:
PARTING OF THE WAYS

Parted, separated, divided, lost
A split in the road,
Adds burden to the load.
Left, right, or should I turn back?
I need you he thinks, but yet he walks.

Love, happiness, stability, sanity, lost
Glancing back, glancing right, glancing left. Alone.
Seeing the sun, he remembers her smile.
Seeing the skies, he remembers her eyes.
Hearing the birds, he remembers her tone.
Remembering makes him feel never alone.

What would have been if he went back to her?
Let it be, forget her, walk on.
Fight it, why give up on love?
Go back.

It was morning in Theragorn city. The city woke up and was alive with the buzz of people rushing to repair the damaged parts of the city. Zanatose had also woken up to see that his team was circled around his bed and Macbeth was there too. Zanatose's injury was still bothering him, but acted as if it did not feel crippling. "You sure you're up for a journey like that?" asked Macbeth. He was shocked that Zanatose had fought against Fang and lived. Macbeth remembered back to the great tournaments in Nijad city, Fang had been the champion year after year. Fang was once part of human society before he turned to the wolfos.

Zanatose sat on the side of his bed instead of standing up because he knew he cannot stand for a long time. "Where are the horses?" he asked.

"Waiting right outside," said Jonathan. "If you would wait a little longer to leave, I could've assisted you Zanatose."

"We might not have much longer until the tarik figure out what we're up to," said Zanatose. He did not want Jonathan with him any longer. "Which way to the war city you spoke of earlier?" asked Zanatose.

Jonathan was about to laugh, but he thought otherwise, seeing Zanatose's stern face. "The Hayvans are a race of aggression and war. If you want their elemental item, you'll have to fight for it to hell and back again!" warned Jonathan.

"I don't care," said Zanatose heatedly. "I'm going to go there. Now I'll ask again, which way?"

"It's in the north, in the desert wasteland," replied Jonathan dryly. The new king was insulted by Zanatose's tone, but dared not challenge him yet. "I hope you can even make it there alive."

"Alright, that's where we're going," said Zanatose. He felt that they should seek assistance from a city with enough strength to wage war against all that opposed them, like the Hayvans. He wanted to prepare for a war. They were in dark times, and he felt a coming war was inevitable. The others in his team disagreed with him.

"I think the Hayvans maybe too dangerous," said Macbeth. "We're not prepared yet. I can take some of the group to the water and earth elemental items instead."

"I'm not going either of those two ways," said Brett. "I need to go there," he pointed out the window and toward a distant tropical jungle.

"That's where the cheetah tribes live," said Jonathan. "Legend has it that their greatest warrior has the wind sword."

"Well, I'm going there," said Brett. There was a deep longing in his stare.

"And I'm going to the Hayvans," said Zanatose defiantly.

"Then I'll take the rest to the water and earth elemental items," said Macbeth. Everyone nodded in agreement.

"Wait a second," said Bill. "That means Brett and Zanatose are going their separate ways, alone! Zanatose in your state I don't think you're fit to go alone."

"I'll be fine," said Zanatose. He was getting annoyed that everyone thought he could not go on alone. "I'm just worried about you guys."

"Same here," said Brett as he glanced at Zanatose with pity in his eyes.

"Well, let's get going," said Zanatose, ignoring Brett's glance. They left the hospital and they mounted their horses. Zanatose limped on one leg to keep pressure off his other side.

"You'll need these," said Jonathan as he handed Zanatose some food and water. "Good luck."

Zanatose took them and placed them into his bag on the strong black horse. "Thank you General Gateman," he said. As soon as Brett mounted his horse he rode off, on his white steed, leaving without a word. Something was calling to him, beckoning his soul, and he had to meet it.

Zanatose stared after him until he disappeared into the distance. "I hope you two guys will be alright," said Katie. "This isn't safe in your state, Zanatose."

"Don't worry, Kate," said Zanatose reassuringly. He

jumped off his horse to talk to her face to face, one last time. Seeing her face made him smile. "If all goes well, I'll be back with an army to help us."

"I'll miss you, Zanatose," said Katie, looking down.

"I'll miss you, too," he said slowly. He took a step forward and she looked up. Their eyes met for a moment, unblinking. Zanatose's eyes showed his years of longing; Katie's eyes showed a new affection that she had never felt before. They drew nearer to each other shyly. Zanatose's eyes started to water. He backed away slowly. "I've got to go," he said suddenly as he shook his head. Katie nodded sadly. Neither one had the courage to express how they felt. Zanatose mounted his horse and rode off toward Bill.

"Zanatose, is there anything I can do to help?" asked Bill.

"Yeah, there is," said Zanatose. "Make sure no one dies, especially Katie. I'm putting you in charge okay?"

Bill was stunned that he was put in command instead of Macbeth. "Thanks man," he said happily. He had never been the leader before, but the fact that Zanatose had confidence in him made him feel more comfortable.

"I've got to go," croaked Zanatose. He looked miserable, and his eyes were shining with tears that he fought back. He quickly turned his horse toward his destination and rode off into the horizon just as Brett had.

"Farewell, Zanatose," whispered Bill. "Alright, let's go," he commanded with a heavy heart. They rode slowly in the direction Macbeth had said they should go. Katie kept looking back with shining eyes, hoping to see Zanatose.

Brett was traveling upon his brand new steed. He rode skillfully and swiftly. Every now and then his horse stopped to graze on the grass. He rode toward the jungle with a purpose that he felt he must fulfill. He was going there to retrieve the sword of light. No one else knew it was there, but he could feel it.

He kept riding until nightfall. Brett decided to stop and rest. He set up a place to sleep and a fire. After tying his horse down to a nearby tree, he thought of his difficult task. This made him feel nervous and a little jumpy.

"Maybe a good story will help," thought Brett. He rummaged through his bags until he found the only personal item he had brought. It was a thick book, with a few tears, an heirloom. He turned its pages until he reached a legend about the chosen one of the light sword.

He read the story: There once was a brave knight who was soon going to up his class to a hero and he did not even know it. He had just returned from the trials of the desert and was summoned to the court by the prince of Nijad.

"My father has been killed by the dark beasts and his sword was lost in the jungle shrine," said the young and handsome prince. With every word, his chiseled mouth moved gently with the grace of a true prince. "The tribe of cheetahs has also lost their king. The blessings of the four winds have brought them a great hero. You are our only hope. Go retrieve my father's sword and make Nijad proud!"

The knight accepted and headed off. He traveled until he had reached a lush jungle. He looked through the thick trees and bushes and saw a place where the trees had been uprooted, the dirt still hung off the tree roots. He went there and found the towering shrine of light. He walked in through the heavy doors. He saw a glowing blade with some kind of magical properties. It called out to his very soul from first sight. He ran to the sword and raised it. As he raised the sword, the shrine darkened. The shadow beasts had come to end him.

As he fought the onslaught, the many shadow beasts struck him down. The hero refused to fall and allow them to win. He wanted to bring back the light to the world and stop the darkness no matter what, even if it meant his life would be lost in the pursuit.

With these desires in his heart the sword transformed into a sleek, sharp, and crystal elemental sword. It was the birth of the light elemental sword. Its presence brought light to the room. It was a pure light that made the shadow beasts leave.

"*That was a nice story to liven the spirits*," thought Brett.

Brett was about to call it a night when he saw a strange, shadowy figure moving toward him from in between two trees. Brett dashed to his horse and unlaced his sword from its saddle. He quickly fastened it on his waist and took out Blazer incase it was an enemy. He could feel cold sweat inching down his brow as he stared into the foreboding darkness.

The figure's snake like eyes gleamed in the night as it approached. "Hello, Brett. It does not do you good to be alone in such times," said Fang.

"Fang!" yelled Brett as he raised Blazer. "Leave or else," he challenged Fang to a fight, hoping he could beat the snake.

"I come to offer safety. We can get the swords together as one combined force. We can defeat the shadow beasts together. Why don't you join the wolfos?" asked Fang in conclusion.

"Join you?" Brett laughed, "Never! Is this what Zanatose was keeping from us?"

"This is part of it," admitted Fang. "I wanted him to be the commander of a small platoon of wolfos. I want the same for you. You have shown me that you are worthy to join me," said Fang as his face gave a wicked smile. "Just think of all the wolfos under your control! You could easily defeat the shadow beasts!"

"You may be able to trick Zanatose, but not me!" said Brett firmly. "I am an elite soldier of Nijad!"

"You are such a fool. I offer you peace but you refuse it," said Fang through grit teeth.

"You are evil and to join you would be against everything that I believe in," said Brett.

"You are strong, but you are on a drowning boat, and you don't even realize it," said Fang as he swung at Brett with his staff. Brett ducked and countered back with a swift stab at Fang. Fang jumped over it and landed behind Brett. "Impressive attempt to fight me, but it's still not good enough. Just like our little tournaments isn't it?"

Fang stabbed back straight at Brett and continued his ferocious assault. Brett dodged and weaved as well as he could. He agilely dodged Fang's swings until he caught his leg on Fang's staff and fell. "An elite soldier?" asked Fang as he stood over him. "Pathetic," he muttered as he stabbed down at Brett.

Brett rolled out of the way and Fang stabbed down, trapping his staff in the dirt. Brett quickly got back on his feet and Fang dislodged his staff and swung at him. Dirt flew off the staff's end and some of it hit Brett in the eye. He winced from the pain as he ducked and swung blindly toward Fang. Brett rubbed the dirt out of his eyes and once he opened them again he saw Fang's staff inches from his cheek.

Brett blocked the attack with Blazer. He replied Fang's attacks with his own swift stabs. Fang gave a strong blow from above coming down, but Brett quickly blocked and push kicked Fang back and ran at Fang. He gave a mirage of several quick blows coming from every direction. Fang blocked them effortlessly until one caught him off guard and slammed against his chest plate.

The hit was hard enough to pierce through Fang's chest armor and penetrate his skin. Fang groaned softly then stood up again. "Well done," Fang said. "Now I want you on my side even more."

"I will never join you!" Brett yelled at him as he disappeared back into the trees clutching his bleeding chest. Brett stood there, staring at where Fang last was, thinking about how Zanatose had fought Fang twice, and lived.

"Zanatose is gone," muttered Katie desolately. She looked like she was close to tears and depressed from atop her white horse. He was gone, but there was still so much she wanted to tell him. So much was left unsaid between them.

"I'm sorry for all the things I've said, Zanatose," muttered Edwin to himself. "I wish I'd told him before he left." He hung his head in sorrow.

"I wish Brett was by my side to help me lead you guys the right way," said Macbeth. Brett had always been the one for directions, having led reconnaissance missions for the city.

Bill was now the leader and he decided not to join in with the grief. He rode ahead of them all on his brown horse. He pulled on his horse's reins to turn and look at the group. He watched Anton, Macbeth, and Edwin on their brown horses, and Katie from atop her beautiful white horse as they approached slowly. He tried to ignore the fact that Zanatose and Brett were gone, but he could not. "*Our two best men are gone…and now, we're stuck with me leading the way and the weakest of the team. How are we going to get the elemental weapons, alive?*" thought Bill. He doubted the capabilities of everyone he was leading, including himself.

As he followed Macbeth's directions he noticed a strange beady eyed crow watching them from a distance, from a tree branch. He tried to ignore this, thinking he was paranoid to think a bird was watching them. Bill thought back to the hospital; he found it odd how Brett and Zanatose fought to

travel alone. Bill thought maybe Zanatose and Brett felt they
had something to prove.

Bill became lost in his thoughts as the crow flew away
toward a snowy summit in the distance and past a man on a
black horse heading toward the dessert, followed by a strange
wavering shadow.

CHPT 16:
OCEAN VIEW INN

B rett had been awake most of the night after Fang's appearance. He was leaning against an old tree and staring into the darkness with his sword on his lap. As he stared into the darkness the sun soon came up, and it brought the light of day with it. *"Finally ... dawn I can move ...now,"* thought Brett with difficulty. His mind felt numb from being awake and thinking all through the night. He thought about Zanatose and about Katie, and then about Fang, and then everyone else. His eyes burned from the light and exhaustion. He stood up like a weary drunk and waddled to his horse, mounting it lazily.

He trotted slowly and dizzily on his horse toward the lush jungles ahead. He could hear loud booming sounds from within the jungle. They may have been drums, but Brett was too drowsy to pay attention. All he could think about was the light sword waiting for him.

The morning soon grew to mid afternoon before he reached the lush jungle. Once he rode in, he saw various, different flowers and trees. They all had different colors. He was afraid to go near a few of the flowers because he knew they were poisonous, noticing the strange purple fuzz on their petals.

As he rode on slowly to admire the sights he noticed a strange tree branch with many peculiar patterns. He dismounted his horse and walked toward it. "I've heard something about this pattern. What was it?" he asked himself. After a few more steps he felt a sharp pain on his shoulder and he remembered. "Oh, it's a snake."

Brett wheeled around and saw the snake face to face. Then he tracked its body and saw that the tree behind him was part of this gigantic snake. "Oh great," he mumbled sleepily as he tried to take out his sword. Before he could take out his sword, the snake wrapped itself around him from behind. It started squeezing the life out of him. He could feel his lungs being crushed, and he could not breathe any more.

He struggled, but the snake's grip only tightened. The snake brought its face level with Brett's. The horrendous snake had a hungry look in its black eyes as it drooled on him. It showed its sharp poisonous fangs as it neared Brett. He yelled out for help with his last bit of air, and then like a flash of lightning something with golden fur came to the rescue.

It sliced Brett free in seconds, from its sword came a great gust of wind, blowing the snake away. The cheetah turned to Brett and spoke in a slow, grim voice. "Come with me," and it braced his long silver sword.

Zanatose had been riding since dawn and it was mid afternoon. The accursed crow had returned again and it was very annoying as it kept circling him and calling out into the distance. On top of that, whenever Zanatose rode at a moderate speed his wound would begin to burn as if it was just slashed through recently. The more the lone warrior rode, the more the heat grew and the trees diminished.

"I hope Katie's alright. I shouldn't have left her side. This wound is killing me!" he thought. He rode on very uncomfortably.

Soon, he caught sight of the desert wasteland. There was a wooden, hut like in appearance, stand before the desert. "Hello there," he called out to the salesman.

"You approachin de dezzy sire. You nee di camol ya? Orse do you no good in di dere dezzy," said the old, foreign sounding, market man. The old sunburned man was bald and was missing several teeth. "You give me de orse I give dee de camel, ya?"

Zanatose looked at him questioningly, but then understood what he had said. "Alright good sir, I'll trust you. De orse por camol," said Zanatose as he laughed. The old tanned market man laughed and Zanatose saw that he had very few teeth.

"Ya arry pig orse. You breed em vel ya?" asked the merchant as he handed Zanatose the reins of a sad looking camel, bald in a few spots.

"He was a present from an acquaintance," said Zanatose as he mounted his camel painfully. "See you later," he said as he rode off, at a snail's pace, after he placed all his remaining water on the camel's belt.

The group continued on their journey slowly with hearts filled by sorrow. Katie was moving slower than most of the group. Bill saw this and decided to try and comfort her. He redirected his horse gently toward Katie and trotted along besides her. "Don't worry about those two guys," he said. "They probably have the best chance on their own than anyone else."

"But those guys aren't safe!" she argued. "And Zanatose has an injury," she said in dismay. Bill decided that she was not in a rightful state and continued silently.

As the group continued on, they started to approach a desolate canyon. "Once we get through here we'll be near the beach," stated Macbeth, seeming untroubled. He was either confident in Brett and Zanatose, or was unconcerned about their lives.

The sun was at its peak for the day and the hot and humid air of the canyon was a great nuisance. They rode their horses into the canyon, figuring out too late, a canyon was not a good place for horse riding. When they rode in, almost immediately, they fell into a quagmire. "How do we get out?" asked Edwin in a panic as his horse cried in alarm and kept sinking deeper in.

The horses and their riders were starting to sink into the quagmire. "We have to jump off," yelled Macbeth through all the panic. They all jumped off their horses and onto the hard earth of the canyon. The landing was a little painful because their horses were so tall and the ground was rock hard.

"That was way too close," said Bill. Everyone was a little nervous after the quagmire. "We should probably watch our steps. I'll lead the way to make sure that there aren't any more quagmires." Bill led the group ahead in the canyon. They were sorry for the horses but they were glad that was their only sacrifice, along with the food. The earth was moist in some places and would easily start sinking, but for the most part the canyon floor was dry. "There must be an underground spring here," suggested Bill.

Eerie whistling sounds echoed through the canyon, but there was no other living thing there other than the group. There was no sign of life anywhere throughout the canyon. They looked around at the ledges and saw nothing but jagged rocks. "Isn't this a nice quiet place?" laughed Edwin.

"Yeah, I agree Edwin. It's real nice and cheery," said Anton with a impish smile.

"The ocean isn't much farther," remarked Macbeth.

"This place gives me the creeps," said Katie. She was anxious and felt like something awful was about to happen. As she stared uneasily at the jagged rocks she noticed a cave entrance that no one else bothered to observe. They walked on and a cloud blocked out the sun, and everything grew dark.

"Seems like lots of things have died here," whispered Edwin. He had just seen a corpse lying on the ground which he had almost stepped on.

"Yes, there's a list of things that died here," said a familiar voice. The group looked up and saw Zanatose. He was standing on the edge of a ledge, above them. He jumped down in front of the group, blocking their path. He landed perfectly, catlike. "That list will include all of you," he said coldly.

"Zanatose, what are you doing here?" asked Bill. Zanatose started to approach the group.

"Zanatose is back," said Edwin happily.

Bill stared into Zanatose's eyes and saw nothing there that he recognized. He did not see any warmth in Zanatose's eyes. He was convinced that this was not the real Zanatose. Bill rammed Zanatose back, away from the group. "You're not Zanatose," he said. "Get back or else." Bill took out the Sholkon sword and his shield.

"What are you doing, Bill!!" screamed Katie.

Zanatose brushed the dust off and took out both of his swords. "You think you, of all people, can defeat me?" The group gasped as Zanatose dashed at Bill and slashed with both swords. Bill blocked with his new shield. The crash of sword against metal reverberated through the entire canyon, leading to a dead silence as the two stared each other down.

"I will keep my promise to Zanatose and I will protect this group," said Bill as he crashed against Zanatose again, struggling against Zanatose's force.

"Come on, can't you do any better?" laughed Zanatose. He turned into his dark form and rushed Bill with a flurry of hard blows. Every blow felt like dropping boulders against his shield. Everyone stared breathlessly as the two dueled.

Bill's arms were starting to burn from the weight of returning those blows. He bashed Zanatose in the face with his shield then he stabbed Zanatose in the stomach. Katie grabbed Anton's staff and was about to charge at Bill until she saw that Zanatose was not gasping from pain. He fell back and he changed into Abigail as he stepped back. "I didn't expect you to attack your own friend," she said with a bemused smile.

Everyone's initial joy at seeing Zanatose had disappeared. It was replaced with a nasty cold feeling in their hearts. Abigail was back...

"Zanatose was my best friend, and I knew that you were an imposter," said Bill angrily. "Now leave, or else I'll finish what I began," he said as he raised his shield and sword.

"It... It's Abigail..." said Katie with great disappointment. She had really hoped that it was Zanatose. She felt a choking feeling in her throat from her frustration.

"You can't stop me from reaching my revenge this time. Not without precious Zanatose's help," said Abigail mockingly.

"You'll have to get past me," said Bill as he stepped in front of Katie. She grabbed a dagger on Bill's belt, unnoticed by the others.

"And me," said Macbeth.

Anton and Edwin looked at each other and nodded. "And us," said Edwin.

"You lack your great warriors for this encounter," said Abigail with a menacing laugh. "I will easily get past all of you." A bright light blinded them for a second and when they opened their eyes they saw that Abigail had summoned her zombies.

Anton took out a hidden spear, inside his thick cloak, and threw it into the nearest zombie. He used his magic powers, by blasting fire balls, to fend off the brainless zombies until he reached the spear which he used as a pike. Edwin also assisted him and had his back. The two friends fought back to back. Macbeth had taken out his broad sword and was hacking away at many of the zombies at once with long, elegant slashes.

Macbeth and Bill were both close to Katie at all times so that she would not be abducted, although she did not really need their help. Bill was bashing the zombies back with his shield and then slashing them to shreds. Katie had taken out her bow and arrows that she carried on her back and was firing them at the zombies, slowing the hungry army of undead. Just under her belt was the dagger she had stolen from Bill, ready for anything that came too close.

Abigail was still summoning more and more zombies as the rest fought on. Bill decided to concentrate and keep fighting at the same time so he would use his sword's power. The extra focus made him more effective. He surveyed his surroundings noticing an outlying ledge over Abigail. Once his sword charged up, he blasted at the canyon side and sent boulders falling onto Abigail and most of her zombies.

The boulders lifted themselves, levitated by magic, and combined to form a large rock golem, under Abigail's control. "You'll have to do much better," said Abigail. The towering golem stepped on the zombies as it made its way toward the group. It had a huge figure, did not have any eyes or a mouth. It was a slave and a creation of Abigail's.

"Any ideas, anyone?" asked Edwin with a dazed look. The ground shook with every step the golem took. "I volunteer Macbeth to fight it. You think you can pull a crazy acrobatic stunt, clinging to its hand, like Brett did?"

"Great, I'm just so flexible," Macbeth said sarcastically. He had a distinctly larger build than the light-footed Brett. "Does this thing have any kind of major weakness?" asked Macbeth.

Edwin nodded that there was a weakness. "I've noticed it's much bigger and stronger than you." Macbeth growled at

Edwin. The golem smashed its hand down onto the ground right next to them. Everyone jumped out of the way, except Bill. Bill jumped onto the top of the golem's hand, taking initiative to keep his promise.

The golem raised its hand, Bill stabbed his sword into its hand to stay on, the hand slammed down again. Once the golem's hand went high enough, Bill jumped off onto its head. "Be careful!" warned Macbeth as he dived out of the way of the golem's legs.

Bill ignored him and tried to chip away the skull of the golem with both his shield and sword. He thrashed at it with his sword, and hammered with his shield. It chipped away little bits and pieces of dust from its head. "How do I take this thing out?" he asked.

"Use your head," suggested Macbeth.

The golem started to shake violently to get Bill off. Bill stabbed his sword down into the golem's head as hard as he could. The sword became lodged into the golem and he held on tightly for dear life. Once the golem stopped moving he took out his sword and focused his energy so that he could get rid of the golem. His sword started to glow like a blazing torch.

"Farewell," said Bill as he stabbed his sword down into the golem, releasing the energy blast inside of the golem's head. The golem's head burst open and Bill fell all the way down to the ground. Luckily, Edwin and Macbeth were there to catch him as chunks of rock flew in every direction.

"Oh, my hero," laughed Bill. Edwin quickly dropped him after that and Bill landed painfully on the ground, laughing.

"Abigail is still here," said Anton. After he said that, endless pairs of dead rotting hands reached up from the ground and reached for them frantically.

A pair of hands grabbed Katie's ankles and started dragging her down into a quagmire. "Help!" she screamed out against the others' panic. She took out the dagger and hackled at the hands. She was able to hack one off, but another hand soon replaced it. The guys rushed over and tried not to get caught too as they helped her. Bill grabbed her hands and tried to lift her back up from the ground. She was waist deep by the time they reached her.

Bill tried as hard as he could, but he could not lift her out. From all sides the hands raised themselves out of the dirt. Katie looked at Bill with great worry. "Pull harder!" she cried.

"Don't worry, we're here," said Edwin as he and Macbeth started to help. Anton was turning the sand around Katie blue and the grips of the zombies were loosened by it. She finally started coming back up. The arms reaching upwards for them had stopped trying and grabbed the soil instead, lifting themselves up, out of the dirt.

These zombies were different from before. They barely seemed human at all. They seemed like strange werewolves with glossy eyes and missing fur. Their fur coats were brown and covered with dirt. They seemed similar to an undead army of wolfos. They brought a strange darkness with their presence.

As the strange beasts approached, the canyon became darker and darker. It became harder to see in the obscurity.

The group all huddled together. "I can't see a thing," said Edwin as he listened to the approaching growls of the beasts. Macbeth was getting nervous and was backing away from the group.

A zombie slashed Macbeth in the back with its long claws, and another was about to do the same. Bill heard Macbeth hit the ground and back kicked in the direction. He felt his foot hit one of the odd beasts and he could hear ragged dog like breathing to his left. Bill took out his sword and slashed down into the general direction of the sound, against the unrelenting darkness. He heard a strange unearthly cry. "Good, I got it," said Bill with relief.

They suddenly heard an uproar of barking through the dark, hearing sharp talons scratch against the ground. They knew that the beasts were angry, and they were coming for them. Katie tightened her grip on the dagger. Bill had his shield out and ready. They all heard howling as they felt heavy bodies ram against them. Bill's feet buckled as he felt the heavy body hit his shield. Edwin fell flat on his back from the impact. The hungry hound jumped onto him and opened its massive jaws around his head. He quickly lodged his sword in-between the teeth of the ferocious beast and pushed out, feeling the hot, musky breath of the senseless dog. Through the darkness, Anton could only see the beast's dead, gray, eyes and sharp teeth. He could smell the scent of death in the wild beast's breath as he struggled to keep the sharp fangs away.

"Where's Zanatose when we need him!?" yelled Edwin.

"He's probably miserable from the desert's heat and that wound," yelled back a very angry Anton. His spear was whipped out of his hand. Katie caught it and stabbed it down into the beast that was inches from eating Edwin's face, then she swung her dagger toward the growling behind her and struck a wolfo through the skull.

"Thanks," sighed Edwin as he stood back up onto his feet. Another beast was about to pounce on them from behind. It came running at Edwin, a blur of motion in darkness. Macbeth tried to run with the beast to stop it. The beast began to run on all fours and went even faster, Macbeth could no longer keep up. He did not want the beast to pounce on Edwin and Katie so he flung his sword into the beast's back. The dog collapsed to the floor, motionless.

"Everyone, follow my lead down through the valley!" commanded Bill. He started clearing a way straight ahead toward what he hoped was the ocean.

He rammed through everything that stood in his way with his shield and slashed at anything that would not give up. Macbeth withdrew his sword from the fallen mutt, and covered the rear in hope of stopping the zombies from following them. "They keep following us!" yelled Macbeth in frustration after yanking his sword out of another beast. Every zombie he fought off stood up again and started following them.

Bill used his sword's power again and blasted the side of the canyon. It gave way and many boulders fell, crushing the zombies and blocking off the path.

"Let's see them get through that!" yelled Edwin. Katie smiled in relief and took a deep breath to calm down. She was overjoyed to have escaped Abigail again.

Once they got out of the canyon they heard the sounds of the ocean waves crashing against the shore. They could see some of the vast ocean by the moonlight. The water flickered like a vast beautiful diamond. They had finally reached the ocean. They could just barely make out a tiny inn by the shore.

The group made their painful way there. They were all battle worn and treading through sand. The group kept going on until wet rock and sand became dry dirt and sand. Once they reached the porch of the small inn they looked back at the beautiful ocean waves. The Great Ocean, tall towering waves, filled with huge fish leaping out of the water. The moon glazed the waves and shined beautifully.

They all took a long look at the inn they were about to go in. It looked more like a ship that crashed into land. It was entirely made of wood and had a couple masts at the top deck. They peered through a crack in the wooden boat and saw candle light.

"Good. There's some place to rest at," said Edwin. They were all relieved once they saw that the inn was not deserted.

They knocked and heard someone rushing to the door, with a cane, by the sounds of the clattering wood. The door was swung open by an old bearded man with a wooden leg and a skull and cross bones tattoo on his arm. "Ahoy, maties," said the man's gruff voice. He had snow white hair which was thinning.

The man walked them into the inn that was made of aging wood. With every step they took the old floor boards creaked loudly. It resembled the inside of a ship more than an inn. The old man limped ahead of them into a hallway with a few doors. "Tis free for your first days in the inn, maties," he said amiably.

"Thank you so much!" said Katie. She was looking forward to sleeping comfortably in a nice warm bed. Macbeth was relieved it was free because none of them had money.

They each had their own room except Bill and Edwin which shared a room. They enjoyed this though, finally able to talk and tell stories. "Remember the time we snuck up on Zanatose and he ran?" asked Edwin. It was an old prank they had played on Zanatose back in Sholkon village only a week before everything happened.

Bill, for the first time, noticed something strange. Only a week before the events and Zanatose was not nearly as brave as he is now, and he would never have stepped up as leader. "Edwin, what happened to Zanatose?" asked Bill. "He's changed a lot hasn't he?"

"Yeah, you're right," said Edwin. "I haven't thought much about it. I mean, I've seen him train. He was never as focused as he is now. What changed him?"

"The sword?" suggested Bill.

"Then he'd be evil."

"Hatred for the tarik?"

"He could care less."

"Friendship?" suggested Bill.

"He left us!" laughed Edwin.

"Katie," whispered Bill. They both nodded then an awful thought occurred to Bill. "He has two dark swords now! And he's left on his own!"

"He's strong, he wouldn't fall to darkness because of a few miles," said Edwin.

"What if she dies like Alexis did?" asked Bill. He hated the idea of Zanatose turning against them.

"Then we shall make sure she lives…. In the morning," said Edwin. They both nodded and went to sleep. That entire night they had nightmares of Zanatose on a White Mountain top, bowing to Wolf Fang.

CHPT 17:
JUNGLE PERIL

"Who are you?" asked Brett with fear.

The cheetah was very tall and stood on two long legs. He had a brilliant gold fur coat speckled with black dots, his fur shined in the sun. Most importantly for Brett, he had an elemental sword in his left hand. "I am Marik, human," said the cheetah in a low growl.

"Um... I'm Brett an elite guard of Nijad.... And thanks for saving me back there," said Brett apprehensively. He was not sure if Marik was a friend or foe.

Brett covered up his wound with an extra tunic in his bag. "So you're from Nijad? I used to be an elite guard of the light shrine until it was taken over recently," said Marik. "Please follow me to our safe haven in this wretched jungle."

"Thank you again, Marik," said Brett as he followed Marik on his horse.

Marik laughed mockingly. "I'm taking you to see our council to be investigated. They may kill you!" laughed Marik. "Why did you venture into the middle of the Roctinian jungle?" asked Marik.

Brett was still trying to get past being killed by more of Marik's kind. "I came here on a quest to get the light sword," answered Brett. He was starting to consider turning and riding far away, but one glance at Marik's legs told him that was not a good choice. Marik would catch him in a heartbeat.

"Good luck with that, human," said Marik glumly. "The shrine holding it has been taken over."

"My friends and I are collecting the elemental items to get rid of the tarik," said Brett proudly. Marik looked like he did not believe him. "I'm telling the truth."

"Ha ha, my little friend, do you really expect me to believe that? Where are your friends? Where are your elemental swords?" he asked in an insulting voice.

"At Theragorn city there was a skirmish. We decided to split up to cover more ground," said Brett.

"There was a battle in Theragorn?" asked Marik.

Brett nodded and told him about how the wolfos attacked Theragorn city. "Wolf Fang tried to kill one of my friends, Zanatose."

"Really, the wolfos, that's not like General Fang," said Marik. He looked morose. Apparently, this was troubling news for him. "The wolfos are an ally of ours against the tarik. They agreed not to attack us."

"You... the cheetahs are allies with the wolfos?" Brett did not expect this. He decided it would be better if he did not say how he felt about Fang.

Marik nodded and said, "Yes, they are our allies. This is mainly because we cannot fend off everything that attacks the Roctinian village."

"Roctinian... Roctinian," muttered Brett to himself. "Where have I heard that?"

"Probably stories of the malicious Roctinian raptors. It's a constant problem. Those raptors keep raiding our village," said Marik angrily as he slammed his fist through a tree they were passing by. To Brett's surprise, he heard it had collided with something living.

Just then they heard a loud booming cry from a raptor, and Brett saw a sharp claw tear through the tree.

Zanatose had been traveling for a day now in the hot, wretched sun. The heavy gusts of searing, dry wind constantly churned the sands. Zanatose held onto the camel as the sand whipped him around and almost made him fall off. He was covered head to toe with sand. His lips were painfully dry.

His throat and wound were killing him with pain. He had scorching, dry sand in his throat even though he covered his mouth and nose with an extra tunic he had. He was almost blind from all the sand blown into his eyes. The sand being blown into his wound on his ribs burned like fire.

As he coughed up sand he saw blue in the distance. "Water..." he moaned as he tried to sit up straighter. The camel pranced slowly to the oasis. It took them a good hour to reach the small oasis.

Once the camel stopped, he fell off onto the gentle sand. The sand flew up like dust when he fell onto it. He could not stand anymore so he crawled to the water and started quaffing it down. His camel also lowered its head and started to drink from the oasis.

"*I hope the rest don't have it this hard,*" thought Zanatose. He noticed his stomach was grumbling loudly, but he tried to ignore that. He had forgotten the food bags on the horse back when he did the trade for the slow, dimwitted camel. He drank the water until he could not drink more. He refilled his water canteen then climbed onto his camel and trudged into the bright, blazing desert sun.

The entire group awoke suddenly as the inn shook violently. "Wha... what happened?" Katie stuttered.

Everyone was awake and in the hallway as the inn shook

again, they heard a loud crack outside. "Don fuss maties," said their pirate host. "Tis only a wee bit o' a storm."

They looked at each other fretfully as they checked their pockets. At last Macbeth stepped forward.

He cleared his throat to get the inn keeper's attention. "We need to stay a while. Our business is at the sea. And we don't have any money," said Macbeth. He was relieved to see the old man crack a smile.

"Aye, den you'll swab di decks maties! I need di 'elp after dis storm," he said.

"Great. Cleaning duty," moaned Edwin. Bill elbowed him in the rib to be quiet.

"Macbeth, where exactly are the water and ice elemental items?" asked Anton.

"Deep under the ocean," said Macbeth. Anton looked at him with some annoyance.

"How are we supposed to get that?" he asked angrily.

"I haven't thought out that part yet," said Macbeth.

"Dis storm, she makin leaks in dee ship. I need you hopeful maties to swab dee decks for me," the pirate said in his croaky voice through his silver mangled beard.

"Aye aye, sir!" said Bill as he saluted the pirate. Katie could barely suppress her laughter.

"After dis storm blows over mate. Dat'll give you enough time ter rest," he said over the loud booming thunder. "Dis storm maties… she reminds me 'O me last voyage wiz me pops," he said slowly.

Brett flew off his horse and onto the jungle ground with a painful impact. Two Roctinian raptors towered over his fallen body. The two raptors seemed overjoyed by his miserable state. Their greedy red eyes were ready to strike once more.

As one snapped at him, he quickly put his feet under it

and kicked it off. The second cocked its head back, preparing to strike, but Marik was too quick. He elbowed the raptor's head. The raptor shook it off then rounded on Marik. Brett had finally regained his breath; he swept the raptor's legs with a tree branch he picked up. The two dismal raptors got up roughly; they ran off, back into the depths of the jungle.

"Are you alright?" asked Marik. "That was a close call for you," said Marik as he looked at Brett's cut on his shoulder.

"This place is awful; just get me to your village as soon as possible. Before I'm killed on the way please," moaned Brett as he struggled to mount his white steed.

"Then let's start moving," said Marik.

"I'm supposed to let this slide? I could've died if you waited any longer!" yelled Brett. The pain in his arm was causing him frustration and anger. He felt agitated so he brought out his sword to attack Marik.

Marik did not unsheathe his sword; he calmly punched Brett in the gut to make him fall again. "If I am harmed, you will most definitely not receive a fair trial!" warned Marik.

Brett was still a little frustrated, but understood Marik meant him no harm. The pair continued on and Brett mounted his valiant steed once more.

The two continued on in the heavy humid air of the jungle and rested every now and then to drink from a near river. As they kept traveling they began to become better friends as they laughed together and told stories. By sunset they were close friends when they saw the tall walls of Roctinian village.

There was a high wooden wall that separated the village from the outside world. On the outskirts of those walls were very small modest cottages for the poor.

Marik knocked against the wooden wall. Two leather clad sentries at the tops of guard towers saw him. They blew their horns as a signal to others who operated the gates. The loud horn was played in an odd pattern that seemed to mean something to the gate operators. The gates were slowly cranked open by a lever on the other side of the wall.

Once they entered, the gates immediately closed behind them. Seeing so many of Marik's people at sunset was a frightening sight. They were all tall cheetahs on two feet, just like Marik. They all growled and braced their teeth at Brett as he passed. The setting sun made their teeth seem blood stained. Many of the cheetahs wore colorful bandanas on their furry heads, symbolizing various tribal alliances.

As Brett passed, they all glared at him, and a few whispered to each other. There were only a few shops with different poorly made weapons and exotic fruits that were scarce at Theragorn city's market. The different houses had vibrant paintings of several animals from all over the globe. There were fish people, painted in blue, lions, painted in red, and cheetahs, painted in a beautiful gold.

"So am I... um... welcome here?" Brett asked nervously. Although he needed the light and wind swords, he did not want to disturb a small village that was already in turmoil.

"Of course not!" said Marik gently. Brett's heart dropped at the thought of an entire village of cheetahs wanting him dead. "You were discovered by a wide patrol. Then I was sent to fetch you so we can hear what's going on outside the jungle. We need that information because the tarik have taken the temple and we don't know why. They have been too afraid to take it for decades, and now they are suddenly bold."

"Alright, I'll help, but I need that wind and the light elemental swords," said Brett. Marik turned to look at him. He seemed angry at first, but then laughed. His laugh was a little alarming; it sounded more like a dog's bark.

"Alright, friend then I will be able to meet your friends that you have spoken of," said Marik. The two were now walking down an exceptionally smooth dirt road. Brett looked up to see a large wooden fort with a golden door.

"We're finally here, the council establishment. Our council leaders are waiting to speak with you," said Marik.

"What kind of people make up this council?" asked Brett.

"Our old wise cats, retired Generals, our leader, and I make up the council," as he said this he glowed with pride and joy.

"You think they'll want to kill me?" asked Brett tensely.

"I hope not. They normally don't kill people. Earlier on when I said that I was just trying to scare you," admitted Marik.

"Well, it worked," admitted Brett. He noticed that the gold door was already opened and leading inside into a dimly lit room. Once they reached the door they both stopped.

Brett looked over to Marik, waiting to see what they should do next. Marik gestured to him to go in. When he walked in, he saw a crackling fire and several wooden chairs. There were two empty seats he guessed were for him and Marik.

Soon Marik sat down next to Brett on the uncomfortable wooden chairs. They were sitting in the center of the circular room, and the council members surrounded them. They were mostly old, a few wore glasses, but one was young and bold. He was the leader of the cheetahs as Marik told him earlier on.

An especially old council member with more wrinkles than thinkable spoke first in a slow, boring, dawdling voice. "Well, we are very glad to see you two alive."

"We've been expecting you for a while now. Such a long while, we thought you were dead," said another council member who seemed very stern and sharp.

"Sorry about that," said Marik. "We met some trouble along the way."

"Raptor trouble," added Brett.

"So you know of the raptors?" asked the head cheetah. He seemed like he had many suspicions about Brett. "What is your name? I am Theodore, the leader of the cheetahs, and elite guard of the light sword's shrine." Brett noticed that this cat was far more daunting than the others. He had sharp teeth, long claws, and he was much bigger than the rest of the cheetahs.

"My name is Brett. I'm an elite officer of Nijad city," replied Brett.

"What do you know of the raptors?" repeated Theodore loudly.

This made Brett a little nervous. As all the eyes stared at him he felt himself start sweating. "I know that they want the dark crystals for some cause or another," he said.

A silent murmur arose in the council. "Just as we expected," whispered one to the others.

"Do any of you know why they want the crystals?" asked Brett.

"We do, but we will not tell you until we are sure if you are a spy or an ally," said Theodore. "What is your purpose here?"

"I have come here to retrieve the light and wind elemental swords. I am part of a group searching for the elemental swords to combat the dark beasts that plague this land," replied Brett calmly. He was sure this would have a positive result on the cheetahs, but he was wrong.

This caused loads of loud whispering from the council. Theodore seemed outraged. "*YOU* DARE TO PERSUE OUR SACRED SWORDS!?" he bellowed.

Brett fell over in his chair and gave a loud thump as he broke the wooden chair. "I need the sword for my mission," replied Brett in an attempt to explain what he thought were innocent intentions.

"Theodore, calm down!" yelled Marik as he stood up

bravely. Theodore glared at him then his short temper cooled away.

There were still loads of whispering in the crowd, but with one commanding look Theodore silenced the entire room. "I am not angry because you want the swords. I am angry because you think we would fight against the tarik and then just give it to you!"

Brett stood up and straightened himself up. Then he spoke out bravely, "If need be I will personally assist you in taking back the light shrine against the tarik."

"Then it is settled, we shall leave to the shrine at day break!" bellowed Theodore as he started to laugh. Everyone slowly joined in the laughter.

"Splendid," Brett mumbled to himself. He heard his belly grumble. "Could I have something to eat, if it's alright?" asked Brett. He did not know whether to expect them to give him food or not.

"You read my mind!" laughed Theodore. He was glad that they had a new warrior to combat the tarik, and regain their holy shrine. Theodore led everyone into another room. He opened the heavy double doors to expose a long banquet hall.

They were all seated at a long table full of food. Everyone from the council to warriors of valor was seated at this great feast in preparation for tomorrow's attack. Brett kept in mind that he should try to get some information about the wolfos at this banquet since the cheetahs were allies with the wolfos. One of Theragorn city's spies had informed him about the cheetah's loyalties weeks before he had gone missing in the caves.

After a few minutes, Theodore joined the table and made a toast before they began to eat. "I am glad to announce that we shall finally be taking back our sacred shrine from the malevolent tarik occupants." At that everyone cheered politely as they raised their wine glasses and quaffed down its flavorful contents.

There was roasted chicken, fish, and even some roasted Verona plant which Brett kept away from. There were many colorful fruits and salads too. Brett tried to get information on the wolfos subtly as he slowly ate the questionable food.

He turned to his gold-faced neighbor and asked about the wolfos. "What do the wolfos do for your people?"

"Apparently not much newcomer because we need you!" laughed the cheetah.

From the cheetah's comment, Brett inferred that the wolfos had agreed to protect the cheetahs. Marik saw that Brett was eating mainly salads and a few bites of fish. "Brett, come on! Eat! Have some dragon meat!" suggested Marik as he pointed to a platter of what looked like heavily burned meat. "This meat has been aged for centuries!" Brett laughed and declined the offer, remembering that the last dragons seen by mortal eyes dated back to the time of Ares.

At the end of the feast, Theodore stood up and made another announcement. "Tomorrow, at the break of dawn, I shall lead Marik and the new comer, Brett, to the sacred shrine!"

CHPT 18:

THE DESERT'S CRUEL KISS

The kiss of death waits at all corners
for those meant for it.
Even a hero can't survive when his time comes.
All the riches of the world,
All the wisdom of the Gods cannot save the forsaken.

Zanatose groaned as he spat out sand. "This isn't water," he croaked weakly. He was very thirsty, and he had bad sunburns on his neck, face, and his wound was killing him.

He licked his dry, cracked lips and chuckled. "I know what Bill would say. 'You should have gone with Brett you moron!' He'd probably be right," muttered Zanatose feebly.

He felt miserable and felt like he was close to losing his mind. He kept seeing an oasis, but it was never there. He felt things could not be worse, but he was wrong. As he clung to his camel half heartedly, a huge scorpion jumped out of the sand. The scorpion's hard, glimmering shell dazzled the camel just before it raised its tail and stung the camel.

Zanatose rolled off and watched as his camel struggled. He tried to get up and leave, but he was far too exhausted. The scorpion was the size of a Verona plant, and its hard red body shimmered in the sun's blazing light. Once it was done poisoning the camel, it rounded onto Zanatose.

Zanatose put his hands onto his swords and felt the dark

powers take over. Zanatose stood, slowly with pain, and slashed at the scorpion slowly. He missed, and the scorpion stung him in the shins. He felt the poison seep in through the new wound.

He gave one last slash with all his might that split the scorpion in two. Zanatose fell to the ground and the last thing he said was, "Katie... I failed you...."

Zanatose opened his heavy eyelids and saw he was in some kind of palace garden with lots of sand. He found himself resting in a pool of a strange indoor garden. The whole structure was made of dried sand. It all seemed heavenly; he wondered whether he was in heaven. He looked around and saw his ragged clothes were changed to more lush clothes.

He wore a new red tunic with gold linings. As he admired his baffling surroundings, he was surprised to be disturbed by a sudden sound. "So.... You're alive?" asked a stern low voice.

Zanatose wheeled around and was going to draw his swords. His hands went to his waste, but he felt nothing but soft cloth. When he turned around, he saw a huge Hayvan.

It had a human-like face with distinct expressions, a golden lion's mane, and powerful legs. The Hayvan stood on two legs skillfully and this made him seem very tall. The Hayvan looked amused by Zanatose's presence.

Zanatose stood up painfully and recalled his two wounds. "Where are my swords?" he demanded from the Hayvan. He felt a raging anger bubbling in him, and he struggled to fight it. He gave a shudder as he fought his rage. He did not know whether to fear the rage inside of him more, or the poison that was threatening his very life.

The Hayvan gave an earth-shaking roar and Zanatose stepped back. "You do not make the demands! I am the great king Rezaar! I command and rule over Parikine city, and you dare to question me!" Rezaar glared at Zanatose with bitterness.

Zanatose regained his courage and took a step forward. "You should work on your first impression your *highness*," growled Zanatose. Rezaar laughed at him, and Zanatose noticed a curved sword on Rezaar's hip as he turned to walk away.

"In this war-driven city, we respect strength, bravery, and above all loyalty!" Rezaar barked with pride. Rezaar gave Zanatose a serious look. "We shall see if you deserve to live among us. We saved you from the desert, and we shall find you fit to live on or die."

"And if I refuse?" asked Zanatose.

"Then we shall act as if you never existed," Rezaar laughed as he said this. "Guards, take him to the arenas," he commanded to a few large Hayvan. They went and grabbed Zanatose around the wrists. Zanatose decided it was best if he did not resist.

"Why thank you Ryza..." started Zanatose, but he was interrupted.

"It's Rezaar!" yelled Rezaar.

Zanatose laughed and continued his ridicule. "So you've prepared a show for me?"

Rezaar gave a menacing laugh. "Yes, something of that nature."

"Brett! Brett, wake up!" yelled a slim, young cheetah. He was clad in gold plated body armor and had a small dagger in his leather belt.

"Ri...right," yawned Brett from his small straw-filled bed. He did not sleep too well ever since the journey started, but that night was just awful. He kept having strange dreams, and he was constantly confused about where he was. One moment he was atop a flaming mountain and knew he was in a dream, but the next moment he was fighting Zanatose and it felt so real to him. Brett felt groggy, and he did not want to go out to take back a shrine so early in the morning no matter how important it was.

"Come on sir. You need to get ready and head out," insisted the young cheetah. Brett nodded, and the cheetah decided to leave.

As Brett sat lazily on his bed and started to put on his boots and sheath, he tried to remember his dreams and make some sense out of them. He tried hard, but the memories were already fading. After he tightened his sheath around his back, he remembered his last dream vividly.

He started to remember his deadly premonition: Brett sat in a cold dark palace chamber tightening his armor. He opened a cabin and took out his shield and sword. He left the palace to the cold, black, misty night.

He stepped onto the damp grass and faced an army of men wearing Nijad's armor. Brett swung his sword forward, and the awaiting army charged forward into the black abyss. He watched as his men disappeared. The sun came up and revealed that all his men were lying face down in the ground. He looked around for a cause, but found nothing.

He walked forward, feeling lost, and then he saw a cloaked figure rush at him. He brought his shield up, blacked out, and woke up.

"*What was that thing?*" Brett thought to himself. "*Or **who** was that thing?*" Brett tried to ignore his appalling nightmare and left his room to go into the dining hall for breakfast.

Zanatose stood on a platform in the middle of a lava pit. He seemed to be in some kind of coliseum. Around the side walls of the inside of the volcano were metal stands for the crowds. Zanatose was on one of the many platforms; there were several more which seemed to be used for another purpose. Upon the throne, at the top of the volcano, Rezaar sat with three guards.

A Boar sat in a large stand, alone. The boar was ugly as it sat, fat and muddy, in the stand. He took a deep breath and started to speak with a loud booming voice that reverberated throughout the mountain. "Peoples of Parikine I present to you our next victim..." the boar stopped, thought, and then commenced speaking again. "Oh, sorry for that mistake. I meant our next competitor... Zanatose!" squawked the dirty boar. Its tusks were chipped at the ends. The crowd all cheered for Zanatose, but a feeling told Zanatose that they were cheering for his death.

The stands were full of Hayvans, all cheering for Zanatose to fail. It seemed they would get their wish thought Zanatose, assuming that he would probably have to fight some horrible beast completely unarmed. Zanatose tried to imagine what he may have to fight, first thinking of a horrible fire resistant spider.

The situation looked very grim, and Zanatose realized this as he looked closer at his platform. He noticed that if he looked close enough, there were a few trap doors and several other unknown triggers on the platform.

"I hope you die with honor warrior," announced Rezaar from his throne.

"If I had a weapon I could fight an army. I doubt anything you've got can finish me," said Zanatose proudly, ignoring the poisons that were circulating through his body.

"So you want a weapon?" laughed Rezaar. He grabbed a small sword and shield from behind his throne and tossed them at the center of the platform. The floor on three sides of the spot gave away and it was surrounded by lava pits.

Zanatose's heart sank with the floor as he figured out how hard it would be to get those weapons. He thought about his group, and he found his courage. "I can't and won't fail," he muttered under his breath.

The boar started to laugh at the hero upon the platform. It started to speak in a taunting hiss. "You of all people will not live! You are a mere human, more mortal and weak than any other race upon this land. You will die in the lava just like the rest. You think a sword will change your damned fate?" it asked. The boar glared down at him with its pudgy, greedy eyes. Zanatose looked back at the boar with defiance; no fear was going to conquer him. "Good luck dying you pathetic human… No! Was that bias?" asked the boar, realizing he was hired to be a commentator, nothing more. "I meant… who am I kidding? Yeah, you're gonna die," concluded the boar.

Zanatose was aggravated at the boar's racist remarks. "Can it you dirty pig!" he yelled. He clenched his fists and bore them threateningly at the animal.

"Enough!" yelled Rezaar. "Zanatose you have a challenge to complete," announced Rezaar. Zanatose stood still, and lost most of his courage. "Prepare the platform," Rezaar commanded.

A few of his workers pulled a switch and the platform reacted with showing its traps. It had swinging pendulums, trap doors, and….

"Wow!" yelled Zanatose as the floor beneath his feet gave away. He grabbed onto the ledge and vaulted up quickly before the door closed on him. A dark part of Zanatose laughed at the prospect. "*They think this will finish us?*" asked an odd voice not much different from his. Somehow, the dark powers of the swords were a part of him.

"You will take part in the first of several gladiator matches in these rings and prove you are worthy enough to live," said Rezaar. He looked like he was preparing to watch his favorite play. Zanatose half expected to see actors come out onto the platform and perform some sort of tragic play.

"*Gladiator matches must be their favorites,*" thought Zanatose.

"*I agree,*" said the voice in his head. "*This'll be fun!*"

"Who are you?" Zanatose asked aloud.

"It is time!" yelled Rezaar. Three Hayvans jumped down onto the platform, and they were all well armed with scimitars, clubs, and shields.

Zanatose saw the weapons he was given and made a mad dash for them. A Hayvan stood in his way. It swung at him, but an instinct within Zanatose quickly replied. He grabbed its arm and used it as a support to vault over the Hayvan. Zanatose was a few feet from the weapons when a pendulum swung his way. He jumped to the side and dived at the weapons.

As he grabbed the weapons he rolled under another pendulum. He rolled onto a trap door by accident. The ground fell and he dangled on the side supported by his weaker left arm. He held the weapons tightly in his sweaty hands, gripping the side with his fingers.

It was here that he realized how exhausted he was. When the trap door had given way, he had crashed into the side of the arena and his wound was starting to bleed again. He tried to ignore this as he pulled himself up. A Hayvan was above him waiting. It stabbed viscously down at him. Zanatose rolled behind the Hayvan and stabbed the small sword into the Hayvan's back. It gave a loud roar and Zanatose kicked it into the lava pit and held onto his sword tightly. He coughed a couple times, starting to feel ill from the slow acting poison in his system.

"Who's next?" he asked from the other two Hayvans, straightening himself up. One had a sword, and the other had a huge spiked club. They nodded to each other and charged at him.

He ran in the opposite direction and suddenly stopped. The Hayvans followed him, and once they stopped, one of the two almost slid off while the other skidded on his heel and changed direction. The Hayvan swung at Zanatose with his spiked club and Zanatose blocked with his shield. That one blow shattered his shield; Zanatose staggered back from the impact. His hand stung badly, the spikes had pierced his skin. The second Hayvan finally started chasing after him and jumped over the lava pit between them.

Zanatose threw his sword into the first Hayvan's heart. It staggered backwards and fell into the lava. Zanatose was now unarmed against the last Hayvan. He felt the voice inside him take over, and he turned into his dark form.

He gave the last Hayvan a bone shattering punch, making it fly into one of the supports for Rezaar's platform. The impact shook Rezaar out of his daze and he stood hastily and stared down at the battle just in time to watch the last Hayvan slide down into the lava. Zanatose turned back to normal, his whole body ached, and he felt the snake burn onto his neck and around his back toward his heart. He staggered forward toward Rezaar's platform clutching his painful wounds on his side.

A metal bridge leading to an exit rose from the lava. "W... well done," said Rezaar. Everyone was stunned to see him alive; the crowd stared in a silent awe.

"He has survived!" bellowed the indignant boar. "I can't believe it folks, there's more than meets the eyes with this human!"

Rezaar was faintly disappointed to see Zanatose alive. "Hmm... Well done Zanatose. You will live on... for now," he added quietly. "You may roam upon our great city while you await our next test. One of my soldiers will follow you and help you, like a chaperone as they say in your human schools." A soldier opened the door, he was awaiting Zanatose.

Zanatose clutched his sides tightly, trying to slow the bleeding. He staggered along the metal bridge, over lava, slowly toward the soldier. His heavy steps echoed off the metal. Zanatose felt the pain of his wound. He was starting to doubt his plan and himself. *"I'm too weak. Poison eats away at me, the darkness eats away at me, what's left of me?"* he thought sadly.

"Well done out there," said the young soldier. His mane was not fully grown out. He held out his paw to shake hands. "My name is Amir; it's nice to meet you Zanatose." Zanatose removed a hand from his bleeding wound, and he shook Amir's hand. "You were wounded?"

Zanatose shook his head. "It was... an old wound that started bleeding when I slammed into the side of the stadium," explained Zanatose. He was in terrible pain, and he just wanted to rest. "I need rest."

"Really? I'm a great warrior just like you, and I hoped we could spar," suggested Amir. Zanatose was aggravated by Amir's foolhardiness, but he acted like he did not care. "I'll take you to your room at once then."

They left the arena through heavy, metal gates to the great Parikine city. The sun shone brightly and Zanatose squinted to see. What he saw took his breath away, making him cough. "This... this is greater than..." stuttered Zanatose. Amir laughed at his reaction.

The city did not have huts, or wooden buildings. Everything was made of some stone. Amazingly crafted pillars stood everywhere, bearing the symbols of the Hayvans. On the top of the pillars were figurines of their great leaders' heads.

"It is impressive isn't it?" asked Amir with pride. Zanatose nodded wordlessly. "You're living quarters will be in that building," Amir pointed to a flat roofed building.

"Thank you," said Zanatose as he started staggering toward it. He started to feel the effects of the battle as he staggered on the paved road toward the building.

The pain was stabbing him from every direction. He felt the hot sun beaming down on him, his sore arms and legs giving up, and he could feel the poison pumping through his veins. It all became too much for him. His eyes rolled in his skull, and he collapsed to his knees, still fighting the pain.

"Are you alright Zanatose!?" asked Amir with an alarmed tone.

Zanatose tried to reply, but he felt the poison take its toll on his body. He choked on his own breath and started to twitch abruptly. Amir mumbled prayers under his breath and started yelling for help. "Someone, please help this man!"

Several Hayvans were about to help until they saw that the "man" was just a human. "Humph, pathetic humans," one passerby whispered to his friend.

Amir did not know what to do to help Zanatose. He knew Zanatose was suffering from the effects of the deadly Parikine scorpion's poison, but Amir lacked the antidote. A Hayvan in brown silk robes and a turban walked by and saw Zanatose twitching on the ground.

"Stand back!" bellowed the large Hayvan in a fierce commanding voice. The Hayvan stood over Zanatose and reached into his robes. He took out a corked vial filled with a disgusting looking green solution. "Hold him down," commanded the Hayvan.

Amir quickly complied and pinned Zanatose's arms to the floor. Zanatose tried to fight back. "Control yourself Zanatose!" yelled Amir as he pinned his full weight on top of him.

The fierce Hayvan uncorked the vial swiftly and poured its harsh contents down Zanatose's throat. Amir stood up, releasing Zanatose gently. Zanatose had stopped twitching uncontrollably.

"Thank you for your help Nima. I don't know what I'd have done without you brother," said Amir. Nima laughed at his little brother's worry.

"What are brothers for!" he laughed happily. "You need not be so fearful my brother. If God had ordained this man to die, then it is God's will, but He still has work for this man."

Nima was a far larger and much more powerful Hayvan than Amir. He was older by one year. Nima's mane was fully grown, and it gave him a fierce yet majestic look. "Your friend won't wake up for a while. We should carry him home," suggested Nima. The two brothers agreed. They grabbed Zanatose and hauled him to his quarters.

Brett had a small breakfast before Theodore and Marik decided it was time to leave. "We have to go now. My goal is to take back the shrine by lunch time. I believe that's very reasonable," said Theodore considerably.

Brett laughed at his proud presumption. "Before lunch!?" he laughed. "We'd be lucky to be done by night fall. These things are stronger than even the wolfos. You shouldn't take the tariks so lightly Theodore," cautioned Brett.

"Theodore's right Brett, this'll be easy!" said Marik. "You have Theodore and me on your side. Even without you, we may have been able to take on the tariks."

What a humble group," thought Brett to himself.

Theodore stopped laughing and made a serious announcement. "The path to the shrine will be very dangerous Brett. The raptors will most likely find us. We shall have to fight them with the best of our abilities. Are you prepared to make this treacherous journey?" Brett nodded solemnly.

CHPT 19:
TRIALS OF COURAGE

Zanatose was at the volcano again, the location of the great Temple of Legend. He took his dark swords out and started cautiously walking toward the tall, white temple. He was almost across the metal bridge when Brett appeared, blocking his advance.

"Stand back or else," warned Zanatose in a strange, dark voice. Brett shook his head. Zanatose raised his sword and was about to stab down, but then everything turned black.

He was at the beach side. He looked around but found nothing except sand, water, and a few trees. He gazed into the open sea and saw someone drowning. He ran into the water and swam toward the person as fast as he could.

He struggled against the waves of the cruel sea. He was almost there, and he could recognize that person as Katie. "NO!" yelled Zanatose as he suddenly gulped down a mouth full of water.

Zanatose sat bolt upright, covered in ice-cold water. He rubbed his eyes so that he could see a little better. He saw Amir standing over him with a bucket. Amir gave a smile and apologized. "Sorry about that Zanatose. I was trying to water the plants by your window. Guess my hand slipped," he said innocently. "How are you feeling?" asked Amir. "You collapsed yesterday."

Zanatose did not know what Amir was talking about. He thought back to yesterday, but he could barely remember it. "I feel alright except for the usual battle scars… did something happen yesterday?" asked Zanatose.

Amir nodded his head. "The poison in your wound acted up. I'm glad that you're in good shape though."

"You saved me?" asked Zanatose. Amir nodded his head in reply. Zanatose slowly started to laugh. "That makes two times you've saved me! Once from poison, then from a bad dream!" he started laughing, but Amir did not.

Amir seemed concerned. "How odd… so you are having strange dreams," asked Amir. "It seems our people can only have nightmares of death and doom these days."

"These are strange times we live in?" remarked Zanatose. "After I survive the trials to gain your king's respect perhaps, your kind, the Hayvans, may come and assist me and my friends in my perilous journey," suggested Zanatose.

"Perhaps we will play a role in this," said Amir contentedly. "Where are your friends, Zanatose?"

Zanatose gave a heavy-hearted sigh and remembered how he left the group. He left Katie, Bill, and all his friends to go alone. "We separated at Theragorn city to find the different elemental items which can help us stop the tarik," explained Zanatose.

"You are sure the elemental swords will help you more than a grand army?" asked Amir.

Zanatose gave a little chuckle then replied. "The swords are important, but perhaps your *grand* army could buy us some time to solve this problem. The point of the swords isn't to destroy the tarik by force. It's supposed to lead us to a sacred temple that haunts my dreams. The answer seems to be in that temple."

"So that is where you plan to head soon?" asked Amir.

He seemed worried. "You would sooner be dead than reach that wretched temple. We, the Hayvans, regard the temple as a forsaken place." Amir drew his large threatening head toward Zanatose's and whispered into his ear. "That place is protected by the tarik, and an occult beast that lives within the lava. No one knows where this temple is because no one could come back alive after looking for it. Some say it doesn't exist."

"Well that's unsettling," exclaimed Zanatose disappointedly. "But I feel I could make it through easily. Nothing can stop my power," he said proudly. Amir started to roar with laughter.

"We will soon see. The next trial is about to start," Amir said.

Brett had left his horse at the village, and he was trudging through the thick vines and scores of trees. He was following Theodore and Marik toward the shrine of the light sword. He was starting to itch from head to toe from all the bug bites. Brett tried to ignore the irritation, but it felt impossible.

"This journey to the shrine will test your courage and valor. Are you prepared Brett?" asked Theodore as he slashed through a few vines blocking his way with a long silver sword.

"I'm sure it won't be too dreadful," said Brett confidently. Theodore was glad to see this confidence in his men. "Why didn't we bring more soldiers?" asked Brett.

"We'd attract too many raptors," said Theodore with a taunting voice. Brett started to feel ill-at-ease as he traveled through the jungle, littered with hiding places for an adversary.

They went through the thick jungle for hours until they felt exhausted and stopped. The sun was slowly setting in the distance, and Brett was relieved that they had not faced any hardships yet.

"We shall rest here for an hour and then we shall continue on," announced Theodore.

They had not eaten since morning, and they were now starving. The group unpacked their food, and they gorged on the bread and imbibed the water. "We should keep moving as soon as possible," said Marik as he eyed the bushes suspiciously.

Zanatose was before Rezaar's throne bowing on one knee. "Your next challenge is to survive a battle against an armored spider. They are strange beasts which posses a hard outer shell, but inside they are weak," said Rezaar. He noticed the angry look on Zanatose's face and added, "Don't worry, you will have weapons."

Rezaar snapped his fingers, and a human servant came and bowed, holding a large chest over his head for Rezaar. Rezaar opened the chest and took out a thick velvet cloth used to contain the two dark swords. He handed them to Zanatose slowly with caution.

Zanatose was glad to see his two old friends again. He grabbed them cheerfully. "How can you hold those swords!?" asked Rezaar suddenly. "A few of my servants were instantaneously killed after touching those *things.*"

"These aren't just any swords. They are the dark elemental swords," said Zanatose proudly. "And I am the one destined to wield them against the tarik."

Rezaar rolled his eyes and spoke again. "None-the-less *destined one;* you have a battle to win, so follow my soldiers, quickly."

Zanatose exited the cozy throne room and followed Amir through the desert city and to the gladiator rings. He was slightly relieved to feel less pain in his sides, but he was sure the old scars would burn again if he was hit too hard.

As he walked with his loyal blades by his side, he felt the snake scar burn, on his back and arm. He walked a little more slowly, but he tried his best to hide the excruciating pain. He flinched after every other step from the pain.

Amir talked very little on the way. Zanatose was guessing this was where he would die because every time he asked about the trial, Amir would look at him gravely and walk on. The buildings were showing signs of ageing as they kept going toward the boundaries of the city. Amir suddenly stopped; they had finally reached the edge of the city and the beginning of the desert.

"This isn't the same coliseum is it?" asked Zanatose. He did not remember having to cross the desert to reach the gladiator matches.

"You've never seen an agrab have you?" asked Amir in a hoarse voice. Zanatose shook his head, assuming by agrab, Amir meant the giant spider. "They are huge vile beasts. I and my brother believe it is wrong to put even the worst people against such a sinister beast."

Zanatose felt like his heart had skipped a beat; he was about to face his worst fear. They went onto a large wagon pulled by five large horses. It was an uncomfortable ride through the desert for Zanatose.

"Well…. Here we are," said Amir as the wagon stopped. They stepped out of the wagon, and they saw the largest coliseum ever built. It was supported by rows and rows of giant marble pillars and was at least twice the size of an average building in Parikine city.

Zanatose slowly walked through the sand in his leather boots. He walked under an arch and through a metal gate which instantly closed behind him. He could feel the hot sun in his eyes as the crowd cheered noisily above.

He was alone in the center, far below anyone else. The

crowd could barely see him they were so far up. "*How are they going to see me or the spider?*" wondered Zanatose. He noticed that the ground around him was full of craters that had traces of hair and blood. "*What could have caused that?*"

There was a loud screeching sound that drew his attention. He looked at the far wall of the arena and saw the tall, black metal bars containing his enemy. "That was a little loud for a spider," thought Zanatose aloud. The bars slowly creaked up, and Zanatose drew both of his swords. He stood perfectly still, waiting for his foe to appear.

He saw a hairy black stick which was twice his size poke out from behind the bars. It began to occur to Zanatose why Amir was so afraid to come, and why the stands were so far above the action. The whole spider now entered, and it was three times the size of any Hayvan; they were already much taller than Zanatose.

Zanatose started sweating and felt his swords slipping. He tightened his grip on his swords and felt the dark powers seeping into him. He thought of his dreams with Katie falling through the water. "I can't let that happen," said Zanatose to himself with determination. "I have to try, I have to fight."

The spider was hairy at the stomach, but on top, he had an almost metallic-looking shell. It stood on its hind legs and gave a hungry screech before it stamped its feet against the ground. The earth shook and Zanatose almost fell to his knees. Its many red eyes glared at him as he stepped away slowly with his dual swords raised.

"Let's begin this," said Zanatose. He used his dark powers and blasted the spider's hard outer shell. It was completely unfazed.

The spider gave another horrible screech. It was not hurt, but it knew that it was attacked. Zanatose was demoralized when he saw that this only made the spider angrier. The spider started crawling toward him, and yet Zanatose refused to turn into his dark form; instead he blasted the spider's feet. He pointed his sword and blasted many dark balls of energy, but none of them had any effect.

The spider started to spit webbing at him. He dodged as quickly as he could. He hastily rolled out of the way of one of the spider's legs as he ran to the opposite side. "*I've got only one last hope,*" thought Zanatose. The spider had webbed most of the upper part of the stadium, and Zanatose was now cornered.

Behind him was a thick wall of sticky spider webbing. In front of him was the huge horrific sight of the spider. It watched his every move with joy as it advanced on him. Zanatose was more afraid than he had ever been.

The crowd half cheered and half booed the spider as it advanced on the helpless hero.

Through his fear, all he could think about was, "*If I die, then things can never change. I'll never be with her. I can't die, not yet!*"

"Then use the true power of your swords!" said a voice in his head.

"The snake at my throat maybe dangerous though."

"It symbolizes my growth and power," said the dark part of him.

Before Zanatose could make up his mind whether he wanted the darkness to grow or die, the spider was about to clamp down with its sharp pincers on him. Zanatose lost control as the dark part of him took over.

"Now the real fun begins," said Zanatose with a smirk. He slashed his sword through one of the spider's pincers; the new sword gave off a wave of dark power. "Your end is near!"

The spider was enraged, and it tried to smash him with its long powerful legs. Zanatose's dark form felt little concern and tried his best to fight back.

He crossed his swords against his chest, preparing for

the impact. The spider stepped down on him with its heavy leg. He pushed out with his twin dark blades and pushed off the spider. The spider's leg was cut deep by his swords, and the spider fell onto its back.

It was disgusting to watch the mammoth spider die. It wriggled its legs helplessly, trying to roll off its back. Eventually, the repulsive spider lay to rest, and Zanatose was declared the victor.

The crowd stopped cheering, struck dumb by the result of the trial. There was a low murmur throughout the crowd and everyone was trying to understand how a human could defeat the undefeatable foe. Above the normal crowd's seats was the king's throne.

Zanatose turned back to normal with a painful shudder. He groaned and almost fell down to his knees with pain. He slowly placed his two dark swords back into their sheaths. He looked at his arm, and he was appalled by the snake's growth. He did not have much time to ponder upon this because the king had come down from his throne and was in the gladiator field.

Rezaar walked around slowly with his fancy red robes dragging behind him on the floor. Rezaar took out his sword and pointed it at Zanatose. "ZANATOSE!" he howled as he drew nearer with a malicious look in his eyes. The crowd held their breath, and Zanatose was struggling to stay on his feet.

"Let's go now," said Marik as he stood up off the soft soil. He kept his eyes on the same bushes.

"Why the rush?" asked Brett in a low whisper.

"We're being followed," replied Marik.

Theodore seemed upset that they had to leave the spot so quickly, but did not really mind. "Fine, we shall start moving again."

They all stood and followed Theodore through the thick jungle. As they continued, Brett noticed that there were less and less clearings. There was absolutely no trace of a path, and it seemed nothing had traveled to the shrine for some time.

As Theodore led them on toward the shrine he abruptly stopped. "Halt," commanded Theodore. He hunched down and examined the dirt closely. After he eyed it skeptically, he sniffed it to try and identify the scent.

Once he arose, he looked around them shortly and spoke to them in a low whisper. "These are raptor tracks, and the scent doesn't seem that old. Watch your backs."

Brett was a little worried as were the other two. They went onwards slowly and silently. Every time they broke a twig, they stopped, looked around apprehensively, and then moved on. After a few rounds of this happening, they lost interest and moved along quicker.

"Guess they aren't here anymore," exclaimed Brett with relief. The other two nodded gladly. "How much further is it?" asked Brett.

"About two miles," replied Theodore. Marik tripped and fell on a loose tree root on the path, in reply, two raptors jumped at him from below the growth on their path.

Brett quickly took action and took out Blazer while Theodore rammed one. The second one turned onto Theodore, and Brett lacerated his sword straight through its head. "Everyone okay?" asked Theodore as he helped Marik to his feet.

"For now we are," said Marik. Marik also drew his wind sword now and they all walked on, ready to fight.

They heard loud rustling sounds throughout the jungle from there on, and they were starting to become weary. "We're almost there," said Theodore.

They heard a loud snap from above, and a raptor fell down from a tree onto Theodore. It pinned him down as many more raptors appeared. Their scales glimmered in the shreds of sunlight that made its way through the trees. Marik swung his sword and sent a gust of wind to blow the raptor off of Theodore. Theodore rose to his feet with great difficulty; he received two claw wounds in his shoulders from the raptor.

The three stood back to back facing the circle of raptors that were ruthless by their nature. The raptors did not hesitate for a moment to pounce on them. Marik used his sword's power, but the raptors were too quick and a few caught him through the ribs.

Theodore used his blade to fend them off the best he could as did Brett. *"Alright, now there's no Zanatose to fight these guys, what should I do?"* thought Brett. Brett swung through many raptors, but it seemed they would just keep on coming.

After he chopped through a few raptors, several more would catch him off guard and stick their sharp claws into his shoulder. He stared into the raptors' cold heartless eyes and saw that they did not even look him back in the eyes.

"We cannot fail!" yelled Theodore as he pushed a raptor into a tree. Theodore lost his temper and started slashing the raptors with his claws. The location was not ideal for a battle since there were tall bushes and trees for their attackers to hide behind.

Brett was kicked down by a raptor that jumped at him. It stood on him with its painful weight and snapped down at him with its sharp treacherous teeth. He shoved his sword in between its jaws and pushed it off with one arm. His left shoulder was so badly gnarled he could barely feel it anymore.

"Can't we do anything to stop these raptors?" asked Brett as they all bumped into each other, trying to back away from the fight in the jungle.

"I'll try my best," said Marik with anxiety. He closed

his eyes tightly and raised his sword high. The raptors ran at them as quickly as they could. He stabbed his sword down as fast as he could and an enormous tornado erupted from his blade. The jungle was torn apart, but so were the raptors.

"Nicely done!" yelled Brett. They had stood in a wooded area before, but Marik's powers turned it into a small clearing void of raptors or trees.

CHPT 20:
TEMPLE OF HOPE

Rezaar lifted his sword high above his head and stabbed down. Zanatose was so exhausted, every bone in his body ached from pushing off a huge spider's weight, and he did not even care to flinch. He looked up into Rezaar's eyes and was relieved to see that he did not see hatred, but admiration. The sword stopped just before his shoulder.

"Zanatose," said Rezaar, in his loud commanding voice. Both of the two had a broad grin on their faces. "I declare you an honored citizen of Parikine city, the greatest warrior, not of a Hayvan decent, and a friend of the royal family."

Zanatose lowered his head to symbolize a bow. "I am truly grateful Rezaar," he said. Everyone in the crowd erupted with applause, moved by his resilience.

"Take him to the palace where he may stay at as long as he so desires," commanded Rezaar to his men.

His men helped Zanatose to his feet. This was a painful process for Zanatose, and his sprained ankle he got from the impact of the spider was killing him. He was strong in his dark form, but when he's back to normal it all hurts. He shortly blacked out from the pain.

Zanatose awoke in the same place he awoke in when he had first woken up in Parikine city. He looked around and again saw Rezaar. "I hope this time I don't have to go to another gladiator match," said Zanatose with a laugh.

"Don't worry about that Zanatose. You are now a friend of Parikine city. We would never jeopardize your life again," said Rezaar reassuringly.

Zanatose was about to try and stand, but he remembered why he *woke up* here. He decided it was best to just lay there for the time being. "I came here to this great city to ask you and your people for help against the tarik. Will you help my efforts against the tarik?" asked Zanatose.

"Perhaps," said Rezaar. "You know the sword Amir has... perhaps he hasn't shown it to you yet. Amir has one of those elemental swords which you most likely need if you want to bring the legends true."

"Which one?" Zanatose asked.

"The sword of flames," said Amir suddenly. Zanatose almost jumped but could not. "And I will be honored to assist you in your cause Zanatose."

"Thank you Amir," said Zanatose.

"What is your plan to defeat the tarik?" asked Rezaar.

"Our plan is to get the elemental swords, so we can defeat the tarik's leader. Hopefully, that'll cause some instability in their forces, or end the tarik," replied Zanatose.

"And, several others of my friends have gone different ways for different swords. We hope to meet at Theragorn city soon and move on from there," continued Zanatose. "But once I'm well enough, I'm going to make a pit stop at Wolf Fang's place and take care of him," said Zanatose with a demonical look in his eyes.

"That's not so wise Zanatose," warned Rezaar. "The wolfos army rivals even ours at their stronghold. I fear attacking him head on would lead you to your grave."

This made Zanatose upset, but he disregarded it. "Amir, you need to start going toward Theragorn city to meet my friends. Their names are Edwin, Macbeth, Brett, Bill, Anton, and Katie. Everyone in Theragorn knows them."

"And take a small platoon of men with you," said Rezaar.

"It is going to be a war after all." He had concerns about Amir's safety in Theragorn city, but he did not want to let Zanatose know about that. Rezaar was well informed, and he knew that Jonathan had recently killed the king.

"We're trying to stop that from happening with the elemental swords," said Zanatose. "Fang thinks that's our best plan. I think he's wrong," said Zanatose.

"Against the tarik, I fear war is inevitable. This time I have to agree with General Fang," replied Rezaar gravely. "Why do you want to confront such a powerful adversary Zanatose?"

"I want something of his other than his army. I'm sure he has it," said Zanatose. *"I need the dark crystal I'm sure he still has it, and some answers!"* thought Zanatose to himself. Rezaar sighed then left as did Amir. Zanatose settled back onto his warm straw bed and fell asleep.

"We're finally there," said Theodore from a short distance ahead. Brett pushed away a branch blocking his view and saw an ancient shrine covered in moss. The white of the shrine had turned gray with age.

Brett peered into the grimy, mosaic windows but saw nothing but darkness. He could not see anything inside. *"Maybe if we go closer,"* thought Brett.

"Well, let's go in," said Marik.

"Everyone, be prepared for anything. I believe there may have been a few traps here and there in our ancient shrine," explained Theodore in a hushed whisper.

All three of them took out their own sword. Brett was approaching until he saw the others were not, so he stopped as well. "What's the big speech going to be now?" asked Marik. He knew this as typical *Theodore behavior*; before anything, he'll make a huge inspirational speech.

"This shrine belongs to us and all of our ancestors. If

221

we will not do this for them, then there are countless other reasons such as revenge! And to build to the destruction of the tarik! This is a battle which we dare not lose. Keep fighting until we get the sword, and then fight some more!" hollered Theodore. They all laughed and applauded him. Theodore wore a smug smile in reply.

The small group filed behind Theodore onto the old worn out steps of the light shrine. Their strength was still drained from fighting the raptors, but they knew they had to do this. Brett felt his destiny draw nearer with every step he took. "*I will finally be able to help stop the tarik,*" he thought to himself.

The thought of facing the tarik again made his mind stray to the rumors he had heard as a child about his father's death. Brett heard about it in an alley, in the day, from a stubby little bald man.

"Yer father chap? He died. The dok mongrels torn hum to shreds in de last mission. Why else do yu tink I'm drinking dis here rum? Clean out de memories o' his death, tats why!" said the drunken soldier with a flushed face as he continued to imbibe the near empty bottle. The soldier had returned from duty just recently and his tattered armor still had stains of his father's blood. The red-faced man sat lazily on a barrel as he drank the dark liquid in the bottle.

From that day forth, Brett began sword lessons in Nijad city and registered to become a soldier. Brett was seven when he heard the news of his father's death and fourteen by the time he became an elite soldier. "*I can't fail,*" he thought as they continued up the steps to the stone door.

The group noticed that there were many scratches on the door and parts were broken off. "Perhaps we should knock," suggested Marik as a joke. They all had a silent laugh before Theodore pushed open the door slowly.

"Isn't that hard!?" asked Brett as he watched the tall stone door creak open. He noticed some vague designs on the door, but they were chipped away and misshapen.

"Not for Theodore," said Marik as he walked past Brett into the dark shrine.

"I thought the light shrine would be more… bright," said Brett as he walked inside. There was absolutely no way to see within the shrine's walls.

"That's what I was thinking," said Marik.

"It's the power of the tarik I think…." said Theodore. "Just follow my lead."

Theodore led them into the darkness. Every footstep on the cold, damp stones echoed throughout the entire shrine. They stumbled every now and then from the worn down steps; some steps were in perfect condition, and then some were completely non-existent.

On their way up, Brett tripped on some kind of thin of wire. "*Why is that there*?" he wondered. He heard something flying at him, and he jumped several steps forward. They heard a loud crash, indicating some large mass had slammed into the wall. Brett had triggered a trap.

A cloud of dust was raised, and they could hear rubble roll down the stone steps, but they could not see what had collided with the wall. "There goes our surprise attack," muttered Marik sadly.

Theodore and Brett both laughed tensely. "With these stone steps we never, had a possible surprise attack!" said Theodore.

The group's nerves were tested as they climbed the stone steps in an endless abyss. They were worried about being attacked in such a narrow place or smashed by another trap. The three stayed close to the crumbling stone walls and were covered with dust by the time they reached the top of the stairs.

"That was too easy," said Brett. He tried to peer into the darkness but could not see anything.

"Nonsense!" said Theodore. He dusted off the door in front of them and turned the ancient gold knob. He turned it all the way and pushed, but it refused to open. "How odd…."

They heard the ground below them creek and they started to fall far below into another black abyss. "I told you it was too easy!" yelled Brett as they fell onto a soft landing far below.

"This is a secret room of some kind," exclaimed Theodore as he looked around.

Marik dusted off the floor to see that their fall was cushioned by some rich, red pillows. "What was this room used for?" asked Marik.

"Beats me," shrugged Brett. He stood up and started to stretch a bit, he heard his back crack as he outstretched his arms. He suddenly had a sensation over take him.

"Something wrong?" asked Marik.

"The sword… it's near… I can feel it," said Brett with wide eyes. He could feel the sword beckoning him through the darkness.

"Follow me," commanded Brett. "I think I know where the sword is." He started to march into the darkness and the other two cheetahs decided best to follow him for his own security.

"I hope you do know where the sword is, because I don't have a clue anymore," said Theodore. "The legends never spoke of traps in this great shrine."

"Then you gave these dark beasts too much time in this shrine," said Brett. They walked into a pitch-black cloud. "Does anyone else feel cold all of a sudden?" asked Brett as he stopped abruptly.

"Yes, how peculiar. What could this be from Theodore?" asked Marik.

"The tarik," said both Brett and Theodore at the same time.

They all took out their swords in a nervous rush. They knew they were only three warriors against countless tarik, and they could only fight so long before the cold gets to them but they still felt the odds were on their side. "We will fight to regain our holy grounds and the great light sword. And for this propose we shall not fail!" yelled Theodore into the darkness. They could hear scratching against the walls, and they knew that the tarik now knew they were there. "We will fight for our pride!" exclaimed Theodore loudly as he saw his own shadow move. "We will fight till we die!"

Brett broke into a cold sweat and could feel himself becoming numb with cold fear, but he knew he must not fail. He was terrified by the daunting prospect of facing so many tarik. He started to shiver and held his sword tightly for dear life.

"Here they come," whispered Marik nervously. They saw shadows on the floor approaching them. The shadows morphed into the tall, amorphous, and frightful figures of the tarik as they neared.

Brett felt his fellow fighters lose their edge so he decided it was best if he was the first one to strike. He quickly swung at the nearest tarik with his sword.

He swung with all his might and his sword pierced through only half of its body. He could not make it all the way through. Brett withdrew his sword with disappointment. "Well…. That's unsettling."

"Our turn!" yelled Theodore as he and Marik slashed at the tarik. The tarik seemed very unconcerned and allowed them to cut into them just as Brett had.

The one Marik slashed at showed defiance. It dodged and slammed Marik to the ground with a flying tentacle to the back. The horde of tarik seemed bored at this point and started to go on the offensive to end their hapless lives.

The warriors felt the sting of the tarik from every direction as they fought with all their might. Through the darkness it was impossible to tell a tarik from the dark abyss. Marik used his sword's power against them, but his sword alone was not enough.

With every passing second, they all grew weaker from all the cold that chilled them to their very souls. The heroes were slammed into the wall with a force which shook the entire temple. All that the non-elemental swords could do was cut off the tentacles that would grow back anyway. Brett was starting to realize that the tarik they were facing were far more powerful than the ones in the cave.

As his eyes became better accustomed to the dark he started to see the tarik more clearly. These tarik were just as big as the others, just as dark and gruesome, but they could morph their darkness. Brett ducked as a tentacle came at him. He coughed as debris fell. He looked up at the tarik and saw several of its tentacles turn into large clubs.

"This is enough!" yelled Brett as a tarik slapped him in the face. He could feel blood dripping down his chin as he tried to talk. "You guys, try to cover me while I search for the sword!"

Brett did not wait for a yes or a no. He just rammed the tariks blocking his way and ran blindly toward the direction he sensed the light and the warmth of the elemental sword.

"Please, find it quickly!" yelled Theodore as he fell to his knees and fought the tarik. He could no longer stand and was struggling to block the flurry of attacks. Theodore felt a sharp pain as one of his rib cages snapped.

Marik was in horrible pain as he struggled to stand. He kept getting hit against his knees and face. A hope in his heart told him to stay on his feet and that the pain would end. He only hoped it would not end in death. Looking to his side at Theodore, he saw the great leader disappear under a cloud of darkness that looked more like a large swarm of bees encasing him.

Brett was still running as fast as he could and was being hit on the way. He felt the sword near him, but he felt death just as close to him. The cold clammy hands of death had their grip around his fading spirit and they were squeezing away at his heart.

He felt his sword whipped out of his hand, and he fell against the hard, cold marble painfully. He felt his ribs become crushed under of the tarik that swarmed onto him. He could feel the last breathe leave him.

His arms went limp and he gave up hope until he felt what his hands had hit. He felt the smooth handle of a cold sword. As cold as the sword was, it brought the warmth of life back into his body. He took a large breath of air as he wrapped his numb hands against its cool handle. Unlike leather, it gave way to his grip.

Brett had finally found the sword of legends and knew the battle was far from over if he could awaken its powers like Zanatose awakened Shadow's powers. Brett just hoped he would not lose himself to the powers like Zanatose did.

Brett felt his courage awaken his last bit of strength as he suddenly stood against the tarik and shook them off his back. They fell off and slithered around for a few moments before they took form again to fight him. Brett still had his hands wrapped around the sword's handle. He lifted the sword into the air, and the room was lit with the light of the sword and they could finally see.

The sword's light illuminated the room as much as it illuminated their souls. It was a symbol of hope and it brought the temple's beauty to sight. Brett was astounded by the crystal roof and luscious red rugs under their feet.

He turned to the tarik with the sword resting against his shoulder. "Time for round two!" he said as he brought his sword down into a tarik that was trying to attack him. "Who's next?" he taunted the tarik even though he still had not learned how to use the sword.

The tarik seemed to be blinded by the sword's light. The tarik did not approach Brett and backed away blindly. The tarik left the temple, gliding up the walls. Brett was ecstatic and relieved that the fight was over. He leaned on his sword as he watched Marik stand and look around with a frustrated face and then see Brett's sword. Then Marik's gruesome face lit up.

He limped over to Brett. Every few steps he made a face from all the pain. "You finally got the sword!" he said excitedly. He looked Brett's torn clothes up and down and asked, "What happened to you?"

"You're not looking so well either. Wait... where's Theodore?" asked Brett. The pleasure of retrieving the sword was being replaced by distress.

"Ov... over heh... here," said a soft fading voice in the corner. They looked over to see Theodore pressed against the wall. Theodore sat there with his head down.

It did not seem as if he was going to even try and stand up. Brett and Marik were alarmed to see their fearless leader in such awful shape. "Can you stand?" asked Marik.

A daunting cloud of darkness covered up the sun above the ice mountain. At the top stood Wolf Fang and at the bottom was Zanatose with both swords on the floor. His face was down with regret. There was a pit in his stomach that kept eating away at him. The darkness came up from the ground and engulfed him.

He was plunged into the deep sea. He kept falling, even though he struggled to swim, drowning as if a lead weight was tied to him. He looked around and saw Katie sinking too.

Her blond hair was flowing around her beautiful, sleeping face.

> He reaches out but fails.
> Watches life slip,
> Watches hope die.
> He tries harder, but still fails.
> He loses hope,
> He loses his love,
> He loses his beautiful dove,
> He loses his strength to try,
> The great hero dies.

"*NOOOOOOO!*" Zanatose yelled loudly. His voice rang throughout all of Parikine city. He stood bolt upright, covered in cold sweat. His eyes were wide open, scanning the darkness. He looked around and saw the plants on the windowsill and heard footsteps. Zanatose began to realize where he was again. "I'm safe in Parikine city, but Katie is out at sea and Wolf Fang." He stopped and thought a bit and remembered he had not asked where he could find Fang.

Through the darkness of the room he saw light flood in as a door was burst open. Zanatose squinted against the light and saw Amir had rushed into the room to see why Zanatose had yelled so loud. "What's going on? Is something wrong?" he asked as he drew his curved, crimson sword.

"No, nothing is wrong Amir. How long have I been asleep?" Zanatose asked.

Relieved that Zanatose was alright, Amir began to open the drapes and allow the bright sunlight to flood into the room. "You've been asleep for two days. That's probably why you're able to move again," stated Amir, noticing Zanatose's upright position.

Zanatose still had a lot of aches and pains here and there, but he could move. "That's good; I was hoping to leave anyway. My job here is done, and I have to move onto Wolf Fang. Do you know where he is?" Zanatose asked in a casual voice.

"Why would you ask about him again?" asked Amir. Zanatose was about to talk, but Amir started up again. "I know what you're going to do. After the news I have for you I'm sure you'll fight Wolf Fang no matter what I say. I have some misfortunate news about a friend of yours…" Zanatose's heart fell, and he felt an inexpressible pain in his heart. He knew what Amir was about to say.

CHPT 21:
WHAT LIES BENEATH THE SURFACE

WHAT LIES BENEATH THE SURFACE?
AN ECHOING DARKNESS THAT CHILLS THE SOUL,
OR A WARM LIGHT THAT MAKES YOU WHOLE.
ON THE SURFACE, SO CALM.
BENEATH IS THE TRUE BEAST.

"De sea was a raging witch dat day. Me pops was mid way out in ter de sea. He saw dark movements under de water. He too was searching fur dem elemental swords," said the old man. He saw the sadness in his audiences' faces. "Yep, yu all guessed right. Me pops told me ter take de extra boat and paddle back ter dis spot, and that he was righ behind me. In an instant maties he disappeared. Ye old sea swallowed im whole!" He shook his head sadly as he recalled the terrible memory.

"We're sorry about your pops," said Macbeth forlornly. "My father was said to have been killed at the hands of the tarik leader." A strange fire burned in his eyes as he said this, "I will avenge my father, but to do this I need you to help us get the swords."

The old man had a few tears in the corner of his eyes. He shook his head in agreement. "Aye old matie, I'm a great navigator in de sea, and I know where ta spot de treasure of water."

"Then let's start the search tomorrow bright and early," suggested Macbeth.

"Great, another adventure that has to start in the morning!" complained Edwin. "Why can't these artifact hunts be in the afternoon?"

Bill slapped him in the back of the head and everyone laughed at him. "Come on, where's your sense of adventure? Maybe we'll find the jewel that goes into your sword to give it power like me and Zanatose's swords."

"I hope they're not like Zanatose's swords," muttered Anton. Katie shot him a heated look. "The swords Zanatose has are pure dark energy. I wouldn't be surprised if the darkness of the swords gets to him eventually."

Bill and Edwin gave each other a little look and decided they should change the subject. "We should all go back to sleep so we can wake up early for the adventure," suggested Bill.

"Aye aye maties, yu'll need yer sleep fer tomorrow's long hike," said the old man. They all decided to go back to sleep for a few more hours until sunrise.

"No, I... can't get... up," moaned Theodore. "Just leave me here. I'll only sl..slow you down."

"You're our leader," said Marik. He was not in much better shape, but at least he could stand. Brett was also badly injured, mostly bruises except for a couple cuts.

"We're taking you with us Theodore," said Brett through his pain. He used his new sword as a cane to support him as he tried to pick up Theodore with Marik's help.

This was no easy task for the two of them. Theodore was a large, fully-grown cheetah, and he was not as light as a feather. "Come on Marik, lift him!" yelled Brett as they struggled to raise Theodore off the ground. After a few tries, they succeeded, and they started gradually staggering forward.

Theodore led them out of the temple by pointing which way to go. Unfortunately every now and then they would bump Theodore's head into a brick wall and he would go silent for short intervals. After a while they found their way back out of the temple.

"Finally, the light of day," sighed Marik.

"Tell me about it man. It was dark in there, and it was really cold," said Brett. Theodore had no input because he was still unconscious from the last collision he had taken.

They were dragging him with his hands on either one of their backs. "Well, he's still out. I hope you know the way back to the village because I sure don't," exclaimed Brett as he swayed under the weight of the bulky cat.

"Of course I do," replied Marik. He was exhausted and breathing with some difficulty due to his injured rib cage. "Maybe before we move on, we should take a break."

Brett sighed with relief as he drank some water and had Theodore lying on the ground near them. "Theodore is heavy! What do you guys eat normally?" asked Brett.

"People," said Marik very naturally. Brett did not feel very comfortable, and it was evident in his expression. "No, I'm kidding. We eat other meats from the jungle."

"Oh, okay. That's good; you had me worried there for a second." Brett saw that night was quickly falling. "We should set up camp soon," suggested Brett.

Marik nodded in agreement. "We don't have the resources to set up a full camp, but we can just lay out sleeping mats and make a fire. Hopefully the fire won't attract too much attention," said Marik. The two began unpacking their sleeping mats and started to gather wood from the forest to start a fire. They comforted Theodore and placed him into his sleeping mat softly first, then they went to sleep as well.

It was an uneasy sleep. The two heroes were battle-worn

and very weary of raptors or the tarik. For them every rustle was a potential threat. Brett slept with one eye open and one hand on his new sword.

Morning came too soon for some of the heroes. Macbeth woke earliest and banged pots and pans to wake everyone else up. Bill, Anton, and Katie woke up without much fuss, but Edwin did not wake up willingly.

"QUIET!" yelled Edwin. He was very disoriented and drowsy. He was almost about to go back to sleep with his messy black hair askew until Macbeth started banging the pots and pans even louder to keep him up. Edwin angrily swung at him and punched Macbeth square in the jaw. "Now will you be quiet?"

Macbeth's jaw hurt badly and he slugged Edwin back out of anger. Edwin glared at him as he fell back and was about to attack him again. He was inches from giving Macbeth another hard one, but Bill and Anton jumped in. "Enough you two," growled Bill. "None of us are happy to be awake this morning, don't make it worse."

"Why are those two constantly at each other's throats?" asked Katie. Anton shrugged obliviously.

"They're just like Brett and Zanatose," said Bill as he stared out into the distance remembering Theragorn city.

"What are you talking about? Those two never hated each other," said Katie.

"Really?" asked Anton with a snicker. "Ha, that's hilarious! Did you already forget their little bout back in Theragorn? Obviously, they don't trust each other. Those two are both hungry for the same thing. I wonder which will reach it first."

Bill sighed as he pondered what could have driven those two to argue with each other. *"I wonder if he knew Zanatose's secret about the swords,"* thought Bill.

The company all decided to leave their thoughts aside and go to the dining deck for some breakfast. They went up a narrow, wooden tunnel. Every step they took echoed through the passage. Bill led the way up and opened the door to the deck. They were all stunned by the beautiful, sunny weather.

There was a breakfast table prepared for them by the inn keeper. "Finally something good to eat!" rejoiced Edwin. They all raced to the table and filled their plates with the eggs, cheeses, fruits, and breads set for breakfast.

After skipping dinner last night, this meal was the best they ever had even though the meat was not very well cooked, and the bread was hard as a rock. As they enjoyed their meal, the inn keeper finally arrived.

"Goo'mornin to yu all! Ope yer enjoying de breakfast. Turns ye'll be followin dis map ter the rock elemental item," he said as he unraveled an ancient piece of parchment from his ragged coat pocket. He flattened out the map and laid it on the breakfast table.

Everyone at the table got out of their chairs and tried to get a better look at the map. The map was old and had a few ink blots that blocked their view and made reading it difficult. "According to this, we're going back to that canyon... goody," mumbled Edwin with sarcasm.

"I hope we don't run into Abigail again," said Katie. She was terrified of facing Abigail again. Last time they had narrowly escaped, and the time before that, they had Zanatose and Brett. "If only one of those two were here now."

"Well they're not, so forget it," said Anton coldly.

Katie looked deeply hurt, Bill decided to try and help. "We've got me and Macbeth though," said Bill encouragingly.

"Hey, don't forget the main hero here," added Edwin proudly. Everyone laughed at this since he had never lasted a full fight before. "Well the next elemental item is mine, so I'll be stronger!" he protested.

"No elemental item could make the weak strong," said Anton with a short chuckle. It was one of the only times he cracked a smile.

The inn keeper was waiting patiently for the argument to end so he could talk again. Macbeth noticed this and silenced everyone. "Everyone, quiet."

"Thank you," said the inn keeper before he began talking again. "While all of you search for dat, I'll call de gods o the sea to bring me de water gem."

"Water gods?" asked Bill.

The inn keeper nodded. "They are the protectors of the seas," said the inn keeper. To him this was common knowledge, and he was disappointed by the group for not knowing about it.

"Alright...... We should leave now," suggested Macbeth. "*What a quack,*" thought Macbeth. He snatched the map and stuffed it into his tunic's front pocket. "Come on guys, let's go!" He walked off the plank and onto the sandy beach and headed toward the canyon.

Anton wordlessly followed as did Bill and Edwin. Katie followed last and stopped to thank the old inn keeper for his generosity before she ran by the unsteady plank and followed her friends. "Thankfully it's sunny so Abigail can't sneak up on us," said Katie as she looked back at the breath taking ocean.

"Let's hope she doesn't come at all," said Macbeth. Macbeth had never encountered Abigail before the last encounter in the canyon, and he did not want to see her again. Abigail and her zombies terrified him.

The group soon reached the canyon, and they all stopped so that Macbeth could read the map. "We should be looking for a cave entrance to our right," he said.

"It's kind of cold, don't you guys think so?" asked Katie.

As they neared the cave, the temperature had substantially fallen.

"Yes, it is a little cold, I guess. Do you think it's the tarik?" asked Bill.

"We can just hope and go on," said Macbeth. They reached the cave, and Bill decided to lead the way in.

"It's dark, but there's nothing in here," called Bill. He had gone into the cave as a scout. The cave was dark, but still bright enough to see. There were many dull, jagged rocks and pits leading down into a dark abyss.

"Alright let's go in," suggested Macbeth to the others as he followed Bill. They could hear dripping water somewhere in the distance, and they also heard whispering.

"What is that sound?" asked Edwin.

"Probably the wind… I hope," added Macbeth in an under tone.

Katie was turning a bit pale as they kept walking. It reminded her of the cave they met the tarik back at the beginning of their journey. They would all have been goners if it were not for Brett's swift thinking and Zanatose's strength.

They heard a path in the cave crumble somewhere ahead of them. The crashing sound echoed throughout the cave. "That can't be good," said Bill.

"Thanks for the obvious!" yelled Edwin.

"What could that have been?" asked Katie as she whirled around to face Macbeth. He shrugged and kept walking, trying to ignore the thoughts of what it might have been.

Every so often, they slowed down for Macbeth as he examined the map for which way to go at various forks in the road. "Feels like every step we take, this cave gets colder," said Edwin.

"It might be the tarik," suggested Anton.

"I hope not," remarked Edwin.

"I hope so. I want some revenge for my father," said Macbeth.

Macbeth took out his sword and was ready for battle. He held the map in his left hand, and he took a look at it every so often. "We're getting pretty near to the elemental item."

"Good cause it seems the cave is falling apart," said Edwin as he looked at the moving cave walls.

"That's ridicules! Why would the cave be falling apart?" asked Bill. He took a closer look at the cave walls and noticed they were moving. "They're not falling apart; they're moving and following us."

He was not paying close attention to what he had just said, but the others did. Everyone stopped and turned around to face Bill. "You heard what you said right?" asked Katie.

Bill nodded then reflected upon his past statements. His eyes widened and he drew his sword, and readied his shield. "So the tarik were following us?"

"Well this is better than facing Abigail," said Edwin encouragingly.

"You fool, the tarik are far more powerful than Abigail!" yelled Macbeth angrily. Macbeth closed in on Edwin and the two stared each other down.

"Guys… hate to break up your moment, but the tarik are attacking!" screamed Katie as she ran and hid behind Macbeth and Edwin, helpless without a bigger weapon.

They turned and saw that Bill and Anton were fighting fiercely against a large mass of darkness. "That's *a* tarik…" murmured Macbeth. The anger for revenge he had for his father diminished and so did his bravery. He had never seen a tarik and seeing so many at once was chilling.

Macbeth looked at the tarik Bill and Anton were fighting and saw a huge dark cloud which was a tarik. Macbeth's face turned white, and he started shuddering. "You okay?" asked Katie nervously. Macbeth fell unconscious.

"Great... one of us down already," said Edwin as he drew his sword.

Anton was also starting to tremble from the cold, and he was starting to take more painful blows than he could handle, and his reflexes slowed. This was his first battle against the tarik, but fear was not an option for him.

Bill was fighting with more and more anger for every blow landed on him from the tarik's ferocious tentacles. He kept blocking rounds of blows with his shield and slowly his knees would give up more and more. With every blow against his sword, he would be pushed toward the cave wall.

Edwin was starting to get into the action. He stabbed at a few tariks, but it did not do any good. "How am I supposed to get rid of these things!?" he yelled from a hard hit in the gut.

"I won't let them win!" yelled Bill. He was furious that for every tarik he got rid of with his sword several more appeared. The tariks in front of him all slammed their tentacles down on him at once. Bill quickly turned and blocked them with his shield.

The force of their hits shook him to his core and made his feet break into the cave's rock ground. He was hurting all over and was trembling from the impact and the cold. One more hit in the back of the head, from a tarik that was hiding in his shadow, knocked him out.

Anton was already out, like a small spark on a windy day, only Edwin and Katie were left. Neither one planned to stay put and fight. Katie was running along as fast as she could, attempting to find the sword, and evading the surprise attacks from the tarik. Edwin was following close behind doing the same and swinging his sword at a few tariks every now and then to keep them back.

"That elemental item better help or else we're doomed!" he yelled.

"Found it!" yelled Katie. She grabbed the shiny brown gem off a moss covered pedestal and tossed it to Edwin.

Edwin stopped and reached out his arm to catch it. A tarik swept his feet and he fell hard against the cold dirt ground. "NO!" yelled Edwin. His sword flew straight up, out of his hands, and the gem went perfectly into its slot on the sword's handle.

A tarik stood above him and stared down at him with its cold, red eyes and gave some kind of echoing call that sounded like someone coughing. It morphed its tentacle into a sharp spear and was about to stab down. Edwin's sword fell down right through its heart.

The tarik was immediately vaporized into dust and the sword landed right next to Edwin's head with a clink. "That could've been ugly," sighed Edwin. He stood up and grabbed his sword.

He stood up against the army of tarik and simply dusted off his tunic as they approached. The barbaric beasts staggered as they flew at him with ferocious speed. Edwin braced himself against the tarik, defending Katie. "You saved me, so I'll save you now," he said to her.

She held her breathe as the tarik left the still bodies of their comrades and dashed mercilessly at him. He could feel cold fear wrap itself around him. He stared at the cloud of darkness and saw his whole life fly by.

He could see his mother lift him and hug him after he brought in a finger painting from his second year of school at Sholkon village. He was half the size he is now, and he was half the age. He smiled proudly as his mother whispered into his ear with her soft voice, "Reach high, for stars lie hidden in your soul. You will be a great hero someday."

CHPT 22:
TURNING TIDES

A hero is the light to shine through the fog.
A hero is the burning star of hope that shines against all odds.
A hero is the lion of courage and cunning.
And the hero's creed is to never give up.

Flurries of whipping tentacles poured down onto Edwin. He raised his sword and blocked several, but many landed painful blows. The cold was getting into his soul, and he staggered with his heavy sword dragging against the ground. It gave a horrendous scraping sound against the ground.

The tarik gave loud echoing sounds that made it seem like they were laughing at him. His arms were so numb and tired that he could barely move his sword. "I can't give up," murmured Edwin. He stopped backing away from the tarik and lifted his sword with great effort.

"I WON'T GIVE UP!" he yelled at them. He raised his sword over his head and stabbed it back into the ground. His yelling startled the tarik, and they stood transfixed by his still persevering soul, attempting to survive them. The entire cave began to shake and the ceiling was beginning to crumble.

The ground crumbled starting from Edwin's sword toward the tarik. The cracks stopped right under the tarik and then the cave's rocks spiked through them from the ground. The tarik gave a high pitched screech right before the jagged rocks pierced through their bodies.

Their last call echoed throughout the cave as the shaking stopped. Katie was silent and gazed on at the sight with her wide blue eyes. Edwin was still on his knees with his hands tightly wrapped around his sword. His head rested on its handle, covering it with sweat. He opened his eyes and looked up to see that the tarik were gone and in their place were spiked rocks.

"Good, it's over," he sighed and rested his head back on the sword.

Katie shook her head and ran to Edwin and shook him vigorously. "EDWIN, EDWIN! YOU DID IT!" she screamed into his ear as she kept shaking him. It was unbelievable that Edwin would be capable of such raw power.

He flinched from her yelling and groaned a little. "Don't yell please," he said weakly.

"Are you okay?" she asked sympathetically.

He used his sword as a support and slowly, but gradually pushed himself back up to his feet. "It was kind of hard to take all of those blows and then use my sword's power. I think I'll be fine though," he said with stiff breathes. "How are the others?"

Katie shrugged, leaving his side to tend to the others. "They're coming around!" she yelled back. Anton and Bill were both back on their feet, wondering what had just happened, and Macbeth was surprised to be in the cave.

"What happened?" asked Bill.

"Where are we?" asked Macbeth in a groggy voice. Anton laughed at him.

Katie nodded then pointed back to Edwin who was still struggling to lift his sword out of the ground. "He saved us all with his sword's new powers," she said excitedly.

"Really? Edwin fought against all of those tarik and won?" Macbeth laughed at the thought of it. She nodded enthusiastically.

"Is that so hard to believe?" asked Edwin. He finally had

taken out his sword and used it as a cane. He was covered head to toe with bruises, but he wore a champion's smile as he looked at Macbeth's dismayed face.

"We should start going back while there's still some light for us to navigate by," suggested Bill. The others nodded and slowly followed him out of the cave.

As they walked toward the cave's exit, everyone noticed that there were lots of cracks along the cave walls, ceilings, and even the ground. "What happened here, an earthquake?" asked Anton.

Edwin chuckled and shook his head. "Nah, it was my sword's powers," he said proudly.

"Nice, man!" said Bill. He gave Edwin a congratulatory pat on the back.

Edwin squirmed at the touch. "Owe… please don't do that," he said through gritted teeth.

"Sorry, I forgot about your modest battle back there," laughed Bill.

Brett yawned and stretched out his back before he stood up and started his short hike back to Theragorn city. Theodore, Marik, and Brett had reached Roctinian village safely and without resistance. He was back in the same guest room and went to the same dining hall for breakfast, except this time it was for his goodbyes.

He sat down at the table; at the head, as usual, was Theodore with a happy grin and a large mug in one hand. He raised the mug high into the air once Brett was finished his breakfast of cheeses and breads with assorted nuts all in one delectable sandwich.

"I would like to proclaim a toast to our special guest!" he announced. Everyone, including Marik, stopped talking to his neighbor and listened intently.

"*I should ask these guys for their help in our efforts,*" Brett thought to himself.

"You have come to us in our time of weakness and brought us back into a time of security! You have helped rid our enemies from our sacred grounds and for that we are forever in your debt."

"I have taken the liberty of assigning guards to our shrine so this incident will never again take place. Now let us drink! Unless our guest of honor wants to say something," added Theodore.

Everyone looked down the table at Brett. Brett decided that this was the best time to ask the cheetahs for their help.

"Actually, I would like to ask a favor of you, Theodore," said Brett as he stood up to speak.

"Anything you so desire my good friend," said Theodore as he took a sip from his mug of breakfast wine, a less alcoholic wine.

"As you know, I am part of a small union of people who are setting out to get rid of the new tarik problems. As you have most likely deduced, in this year alone, the number of tarik appearances has increased to a threatening number. I and the empire of Theragorn with the support of Nijad city feel that we have to stop the tarik once again."

"I fear that I can't do this with my small group alone. I ask you to aid me and my friends in vanquishing the dark forces of the tarik," concluded Brett.

Theodore's grin vanished, and Brett took a seat once again. Theodore set his mug onto the table slowly with a pensive look. "We shall help, but we are not prepared to help yet... obviously. For now, all I have the power of doing is allowing my best warrior, Marik, to go with you and help. I will reinforce your efforts with my army in a month if we conclude that we can trust the humans."

"Thank you," said Brett with a bow. "Are you up for another journey with me?" he asked Marik.

"It would be an honor to help you, but will this village be safe without me?" asked Marik. Brett nodded and pushed his seat out from under the table. Brett exited the building after many farewells.

He was glad to see that the cheetahs did not seem as angry or hateful toward him anymore. When they looked at him, he no longer saw anything to fear. The sun was high in the sky, allowing him to realize the beauty of the cheetahs and their feline eyes. Their no longer looked soaked in blood, they were white like ivory.

Marik was still inside waiting for Theodore's reply. "I have been the warrior who has saved this village from most dangers since I was old enough to raise my sword," said Marik.

Theodore sighed as he slouched in his seat, resembling an aged king who had lived through too much. "We will make do. You on the other hand should be careful. Brett has a point; the appearances of tariks have become more common. If any of us can help his cause, it is you," said Theodore softly with a toothy smile. "May the four winds bless your every step, son."

"Thank you, father," said Marik. He went over to Theodore and hugged and kissed him on the cheek. "I'll miss you father."

"I'll miss you too son, but I feel this is part of your destiny. You have to help this boy save all of us from the scars of the past. We were part of the awful war that created the tarik," said Theodore. Marik nodded and left to meet Brett. He knew he would not have to worry about his father.

"You ready now?" asked Brett once he saw Marik leave the building. Marik nodded solemnly. A farmer was waiting for them at the outside of the wall with two large horses.

They were huge hazel horses with muscular legs and flowing white mains.

The two of them secured their small pouches of food and their swords to their horses' straps and mounted. "Let's go to Theragorn city," said Brett.

Marik agreed and mounted his horse as well. "I hope your friends have reached the meeting point safely," said Marik hopefully.

"I hope so too," replied Brett as they both started riding swiftly back toward Theragorn city. Brett rode with a heavy mind. His mind started to stray back to his friends. "*Katie is at the sea without Zanatose or me. I hope those guys didn't let anything happen to her,*" Brett thought.

"We'll be there in one day!" yelled Marik happily as they rode. "We're making great time!" The two of them raced each other to Theragorn city as fast as they could. Brett was in the lead thanks to his riding experience from Nijad's tournaments.

It was dark outside and they had finally reached the peaceful beachfront. "We're finally back," sighed Katie. They had to make many detours in the cave due to the cave-ins. The heroes were thoroughly exhausted from their long day.

"I hope the inn keeper has something good cooking because I'm starving," said Macbeth.

"I hope I can get a good night's sleep," said Edwin. It started to rain in the night, and they could hear thunder rolling across the ocean, approaching them.

"Great, more rain," said Anton dully.

They could hear crashing noises down the hill at the inn. "NO!" they heard the old man yelling, then a huge crash and the sound of shattering wood. The lightening crashed with a loud bang against the ground to reveal that a huge, many armed, beast had destroyed the inn with its tentacles, and armies of strange amphibians were washing in from the ocean. Every wave revealed more and more of them. They were lined up one after another like an organized army. It went dark. They could hear moans from all directions.

They stood transfixed with horror. Each of them stared into the black rain in random directions. None of them could see anything in the blackness of the night, but they were all too afraid to move in any direction in case there was something there. "What... what... what was that?" Katie whispered almost soundlessly.

"Our demise," guessed Anton.

"I hope not," moaned Katie. The moaning sounds increased in volume and they could hear the unmistakable sounds of the inn being smashed to bits further down the hill.

"Why can't Zanatose be here? We need him," thought Bill. "Even if we survive this we have nowhere to go except back to Theragorn city," said Bill.

"Good idea lets go back now!" yelled Edwin.

"Quiet!" hissed Macbeth. They heard a large mass of the amphibian things start marching up the hill to them. They saw an army of the undead appear through the darkness and rain. They were as ugly as ever. Their blood-shot eyes stared blankly as they staggered forward, their mouths gaping at them.

The lightening kept crashing against the ground to reveal them all, and the approaching army of armed and armored fish-people. They looked like pale, ghostly people except with fins and gills. Some of them seemed to have tentacles and sharp teeth. Through the darkness, they could see a large mass of some kind diving back into the ocean.

"And so it began, and so it ends," muttered Macbeth hopelessly.

"What's that supposed to mean!?" asked Katie furiously.

"It means we are doomed!" yelled Anton.

"Edwin, can't you use your sword's powers to stop these things?" asked Katie hopelessly.

The undead army started to try and bite at them; Macbeth and Bill had their instincts about them and started fighting back.

Bill rammed at several zombies with his shield, trying to push them back. They kept trying to push past his shield. He was slashing and hacking away at a handful with his sword, but they kept coming no matter how he sliced them. Macbeth was by his side trying to stop their advancing army. "You guys, wake up!" yelled Macbeth angrily from a cut he got on his arm from a zombie's claws.

Edwin and Anton snapped out of their daze and drew their weapons. "Help me!" yelled Katie desperately. She stabbed her dagger into a few of their heads and pushed them off. Soon too many were advancing on her and she started backing down the hill, toward the inn.

Anton twirled his staff and tripped several zombies, slowing their approach. This gave Bill and Edwin time to use their elemental powers while Macbeth and Anton held off their approach. "Hurry up you two!" yelled Macbeth in distress. A zombie was biting at the air just inches from his face. It was so close to getting him he could smell its rancid breath. He struggled to hold it back with his sword.

Edwin and Bill both took deep breaths and concentrated hard. "*I know what I want to do, but am I able to do it again?*" thought Edwin to himself. Bill let out a great roar as he rushed at the zombies with his illuminated blade.

After every slash a bright light continued from his sword and illuminated the surroundings as the beam shredded through rows of the undead. Bill finally started to discover more of his sword's powers. Edwin was still trying to gather the strength to lift his sword. Down the hill, they heard Katie scream. "NO!" yelled Edwin in frustration. "There goes my concentration."

Edwin whipped around toward the hill and stabbed his sword into the ground. The entire hill started to shake. "WHOA" yelled Macbeth as he fell from the tremor. The zombies even fell from the quake.

"Let her go!" Edwin yelled as he ripped his sword out of the soil and started to stagger down the hill. He dragged his mud covered sword as he ran.

His whole body ached, but all he could think about were his mother's words. *"Reach high, for stars lie hidden in your soul. You will be a great hero someday."*

"Be careful!" yelled Bill as he helped the others back to their feet before all of the zombies could rise and fight.

Edwin was still cold from the fight against the tarik, and the rain felt like needles against his numb legs. He could barely see through the veil of darkness. Compelled by his mother's voice, he kept going.

As he kept going forward, he suddenly felt a sharp sword cut across his cheek. He groaned in agony as his cheek started to bleed. "If you have come to save her, she is already gone. Leave now hero or you shall have to fight us," said a low, dry voice.

The figure from which the voice came from was still invincible in the dark, dreary night. "Why?" wheezed Edwin as he struggled to stay conscious. The blood loss he was suffering and all his battles before were taking effect.

"Because the *dark one* threatened to kill my daughter if I hadn't," answered the voice dejectedly.

"Abigail?" asked Edwin as he tried to crawl toward the creature's voice. He fell to his knees from the pain of his wounds.

"No, the *dark* one," he replied. "I'm sorry it had to come to this hero," said the voice.

The creature started to walk toward Edwin's body.

Edwin tried to look up, but before he could, he felt the wet, cold handle, of the creature's sword against his head. Edwin's head dropped into the bitter sand.

A rod of lightening hit the ground inches from Edwin. Bill, Anton, and Macbeth looked up from the zombies they were fighting and saw Edwin lying face down in the sand and a tall entity with strange fins standing above him. It turned its head to look at them. Everything went dark, but they could still see the thing's green eyes until it turned around and left.

"We have to go help Edwin!" yelled Bill, covered with mud. He looked back down at a zombie he had just slashed to bits and saw that nothing was there. He looked out at the ocean and saw the moon glint maliciously. "If Edwin's down and they're gone, then we failed," he concluded grimly.

CHPT 23:
APPROACHING DOOM

"We've heard from a scout that Ocean View Inn was been smashed to bits. We have also heard that the people of the ocean have taken a girl around your age, nearing nineteen years. They have taken her for an exchange with the *dark* one," said Amir with a heavy heart. He gazed at Zanatose's heartbroken face then quickly looked away. He could not bear seeing the hero's broken face. "I'm sorry Zanatose," he said sincerely. "I shall go to Theragorn city immediately to await your friends and help defeat the *dark* one."

Zanatose was still too shocked to answer and felt a painful gaping hole in his heart. He tried to fight back his tears as best as he could, but the news was more than he could handle. All of his hope was embodied in her angelic figure. His strength came from her soothing voice. He had never understood love, but every moment with her made him wonder if he knew it better than he thought. So much was left unsaid, and always will be. His mind ventured to her kind nature, her fair heart, the blue ocean in her eyes that he would never explore.

"Are you okay?" asked Amir.

Zanatose was finally back to his senses and replied. "Who... who is the *dark one* you speak of? Is it Fang?" asked

Zanatose with a growing rage. All of his sorrow was burning away into an incredible, consuming frenzy for revenge.

"No, Fang is not the *dark* one. We don't know who *he* is, but we know Fang has tried time and time again to find this being. I bet you still want to know where Fang is, right?" asked Amir reluctantly.

Zanatose nodded, but this time he did not want to find Fang for revenge. He wanted to find Fang so that he could help find and defeat the *dark one* that Amir spoke of. "Where can I find him and his Wolfos army?" asked Zanatose. He started to stand up and jumped off his bed onto the hard wooden ground.

Amir sighed and thought it would be best not to tell Zanatose where Fang was, but he decided after the death of his friend he deserved to know. "Fang is at the top of Demise Mountain, to the north of our city."

"Thanks," said Zanatose as he continued to round up his gear to leave Parikine city and head to Demise Mountain.

"Do you plan to fight all of the Wolfos and Fang?" asked Amir with worry in his voice.

"Of course not, I expect him to hand over his army to me," replied Zanatose. Amir stared at him with his mouth open. Zanatose threw on a blue tunic, strapped Shadow to his back, and the new sword to his hip. "If he's ignorant refuse though… I guess I would have to fight him and maybe his army," said Zanatose nonchalantly.

Just then Rezaar walked into the room. "If you truly believe you can take on General Wolf Fang, never mind his army, you are a fool." Rezaar was not very confident in Zanatose's ability to fight an army alone. As far as Rezaar was concerned, Zanatose was deciding to ride off to a definite death. "No Hayvan can defeat Fang and you aren't even a Hayvan."

Zanatose trembled with anger and turned to Rezaar.

"You're right. I am not a Hayvan... I'm stronger than any Hayvan."

Rezaar growled at him, but lost interest. "You are but one man," he said calmly. "You demand from us that we believe you can do an army of men's jobs. If you believe that you must leave and die at Fang's feet then so be it. My army and your remaining friends will be more than enough to finish the job against the tarik."

Zanatose laughed at him. "Don't worry about me, your highness. I promise to you that I will live," said Zanatose defiantly.

"If you are definitely going then let me come too," suggested Amir.

"No, you need to meet my friends in Theragorn and help them. They need a decent warrior," said Zanatose with clenched fists as he remembered Brett and the rest.

"*There were so many of them, how is it that none of them could save her?*" Zanatose asked himself.

"Alright then, I'll leave. Good bye," said Amir. He left the room and headed toward Theragorn city with the awaiting platoon of Hayvans.

"I have a mighty stallion awaiting you just outside our city's gates," said Rezaar. "Ride swiftly and you shall reach him soon enough."

"Thank you Rezaar," said Zanatose. He wore his new Parikine city tunic. It was a royal blue tunic with long sleeves. He walked through the amazing city and admired the sights.

After a short walk, he reached the gates leading to Demise Mountain which he saw in the distance. "*That's about half a day on horseback,*" thought Zanatose.

He exited the city through the pearly gates which shone liked diamonds in the desert sunlight. He saw a black steed waiting for him on the other side. He mounted the valiant beast and kicked it hard. The horse naiad and then started galloping swiftly through the desert's sand.

"I can't believe I left her alone with those incompetent fools. If only Brett were with her, I should've been there for her," he whispered. "Who is the *dark one*?" he bellowed to himself.

He shook his head and decided to stop pondering these questions and to ask them from Fang instead. "This time I will fight Fang until he answers my questions," he muttered to himself.

After a long ride and two very exhausted horses, Brett and Marik finally reached Theragorn city. "Finally," sighed Brett as he dismounted his horse and walked into Theragorn city shakily; he was not accustomed to riding a horse for twelve hours straight.

"I wonder if your friends are here," said Marik. Brett shrugged. "Is that one of them?" asked Marik. He was pointing to a tall well built soldier in very showy armor with a large two handed sword strapped to his back.

"No," replied Brett. "That's just General Gateman."

"Hello there Brett!" called Jonathan. He did not look like his cheery old self. He seemed like he had a lot of his hope drained out of him.

"What's wrong?" asked Brett as he hurried his horse along, dragging it by the reigns, with him toward Jonathan. Marik followed closely behind Brett.

Once they neared Jonathan, Marik put out his paws to shake hands. "My name is Marik, and I am the warrior of the wind. Nice to meet you General Gateman," said Marik with a toothy smile.

"Nice to meet you too," said Jonathan cautiously as he shook hands with the cheetah. He was suspicious of cheetahs and had heard barbaric stories of them on their hunts.

"Is there anything wrong?" asked Brett again. Jonathan nodded his head slowly.

"Ka...Katie is .... She's....Dead," said Jonathan grimly. Brett's blue eyes dimmed and his heart was filled with sorrow and grief.

"How can you be sure? Who told you?" he asked.

"One of your friends died!?" asked Marik.

Anton walked out of the nearby hospital and answered Brett's question. "She's dead Brett, and so is Zanatose, probably," he said in his regular, grim voice.

Brett hung his head down then asked, "Where are the others? Are they okay?"

"They're in the hospital. They fought hard against some unknown creatures and the undead zombies according to Anton," replied Jonathan. By his tone of voice it was evident that he did not believe they had encountered zombies.

"I hope they're alright at least," said Brett.

"Don't worry Brett. They're okay, and I bet you Raymundo is fine too," said Marik reassuringly. Brett chuckled a bit.

"His name is Zanatose, and he's the least of my worries. He can take care of himself," said Brett.

Zanatose was at the foot of the soaring mountain, and it was starting to snow. He had left the desert a day ago, and the temperature had begun to drop. The sun was eclipsed by a tall temple structure in a distant jungle he saw to the east.

He dismounted his horse and started to hike up the snowy cliff. "I'M COMING FOR YOU FANG!" yelled Zanatose at the top of his lungs to the mountain. His voice echoed through the mountain and started a small avalanche.

Piles of snow started falling on him, but he kept hiking up the mountain trail using Shadow as a cane to help him keep his balance against the tide of snow. The only sound

Zanatose heard was the howling wind, echoing throughout the mountain.

He reached a rock side where the path had ended, and he had to climb up. He noticed loads of large animal tracks embedded in the snow. He sheathed Shadow, and started to climb.

The cold snow made his hands numb, but he disregarded the pain. After Katie's death he wanted answers, and he knew the only one with answers was Wolf Fang. The snow gave away, and he was supporting himself from one hand on a piece of ice. He tried to grasp the Cliffside, but wherever his hand reached, it tore out clumps of loose snow. His last hand slipped and he started to fall.

"I won't fail!" he yelled in frustration. He drew both swords and stabbed them into the mountainside's ice. He dangled in midair, holding tightly to his two swords, staying on the mountain and away from falling to a painful death. "That was too close," he muttered to himself. He took a few deep breathes then yanked out Shadow and stabbed it back into the mountain, higher up, pulling himself up again, and again, climbing with his swords. His numb hands shook every time he lifted his swords.

"Are you still trying?" bellowed Fang's gruff voice from atop a ledge just out of Zanatose's reach.

"I came for you," yelled back Zanatose with a heavy, cold breath. His breath was visible in front of him. "Katie died, and I want answers from you, or else!" he yelled to Fang angrily.

Fang laughed at the haughty boy. "You are demanding answers from me… or else? You do understand my entire army resides in the mountain you are struggling to climb?" asked Fang.

As Zanatose neared the ledge, he saw rows of the hungry wolfos staring, unblinking, at him, hungry eyes atop mounds of snow and ice. It would have brought a chill to his soul to see so many rows of the barbaric beasts, but he was so consumed with the death of Katie that none of it mattered. "I will fight them and anyone else I have to for my answers," Zanatose mumbled stiffly. "I won't let her die in vain." He was close to the top and decided to use his dark powers to vault up and onto the ledge above him. He landed perfectly on his feet on the soft snow. He drew his head up and snarled at Fang; his restraint was falling apart and he could feel a primordial fury overtaking him. His months of hardship had shaped him into an imposing warrior with broad shoulders and rippling muscles.

Fang backed away into the ranks of his wolfos. "So you have finally learned to use your dark powers," he said with a smirk.

"Yeah, I have a great handle over my powers. I also have enough strength to destroy you and your army," Zanatose replied confidently.

"Let me fight that arrogant child," suggested a wolfo in his low, hoarse voice. This Wolfo was different from the others though; it was blue with yellow eyes and wore armor similar to Fang's.

"Who's that ragged dog?" asked Zanatose. He tightened his numb hands around his sword as the snow kept falling. He was freezing.

"Him… He is my second in command, Fenrir. Of course if we cut to the chase and you join me you shall take his place," added Fang with an enticing tone.

"How about you join me?" suggested Zanatose. He caused Fang's army of wolfos to explode with barks and howling from their outrage.

"Calm down," commanded Fang. With a small motion of his hand all of the wolfos immediately heeded his command. "If you still won't join me then you give me no choice but to kill you."

"Just try," growled Zanatose. He prepared himself

for combat, his swords' dark energy engulfing the blades. Zanatose could feel the darkness rushing through him and taking control.

The two stood glaring at each other. Fang's army was trying very hard to contain themselves. They each wanted to fight and rip Zanatose to shreds on their own. "This child is a pipsqueak, General. Let me take care of him for you," pleaded Fenrir.

"No, I'll take care of him." Fang took out his bisento and inserted a dark crystal into it. "I won't go easy on you this time," warned Fang as the dark crystal's powers engulfed his body like a tornado.

"You think you scare me?" asked Zanatose.

"Come on! Fight me unless you're a coward!" yelled Zanatose in a darker voice.

"Temper, temper Zanatose," said Fang with a chuckle. "Now let me teach you a lesson in superiority." He lunged at Zanatose with his staff pointed out at him. "Lesson one, I'm superior to you!"

"Wrong!" yelled Zanatose as he did a back flip onto a higher ledge, dodging the fatal attack. His dark powers had taken full hold on him. There was no longer any resistance, he felt its power and he liked it. He jumped down and stabbed his swords down at Fang.

Fang jumped to the right, but Shadow caught his shoulder, slicing off the shoulder plating Fang wore. "You've improved. I'll give you that, but you are still not as powerful as I am," said Fang. He turned into his dark form, as did Zanatose.

The two of them bore fangs and were pale with beady black eyes. Zanatose had also sprouted long talons from his hands. "Tell me who the dark one is or I will **destroy you!**" he yelled in a callous voice that was not his. Zanatose ran at Fang with his swords held over his head. He hammered his swords down, but Fang blocked both with his long bisento.

Fang tried to retaliate with a sweep of his blade, but Zanatose slapped the bisento away and drove his sword at Fang's heart. Fang shocked Zanatose with a current of black lightening out of desperation, at a loss for anything else. Fang could sense something different in Zanatose, as if a mental dam had broken. He knew he could not fight the strength of such a river.

"This all about the *dark one*?" Fang asked. He took a deep breath and turned back to normal. Reason was his only hope, if he could appeal to Zanatose's reason, he could survive this fight.

Zanatose did not back off so easily though. He slashed from one side with Shadow and from another side with his other dark sword. Fang blocked Shadow with his staff and caught the other with his hand; a line of blood began to trickle down his arm. "I am fighting to find and take down the *dark one*. He is the legendary leader of the tarik. No one has ever seen him," continued Fang solemnly.

The hungry look in Zanatose's eyes vanished and they were replaced with the same sorrow of when he found out Katie was dead. The dam was healed, and the river stopped rushing out. "The *dark one* is… the leader of the tarik?" he asked. Fang nodded.

"Join me Zanatose! Trust me when I say we, the wolfos, are not evil! We are, like you, fighting to stop the tarik," said Fang.

Zanatose fell to his knees in front of Fang and dropped his two swords. His head bowed down before Fang. "So you are fighting the tarik… and they killed her…" his voice was starting to shake and the look of sorrow was being replaced with anger. His pupils shrank and a ferocious rage was seen within his eyes. The snake was burning into his skin, deeper than ever before. Its fangs drew nearer to his heart, but he did not resist. The pain was too deep.

"Join my side Zanatose. Join the side of justice," said

Fang. He put out his bloody hand to Zanatose. "The two greatest warriors will work together to defeat the dark one… for Katie."

"For Katie," agreed Zanatose as he took Fang's hand with an iron grip. Fang helped him back to his feet and raised his hand far above his head and turned him around to face the wolfos.

"Say hello to your new family and army," said Fang with a triumphant smile.

Zanatose nodded approvingly of his new army and laughed at the possibilities that have presented themselves with such a grand army. There were rows and rows of these large, loyal, cunning beasts waiting to obediently serve his every command.

"My revenge is nearing," thought Zanatose.

"As a reward I shall give you my last dark crystal," said Fang with a devious smile. He yanked out the dark crystal from his staff and handed it to Zanatose. "I have enough dark energy for myself, but this will make you invincible."

"Thank you, Fang," said Zanatose as he grabbed the dark crystal. The crystal immediately engulfed him with a current of dark energy from the first touch. Zanatose felt a sharp pain, closed his eyes, and took the agony silently. Once he opened them again, he felt a rage that replaced the agonizing pain.

"We must begin the search for the temple into oblivion straight away," said Zanatose with a new voice. His new voice sounded like his dark side was speaking at the same time as his normal voice. The Wolfos and Fang saw a black snake in his eyes.

"You are now one of us," said Fang victoriously. He had finally made Zanatose join him. The dark one would no longer stand a chance against their combined forces. Nothing could stop him, and he would soon teach Zanatose everything about his powers. *"Zanatose will become a leviathan that even the dark one would not be able to defeat,"* thought Fang with a triumphant smile.

"And the inn was destroyed. The poor innkeeper was nowhere to be found… we took any supplies we could find in the rubble and well… there weren't any. We starved until we reached here after that big fight and that's why we're in the hospital," concluded Macbeth to Brett and Marik.

They were listening intently to Macbeth's story of what happened, by Macbeth's bed. "Zanatose's really running late for the reunion," said Edwin grimly. Edwin looked like a mess. He had many deep crimson wounds and a fresh scar across his cheek. He was still devastated by the fact that he could not save Katie no matter how hard he had tried. "I'm sorry I couldn't save her," he said as he saw the sorrow in Brett's eyes.

"It's not your fault Edwin," said Bill. "I should've tried to save her too." He was in better shape, but he still had a bunch of scratch marks on him from the vicious zombies.

"He was the only one to try and save her!?" asked Brett. Everyone nodded. "What were you guys doing?"

"We had an army of zombies to fight," said Anton. "They had us surrounded."

"I wonder if Zanatose is still alive…" thought Edwin aloud.

"I don't care that much," said Brett. "If he is, I'm sure he'll be as devastated as I was to hear that Katie is dead."

They all stared down at the ground glumly without a word until they heard a hard knock at the door. "Come in," beckoned Marik.

As soon as the door opened to reveal a large Hayvan, Marik jumped to his feet and drew his sword, as did Jonathan. "What is your business here?" asked Jonathan. He was very disgruntled to see a Hayvan in his city. The last time they had a Hayvan in their city it was because they had declared war. After the king's death, he was paranoid about turmoil.

Amir raised his hands and smiled innocently. "I was told to come here by Zanatose," he was glad to see the two lower their arms and the rest gasp. Jonathan stared at him questioningly. "And yes General Gateman. He did survive our gladiator matches, even the cruelest one," he said in a side note.

"He's alive!?" yelled Bill. He was about to sit upright from joy, but the scratches burned as he moved. Instead he winced painfully and fell back again against the velvet cushions of his bed.

"Where is he?" blurted out Edwin.

"Is he alright?" asked Brett.

Amir lost his smile and replaced it with a grim face. "I know the answer to only one of those," he said with disappointment. Everyone's joy of hearing that Zanatose was alive vanished with all of their hope. "I only know where he's gone. After he learned that the girl with your forces died, he was kind of disgruntled and demanded to know where Fang and his entire army resided." Bill and Edwin both painfully sat up to listen. They gave each other a sideways glance of worry.

"He didn't actually go to fight Wolf Fang and his Wolfos army... did he?" asked Edwin in a small voice. He already knew the answer, but he was certain even Zanatose could not defeat an entire army. Amir nodded.

CHPT 24:
A New Road

The wolfos stayed outside in the snow and sparred with each other to practice for the next real battle. Wolf Fang led Zanatose and Fenrir into an icy cave away from the others. They walked carefully over the icy ground to a part of the magnificent cave that was not frozen, aside from that one non-frozen part of the cave the rest was frozen in ice. Even the walls were beautiful mirrors of ice.

Fang gestured to a few chairs for the others to sit in while he took a seat at the head of an ancient stone table. Fenrir took a seat in the fine crimson chair; Zanatose leaned on a wall near Fang and refused to take a seat.

"Why are we meeting so formally?" asked Zanatose. He kept rubbing his hands together to stay warm. He was absolutely freezing and would have rather made a fire than go in an icy cave and listen to a speech.

Fenrir gave him a look full of hate and Fang laughed at him. "My apologies, I had forgotten you aren't accustomed to the cold. Does this help?" he asked as he grabbed a wrinkly pile of fabric from under his chair and tossed it to Zanatose.

Zanatose caught it and unfolded it. It was a thick, dark blue sweater. He quickly put it on top of his thin shirt. "It's a little better I suppose... thanks," he said. He went back to comfortably leaning on the wall. "When's this snow going to let up?"

"Well, that's just what I wanted to discuss. Once this snow lets up we have to move out and start our counter attack against the tarik," said Fang.

"Brilliant sir!" added Fenrir. Zanatose laughed at him.

"There's nothing brilliant about that, or are you just that dumb that you couldn't figure that out on your own?" laughed Zanatose. Fenrir growled menacingly at Zanatose from his seat. The pile of fur shook with restraint.

"That's enough, you two!" commanded Fang calmly. "I wasn't done, there was a reason I asked for you two to come and attend this meeting. I am at a loss. There is too much to do and I alone can't execute all of the necessary steps to the downfall of the tarik quickly enough."

Zanatose's interest was piqued and he decided to listen more closely. Fang took out a map from his pocket and laid it down on the table. It had many scribbles and large numbers written all over it. Zanatose walked over to the table for a closer look. He stood over them and gazed down at the map.

"All over the numbers of the tarik have jumped!" said Fenrir with panic in his normally threatening voice.

"Yes, this is our biggest problem. It also means we are running out of time, and it is great news that we have one more commander in our ranks," said Fang as he smiled at Zanatose with pride.

"Thank you General Fang," said Zanatose with a small nod. "What do you think the cause of this sudden increase of tarik is?" asked Zanatose calmly. With his new dark crystal added to his powers and an army of Wolfos behind him, he no longer feared the tarik.

"We don't understand either, but locations which were once void of the tarik like the Roctinian jungles are now filled with them. Until recently their shrine had been ruled by the tarik, and then Brett went there and got the light sword and Marik with his sword of wind," said Fang.

"Brett? So he did succeed - how do you know all of this?" asked Zanatose.

Fang whistled loudly. His whistle echoed throughout the cave, and a shrill cry replied. A beady eyed black crow flew into the cave and landed onto Fang's shoulder. "This is a bird which you may recognize," said Fang.

Zanatose stared at the bird's gazing eyes and saw visions of himself and his friends in the woods, and suddenly he remembered the bird. "That bird's been following me and the others," said Zanatose. Fang nodded.

"From the eyes of this bird and my special scouts, I am able to know a lot about everything going on in this land. Somehow though, I am yet to find the gates to oblivion," said Fang disappointedly.

"Our master is so wise and powerful," said Fenrir. Zanatose ignored him.

"So there is no news on the death of the others?" asked Zanatose.

"No, none of the others are dead as far as I know," replied Fang.

Zanatose pondered these new revelations. "Do you or anyone in your ranks have elemental weapons?" asked Zanatose.

Fang nodded and Fenrir pushed away his cloak. He took out a glittering piece of ice with a hole in the center. "It is an elemental item, but it's powerless. The elemental weapon of ice is useless without the gem of water," said Fenrir.

"Okay, this is very good," said Zanatose. "My old friends have all succeeded in retrieving their target elemental items it seems. Only a few items are left undiscovered. We shall find those items and the gates to oblivion, and we shall hunt my good friends for their elemental swords."

"*Then I can get my revenge from the dark one,*" thought Zanatose.

"*I didn't expect the dark swords to take such a hold on him,*" thought Fang.

"He was once our leader, our last resort, our hope, and our strength," said Bill. "Now you're telling us that he might be dead!?" yelled Bill angrily at Amir.

"I don't know," said Amir forcefully back. "He could be alive."

"Yeah, Amir is right. Zanatose could be alive," said Edwin.

"He could be alright if he decided to turn back and away from Fang's army," said Anton. "But that's not what he did."

Brett sighed and decided that in this time of loss it was his turn to take command with a heavy heart. He stood up straight and spoke to every one of them. "Zanatose may be lost, but our hope shouldn't be. Don't you all remember why we chose this path?" Brett asked of them all.

"To help Zanatose defeat the tarik," said Edwin hopelessly.

"Come on Edwin!" said Brett with a forced calm. "We both know that's not true! We all chose this path to save everyone we care about. We did it save them," concluded Brett.

He looked around at all of them. They still had their heads hung low. The only one with any hope was Marik because he had not met Zanatose or Katie. Brett thought to himself, "*What will bring hope back into them?*"

"Are you all still miserable?" asked Marik with a chuckle. "If you hadn't noticed the odds are more in our favor than ever!" Everyone started raising their heads to listen. Brett hoped that Marik's speech could cheer them up.

"Look outside everyone!" proclaimed Marik. Everyone turned their heads and saw dawn's early light. "A new day, and with that new day rising high in the sky we get a new chance, a new hope! Don't let it slip because you're sad! Grab onto that new hope and make a chance to win this battle!" The sad sorrowful eyes were slowly changed into looks of hope as the light shined in through the windows.

Amir straightened himself back up and reinforced Marik's speech. "He is right! We may have lost two, but we gained not only two but armies with them! We now have the army of the great city of Parikine and the noble army of the Roctinian village!"

Jonathan stood up from his seat with confidence and pounded his chest. "Don't forget the elite army of Theragorn!" he bellowed.

Brett was glad to see hope back in their eyes, but would hope be enough anymore?

"I can't wait to get started!" barked Fenrir joyously. "I remember fighting your group once Zanatose…"

"General Zanatose," interrupted Zanatose.

Fenrir growled and then continued. "As I was saying, I faced your friends before. You tried to stand up to me, but instead you fell like a weakling." Zanatose remembered back to that night with remorse.

He had gone into his dark form twice in that one night. He was unable to defend his friends because his last transformation drained him completely. That was the night that his friends had let him down and allowed Brett to be abducted by the Wolfos. He stared blankly at the rough rocky ground, deep in his own thoughts of the past.

Then he remembered his struggle side by side with Wolf Fang in the mysterious haunted village to save Katie and the others.

She was still alive and he was still pure. Now he fought out of hate and for revenge. Then he remembered the day he found that strange dark artifact with a dark crystal. It was the first time he met the Roctinian raptors.

They were terrible beasts, and probably worked hand in hand with the tarik. He remembered his time alone with Katie ruined by those beasts. He remembered their stand at Theragorn against Fang.

He remembered the parting of their ways. A tear came to his eyes when he remembered that final moment with Katie. He never told her how he felt, that he loved her. He remembered the awful pains of the desert, and the harsh gladiator matches waiting for him in the great city of Parikine. He remembered surviving the trials with Katie fueling his soul.

All that he had done did not mattered a bit. Now Katie was dead, his last hope was in an army of viscous beasts. "Zanatose?" echoed Fang's voice. It seemed to come from a distance. Fang's voice brought him back into reality.

Zanatose looked around and remembered where he was. "When's the snow going to stop?" he asked irritably.

Fenrir and Fang chuckled. "Look outside my new general," said Fang as he gestured outside.

The snow had finally started to stop. The sun finally rose in the glum sky. A new hope rose with that sun. A new darkness eclipsed the hope. A new darkness captured a hero's light. A burning beacon of hope had burned, out and a hero became what he fought so hard to destroy. A new hope was found to counter the heart of *THE DARK HERO.*